WHEN PIGS FLY

JOSIE HARJO BOOK THREE

CATHERINE SEQUEIRA

WHEN PIGS FLY

Published by Barcelos Publishing, LLC, Sacramento, CA, USA

The Library of Congress Cataloging-in-Publication Data is available upon request.

ISBN 9798990323025 (trade paperback)

ISBN 9798990323032 (hardback)

ISBN 9798990323018 (ebook)

Our books may be purchased in bulk for promotional, educational, or business use. Please contact your local bookseller for more information.

First Edition: September 2025

Printed in the United States of America

Novels by Catherine Sequeira

<u>Josie Harjo Series</u>
If You Hear Hoofbeats
The Lady or the Tiger
When Pigs Fly

<u>Stand-alone Novels</u>
The Before and The After

To all the DVMoms.
You got this!

CHAPTER
ONE

No matter how you slice it, airports fucking suck. There's just so much to loathe: long lines, screaming children, grumpy, sleep-deprived travelers, the pervasive scent of stale farts and bad breath. All of it. Airports are truly their own special level of hell.

I sighed and shifted in my seat, trying to find the sweet spot where the metal of the chair would stop pinching my ass.

"Thanks for coming with me, Josie," Laila said, clutching a man-handled bouquet in front of her like a shield. "I know you hate it here."

I reached over and squeezed her arm. "Anytime."

And I really meant it.

No matter how much I hated the hellscape that was Will Rogers Airport, there was no way I was going to let her face her parents without backup. Since her folks had announced their visit a few months ago, the bright light that was Laila had slowly dimmed as the stress of it all ate away at her.

Her hands tightened, and the plastic wrapper around the flowers crinkled. "I'm not sure I could've done this alone."

"I got you," I said, flashing her a confident smile. "They can't force you to do anything you don't want to do." I waved a hand dramatically. "When hell freezes over and all that."

"Um," she started before pointedly looking over her shoulder through the windows. "I'm pretty sure this *is* hell. And it has definitely frozen over."

I looked out at the snow and ice that blanketed everything and barked a laugh, happy to hear her crack a joke despite all the stress. "Okay. How about 'over my dead body?'" I suggested with a smirk.

"Don't tempt fate," she teased back. A smile tipped her lips, but the worry was still there, etched deep in the wrinkles between her eyebrows.

"Seriously, though...." She looked down at the flowers and picked at the plastic wrapper. "I appreciate it. I'm sorry you had to miss brunch with Aunty."

"Psht." I shrugged, trying to appear nonchalant. "It's all good. Tessa is still going, and I'll see both of them on Friday for the holiday."

I patted myself on the back for sounding cool about everything. If I was honest with myself, I was pretty damn bummed I was missing brunch today.

Trying to distract her, I offered, "Want me to grab you something? A coffee? Ice cream?"

She shook her head. "I don't think I can eat anything without puking," she said shakily.

With a twinge of worry, I realized that wasn't hyperbole. Her light brown skin was pasty, even with the layers of makeup she'd applied to try to cover her bags. Her nails had been chewed to nubs. Worry pinched the skin around her eyes. Her throat kept bobbing like she was fighting a rebellious trickle of stomach acid. I wasn't used to seeing her like this, and I felt a surge of protectiveness.

"This is going to be awful," she fretted.

"I'm more than willing to take one for the team," I offered. "I can throw myself down the escalator. That way, you'll have to rush me to the hospital and avoid all this." I flicked my hand toward the zombies shuffling through the doldrums that was the baggage claim area.

The corner of her mouth turned up slightly.

"Just sayin'. It's a sacrifice I'm willing to make," I continued with mock seriousness. "But if I'm immobile in bed for two months, you have to promise to shave my legs. You know how bad they can get."

She feigned consideration and said, "I don't know.... My machete is getting a bit dull."

I put my hand to my heart and tried to look cartoonishly hurt.

"Okay, fine." She was fighting a smile. "But only if I don't have to cut your toenails."

"Ugh," I replied with a shiver. "Please do *not* touch my feet." She knew damn well I didn't like *anyone* near those puppies.

She huffed a laugh, and then her expression turned serious. "I appreciate your willingness to risk life and limb to get me out of seeing my parents. But I'm going to have to face them sooner or later. A trip to the ER would only delay the inevitable."

"Don't say I didn't offer," I said with a grin and threw an arm across my forehead dramatically. "It's just so hard trying to be your knight in shining armor."

Her responding smile didn't chase away the tension around her eyes.

I dropped the grin and gave her arm another squeeze. "Seriously, don't worry. We got this. Your dad can't make you do anything you don't want to do," I repeated, as if saying it over and over again would make it the truth.

The crease between her eyebrows deepened. She looked down at the flowers, and the wrapper crinkled yet again as her hands tightened.

I got the impression her dad was a raging shitass. The way Laila tells it, every call home was peppered with a litany of complaints about the way Laila looked, her home, her lifestyle, her career, and, of course, the reason for their visit: the fact that she wasn't married. According to Laila, her folks weren't going to leave until she was solidly engaged and the wedding was planned.

When I'd first heard about their impending visit, I'd asked Laila how bad her dad really was. "Like Gerald-Richter-bad?" I'd asked. She'd responded with a flat "worse." I wasn't sure how that was possible, and I had to admit I was a little nervous about finding out what that looked like.

I shook off the icky Gerald thoughts. Determined to cheer her up and give her some strength, I deepened my voice and said, "I've come here to chew bubblegum and kick ass. And I'm all out of bubblegum."

I playfully cracked my knuckles.

She snorted. "What the hell movie is *that* from?"

I made a slow turn toward her, eyebrows raised, incredulous. "*They Live*? Don't tell me you haven't seen *They Live*."

She shook her head, the smile finally reaching her eyes.

"What is this world coming to?" I tsked. "Once we chase your folks back home, we're having a movie night," I said resolutely. "*They Live* is required viewing for anyone who wants to be my friend."

"Deal," she said, finally looking a modicum less stressed.

She pulled out her phone for the umpteenth time and let out a heavy sigh. "You know this delay is only going to make things worse."

I nodded but kept my mouth shut. Her parents' flight from Delhi had two stops, and they'd missed their connection in Minneapolis. After almost thirty hours in the hotbox of torture that was an international flight, they were going to be mighty irritable.

"My father is going to be angry before he even sees me," she added, as if reading my mind. The smile she'd had only moments ago was replaced with a deep frown.

My eyebrows crinkled with worry. It killed me to see her this way.

I stiffened my back, channeled my best RBF, and said playfully, "If we have to throw down, I'm pretty sure I can take him."

Unable to resist, she let out a small laugh and said, "I love you, Josie."

Feeling a bit smug, I relaxed in my seat. "How much longer do you think it'll be?"

She swiped down on her phone to refresh the flight times. "About ten minutes until they land."

"Hmm. Ten minutes. Then, they gotta deplane. So maybe half an hour or more?" I calculated.

She shrugged a reply as if she couldn't even be bothered to do the math.

I shifted in my seat again, the incorrigible metal still nipping away at my ass. Despite my best efforts, an irritated sigh escaped, and my sewing machine leg started up.

"Missing him?" she asked.

I looked over at her, surprised. I knew exactly whom she was talking about, but I'd been actively avoiding the topic. It was hard enough being at an airport, remembering that Armand was halfway around the world. I was trying my best to keep those painful thoughts tucked away.

"Yeah," was all I could muster. Even though my thoughts were presently swirling with concern for Laila, Armand's absence was always sitting in the back of my mind, like a painful sore that wouldn't heal.

It was her turn to reach over and squeeze my hand. "Just a few more weeks, and he'll be back," she said, trying to reassure me.

I smiled at my friend. Even when she was facing the wrath of Khan, she had enough energy left to offer support.

"Eighteen days," I said and then quickly added, "not that I'm counting." I waved a hand dismissively.

She smirked. "You've fallen pretty hard, haven't you?"

"Yup," I said, suddenly feeling uncomfortable. I hadn't unpacked what our relationship meant yet and definitely wasn't ready to talk about it.

She caught my eye, sent a soft smile of support, and squeezed my hand again.

Accepting the pass, I tried to stuff the messy feelings back into a tidy box. My relationship with Armand had progressed so rapidly that I'd barely had time to get my feet underneath me. I'd been perfectly content rocking the single life. But when Armand entered the scene, it was like my world shifted, and I didn't even know where I stood on the whole thing. I wasn't sure what the future would look like, and I wasn't sure I was ready to change my life drastically enough to let someone else in.

Trying my best to brush any thoughts of Armand to the side, I glanced longingly at the ice cream shop near the terminal exit. Mint chocolate chip was one hell of a bandaid, and I needed to be on my game when Laila's folks made their grand entrance.

"I'm going to grab an ice cream. Sure you don't want one?" I offered.

She shook her head, and her throat bobbed again. I gave her arm a pat before I made my way over to the booth.

It was still relatively early in the day, and it was the middle of winter, so there was no line. A bored teenager sat behind the counter, eyes locked on his phone, snickering at whatever mindless droll the social media algorithm had decided to feed him. I couldn't blame him; I was sure working in an airport ice cream shop was as soul-sucking as it sounded.

He caught me walking up and unplugged from his phone long enough to get my order, take my money, and pass back a minuscule cup of pistachio ice cream. I was admittedly a bit bummed about the lack of mint chocolate chip, but my current emotional state required ice cream STAT, regardless of the flavor.

With my life-saving treat in hand, I wove back through the crowd and took a large bite. It wasn't the best ice cream—we were in the airport, after all—but it was enough. I could practically hear the trill of the video game music as my health bar powered back up.

Flopping back into my seat, I took another bite and snuck a glance at Laila. Her shoulders were hunched as she dully looked out at the people passing by. I wracked my brain for a way to help her feel better.

You're doing all you can, I reminded myself. *She just needs you to be by her side.*

With that thought, a large blop of ice cream dripped off my spoon and onto my tits.

"Damn it!" I blurted, trying to wipe it away with my napkin and leaving a smear of white across the navy blue of my dress.

Laila's lips quirked into a smile. "I can't take you anywhere," she teased. "You know what that looks like, right?"

"I wish," I huffed.

I licked my napkin and tried again. Small fluffs of cheap paper clung to the smudge of pistachio shmoo.

"Seriously?" I said, feeling exacerbated.

The cleanup effort was clearly a lost cause, so I buttoned my cardigan, pulling it over the incriminating smear.

"There," I said, feeling a bit smug.

Laila raised a doubtful eyebrow.

Before I could respond, the ding of Laila's phone interrupted us, and her face instantly fell.

"They've arrived," Laila half-whispered in dread as if she were announcing the appearance of the four horsemen. Her eyes were wide with panic.

A surge of adrenaline whisked through my veins. *It's go-time.*

I quickly snarfed the rest of my ice cream, crumpled up my napkin with gusto, and dropped everything into the trash.

"We should go wait by the terminal exit, I guess." She tucked her phone away and looked down at her outfit. "Wardrobe check. How do I look?"

She tucked her shoulder-length hair behind her ears, smoothing it out with her free hand. She loved her hair that length, but she'd had a mini-panic attack when her folks announced their visit. She was certain her mom would flip out over how short it was. "One more thing she'll say I'm doing wrong," she'd lamented.

She fidgeted with the edge of her sweater, waiting for my answer.

"You look great," I answered. "How do you feel?"

"I'm freaking out," she replied. "This is going to be awful. Thanks again for coming with me."

"Anytime," I said and gave her a half hug.

Knowing I'd also be judged, I ran my hand over my hair. The dark locks were pulled back into a tight, long braid. Beaded earrings tickled my neck. I'd chosen a modest flared dress and a cardigan. Of course, said cardigan was now covering up my graceless blop. But we won't talk about that.

I gave the fabric of my skirt another brush, trying to get the last few Yersi hairs off. Why did cats always poof all over people at the most inopportune times? Between the ice cream and the cat hairs, I hoped I didn't look too much of a mess.

"Let's do this," I said, sounding way more confident than I felt.

We headed over to the terminal exit to wait as the first few people started trickling through. The regular business travelers led the pack, with their determined speed-walk and practical bags trailing behind them.

"Fuck, fuck, fuck," Laila said under her breath. It was like we were on the rise of a great roller coaster, the front car tipping over the edge of the big drop in front of us.

The slow trickle of vacationers followed, arms full of bags over-stuffed with unnecessary crap, shoulders hunched, and hair frazzled. The hum of luggage bags rolling across the ground was interrupted by the sharp wail of a toddler.

Laila and I exchanged a look.

Said toddler soon came into view. He was in full tantrum mode, face red and tear-stained. His body was like a limp noodle, and his parents were half dragging him as he continued to loudly proclaim his dissatisfaction with the state of life, the universe, and everything. His parents looked haggard and embarrassed as they tried to get him away from the crowd.

"Geez," I said under my breath, grateful it wasn't me. There was nothing worse than being a parent stuck in a tuna can with a child who decided to channel their inner Damien mid-flight. With that little turd nugget on board, I was pretty sure Laila's parents were going to be downright cantankerous.

Laila stood on her tiptoes to look through the crowd. "There they are," she said with a hint of horror. "*Pita*," she called out, waving her free hand weakly.

A man and a woman moved toward us. Laila's mother wore a beautiful blue and purple sari. Her father was dressed in a light tan kurta with loose pants. Her mom had a warm, tired smile. Her dad did *not*; he looked like he'd sucked on a lemon.

Laila and her mom exchanged a few stilted words in Hindi and traded a single cheek kiss. Laila handed her mom the flowers and took her carry-on bag.

Her dad stood there like a gargoyle with a serious case of rest-ing-judge-face. Laila addressed her father demurely in Hindi, and he replied gruffly. I didn't understand a word of it, but I could tell from Laila's flush of hurt that her dad had already struck a blow.

Oh, what sharp teeth you have.

My hackles rose.

"Who is your friend?" her mother asked in English, turning to me.

Laila stepped back, looped an arm through mine, and pulled me close.

"This is Dr. Josie Harjo. Dr. Harjo, this is my father, Rakesh Yadav, and my mother, Ishani Yadav."

According to Laila, introducing me as Dr. Harjo should have afforded me a certain level of gravitas with her folks. Given the way her dad's eyes drifted right over me, I assumed the power of the "doctor" didn't apply to anyone with a vagina.

Yep, borderline Gerald-bad.

Tamping down my irritation, I flashed my best cheerleader smile. "Nice to meet you."

At that point, other travelers had started to give us the side-eye. I wasn't sure whether it was the fact that we'd formed a blood clot in the egress or the palpable tension crackling in the air. Regardless, we needed to get a move on.

"Shall we get your luggage?" Laila offered demurely. "I'm sure you're tired and would like to rest."

"Yes," Ishani answered curtly.

Waves of negativity continued to waft off of Rakesh. I tried my darndest to lock away my own emotions. The best I could do was keep my fake smile strapped on and somehow make it through the drive back home.

We made a beeline to the baggage claim area in uncomfortable silence. The belt started its endless rotation, and the first few bags passed through the flaps. We squeezed into a spot to wait.

The family with the screaming toddler stood opposite us, the kid now sulking and sucking his thumb as one parent wiped his nose. The other parent was eagerly searching for their bags amongst the early releases. I could only assume they wanted to get out of there as quickly as possible. At least the little devil would fall asleep as soon as they hit the road.

Ishani turned to Laila and spoke to her in Hindi. Laila looked like a deer in the headlights as she replied in monosyllabic answers. The exchange quickly escalated, and Rakesh jumped in, barking a few harsh words at Laila. She looked to the ground and pressed her lips together in frustration.

I cleared my throat and took a step forward. "What're your plans when you're here?" I asked, my voice laced with syrupy innocence.

Rakesh turned to me and made a face like I was shit on his shoe. Ishani was polite enough to quickly cover up her irritation.

Channeling my inner Pollyanna, I added with fake cheer, "We just had a pretty nasty ice storm, but there's lots of stuff to do indoors. I'm sure you'll have a lovely time."

Following my lead, Laila spoke up and said, "I was thinking of taking them to the Western Heritage Museum and the History Center."

"Those are great picks!" I exclaimed, hoping it wouldn't sound too false. "You should visit the campus, too. See Laila's lab. She has some of the best equipment in the plant biology department."

Rakesh scowled.

I cleared my throat again as I fumbled for something more to say.

"How do you know Laila?" Ishani asked, her voice neutral but her eyes piercing.

Laila jumped in to answer for me. "Josie is a veterinarian at the school where I work."

"Oh, I see," Ishani replied blandly, her expression dismissive. "I thought you were a doctor."

"Real doctors treat more than one species," I sassed before I could stop myself.

Rakesh's eyes narrowed. "A veterinarian is not a doctor," he said coolly, his tone laced with condescension. He turned to Laila and added, "You are not a doctor either. This country should stop calling people doctors when they are not."

Laila's eyes bounced between her father and me. She licked her lips before saying nervously, "A DVM and a PhD take the same amount of time in school as an MD. Plus, Josie completed a residency, which is another three years on top of that."

I appreciated Laila's efforts, but the comment had come off as weak and defensive. The fact that she'd spoken up for me only seemed to make her dad dig his heels in.

"Doctors heal people," he asserted. "She does not."

I fought the nasty retort that was sitting on the tip of my tongue, trying to convince myself that sparring with him wouldn't accomplish anything.

There was a beat of awkward silence, and Laila shifted uncomfortably. "Well, Josie is a special kind of doctor. She actually cuts up animals to figure out why they died. Like an animal coroner. It's a very prestigious position."

As soon as the words were out of her mouth, I felt my stomach clench. My gaze bounced between her parents, gauging their reactions.

Ishani's eyes widened with horror. "I can't believe your husband allows you to do that," she said, slightly aghast.

Her words blew on the red-hot ember of my anger. My back stiffened, and I felt ready to throw down. It took everything in me to keep my mouth shut.

The arrival of their first bag on the luggage belt saved me.

As I moved to help, Rakesh body-blocked me, grabbing the handle of the bag. He pulled it off the belt and kept his back turned to me.

Definitely Gerald-bad, I thought, heart sinking.

Ishani turned to me and asked, "Do you live in Stillwater?"

"Yes, ma'am," I answered, feeling a tad more comfortable with this type of idle chit-chat. "I live about ten minutes from campus."

"Josie owns her own home," Laila added proudly.

"Your husband must have an excellent job," Ishani said with a slight nod of approval.

I felt a flash of panic. Unsure of how to respond, I went with the truth. "I bought it myself. I'm not married."

Out of the corner of my eye, I saw Laila cringe, and my chest tightened.

Ishani's eyebrows crinkled with confusion. "You should be married. How old are you?"

"Um," I stumbled, tilting on the precipice of a slippery slope.

"But you will be too old to have children soon, no?" Ishani pressed.

She wasn't wrong. Maybe I had another five years or so, and then I'd be pushing the envelope when it came to having a healthy baby. But

I liked my life right now, and I wasn't going to have a kid just because I was getting older.

I cleared my throat for the umpteenth time, unsure how to respond. Laila shook her head almost imperceptibly, and I bit my lip.

"Laila is also getting old," Ishani continued, eyes passing up and down over her daughter. "You will help us, yes?" She looked at me hopefully and leaned forward. "Laila needs to find a husband. She needs to have children before she is unable to."

"Uh," was all I could force out.

"You will help," she added with a nod and leaned back.

I panicked, unsure of how to answer. The last thing I wanted to do was dig myself any deeper.

"I'm here to help Laila find her true path," I answered noncommittally.

Thinking I'd acquiesced, Ishani smiled and looked over to Rakesh as he pulled a second bag of luggage off the belt.

The suitcases were ginormous, and I had a sinking feeling that her folks had planned on staying longer than a few weeks. Given the outside temps, I hoped those overstuffed bags meant they'd packed layers of coats, hats, scarves, and gloves rather than several months of clothing. I wasn't sure Laila could handle them in her house for that long.

I risked another glance at Laila.

See? she mouthed.

I chewed at my cheek, trying to puzzle through the best way to help her. When her parents had first announced their visit, I'd sped over to her house, several pints of therapeutic ice cream in hand. Over tearful spoonfuls, she'd explained the situation; she was happy flying solo and didn't want to get married now. Maybe not ever. She also confided in me that, with absolute certainty, she did *not* want children. I think her exact words were, "Not in a million years."

She just hadn't been able to tell her parents that. She'd already had to dodge a couple of arranged marriages. Thinking she was just being picky, her parents had decided to come here to bully her into finding a husband. And according to Laila, they weren't going to leave until she was engaged.

Her dad is gonna eat her alive.

Goosebumps trickled across my arms at the thought.

I caught Laila's eye again, and her eyebrows crinkled. I gave her a soft smile of support, trying to send her strength through the ether. The smile she sent back was resigned.

She'd said I didn't have to stick around this evening, and maybe I didn't need to. If her parents were as exhausted as they looked, they'd probably take showers and go right to bed. I still didn't like the idea of leaving her alone with them. I'd seen Laila stand up to the biggest of assholes. But with her folks, she was so damn vulnerable; they were her kryptonite.

I needed to be strong for Laila like she'd always been strong for me. Come hell or high water, no one was going to force my friend into marriage and motherhood.

With her parents' backs turned, I flashed Laila a mischievous grin and gave her a wink. This time, the edge of her smile seemed to be genuine.

CHAPTER
TWO

The drive home from the airport had been littered with conversational landmines, and I had come out the other end licking my wounds. I couldn't help but feel like I'd made things worse.

When we arrived at Laila's place, I practically jumped out of the car, eager to get away from the oppressive cloud of judgment enveloping her folks. Laila wasn't too far behind me.

Out of habit, I moved to the back of the Subaru, opening the hatchback to unload the luggage. Rakesh circled around to the rear of the car, glaring at me.

Our eyes locked in challenge, and the theme song of *The Good, the Bad, and the Ugly* whistled through my head. I wanted to stare him down and dare him to pull the suitcase out of my cold, dead hands. After a beat, I realized how petty—and stupid—the whole thing was. I stepped back, trying not to make any waves.

Pick your battles, Aunty's voice whispered in my head.

Even if Rakesh was turning out to be a misogynistic shitass, goading him wouldn't help. I'd learned that lesson a few times over with Gerald.

Trying to brush the whole thing off, I shrugged in what I hoped was a "whatever, loser" kind of way and followed Ishani into Laila's house with only my coat and purse in tow.

There was a hush as Ishani began inspecting every inch of Laila's home. The only sound was the thump of luggage as Rakesh brought each suitcase into the house.

Laila looked like she'd been run over by a train.

I caught her eye. *You okay?* I mouthed.

She frowned but didn't reply.

Her mom returned from her inspection of the front rooms and stared at me expectantly, hands folded in front of her.

I plastered on a fake smile. "Well, I guess I should leave you to it," I said to no one in particular.

There was an awkward silence as Ishani continued staring and Rakesh completely ignored me.

Laila cleared her throat. "I'll walk you out."

"It was nice meeting you both," I said over my shoulder, not meaning a single damn word of it.

Laila followed me to my car, shivering without her coat. Her hands were stuffed in her pockets, and her shoulders were hunched.

She looked up at me and smiled sadly. "Sorry about that."

"Oh, Laila." I folded her into a hug, which she returned weakly. She looked like she was going to cry.

"You sure you're going to be okay? I can totally hang until they go to bed," I offered.

"I'll be fine," she said softly and made a half-hearted shooing motion. "Go home. I know you're on duty tomorrow."

Every fiber of my being screamed to stay and support my friend. But if I didn't listen to her, I'd be just as bad as her parents.

"Okay. Call me if you need anything? Please?" I begged.

"I will. Thanks for coming, Josie. It would've been ten times worse without you. Believe it or not, that was them on their best behavior."

I felt a twinge of surprise. If that was their best behavior, what was it like with no-holds-barred? I couldn't even imagine.

Holding her shoulders, I said, "Remember: I got you. Call me any time, night or day."

She nodded slowly, not meeting my eye. With a weak wave, she headed back to the house, chewing at her lip.

I slipped into the shelter of my car, turned the heater on full blast, and studied her place. It looked cheery from the outside, but I couldn't shake the feeling that it was a facade. Her parents were like an ulcer deep in the belly of the beast. That bleeding hole needed to be surgically excised for Laila to be able to heal completely.

I hated the fact that I was leaving her. Even though she'd practically chased me out of her house, I couldn't shake the feeling that I was throwing my friend to the wolves.

With a sigh, I shifted my car into drive and headed back home.

***

I drove through town, navigating the eerie grayscale landscape back to my place. The clouds blocked the sun, casting a gloom over shuttered homes and naked trees. A layer of ice blanketed the sidewalks and dormant lawns. Thick icicles hung from power lines and eaves like teeth. Even my normally cheery house looked a bit lonely and sad as I turned onto my street.

I hit the driveway a little too fast and felt the tires lose traction on the ice. My whole body tensed, and I braced myself as the Pruis slid right up to the garage door, stopping mere inches from disaster. Heart racing from the near miss, I cut the engine, and the cold bite of the winter air pressed in.

"Stupid ice," I grumbled to myself.

Deep down, I knew that close shave was mostly on me. The morning had been rough, and I was distracted. Being around Laila's parents had stirred up a weird mix of emotions. I wasn't sure if I was thrown off by seeing one of the strongest, most badass professors frazzled by two old people or if it was the fact that Laila's dad reminded me so much of Gerald. I suspected it was a bit of both.

The air nipped my cheeks as I half slid up the pathway to my house. I fumbled the door open, and the artificial heat of my little home wrapped me in a hug.

A cuddle on the couch with Yersi will make it all better, I tried to convince myself. *And hot chocolate. I definitely need hot chocolate.*

Yersi gave me a slow blink from his nest on the couch as I took my coat and shoes off.

"Hey, bud," I said affectionately.

Merf, he replied in greeting. He gave his short black hair a little lick and tucked his nose back under his tail.

I set my purse on the entryway table, careful not to knock over the tower of books to go back to Aunty. I couldn't wait to get settled in with the newest read she'd checked out for me. But first, I needed to get some hot chocolate going pronto.

After a quick internal debate that was lost before it even began, I went with a full circle of Abuelita hot cocoa and added enough milk into the pot to make several cups. With the mix simmering on the stove, I went into the backyard to check on the chickens.

During the warmer months, I would buzz around the garden like Demeter, singing to the plants. It was usually a lovely space when the flowers were in bloom and trees full of leaves. In the winter, however, the plants were scraggly, and the yard felt desolate.

I sidestepped the threatening icicles hanging from the pergola and moved around to the side of the house. Before the storm, I'd rolled the Eglu there to give the chickens a bit of shelter from the icy rain and wind. I'd also piled several layers of hay on the ground and added a heat lamp. I was disappointed to find that the girls were still chilly. They clucked softly when they saw me but didn't bother coming out of the nesting box.

I broke the ice on their water and threw some food into their tray. If the temp dropped much further, I'd need to move their Eglu to the garage. I decided to pulse-check things again tomorrow and make a decision then.

Back inside, I curled my icy hands over the steam rising from the pot. The cinnamon smell of the hot cocoa filled the air. When the circle was fully dissolved, and before the thin lactoderm layer formed, I filled a giant mug with the light brown deliciousness and joined Yersi on the couch.

As soon as I spread the blanket across my legs, Yersi made two circles on my lap and settled down in a donut, purring. I gave him some scratches before cracking open my book.

It was hard to get back into the story despite how good it was. An antsy feeling was making me twitchy. I closed the book and blew on the hot cocoa, trying to settle my whirling thoughts.

I wanted to do something to help Laila, but I wasn't sure what else I could do at the moment. I just hoped her parents had gotten off her back and gone straight to bed. I fought the urge to head back over to her place to check in and make sure her dad was behaving himself.

I might randomly stop by tomorrow. See how they're treating her.

Even though I'd volunteered to cover necropsy duty for the two weeks over winter break, I could easily cut out early tomorrow. It was typically a slow time of year, and most of the staff was on leave.

Except for Gerald. You can't ever get away from that troll.

Trying to stay away from those dark thoughts, I blew at the steam over my cup of hot cocoa. The rich smell relaxed my shoulders. I wanted to take a sip so bad it hurt. But I also didn't want to burn the holy hell out of my mouth. Deciding to take the cautious route, I set the cup on the end table and opened my book.

Several chapters later, I was still feeling off. I headed back to the kitchen to top up my mug and was surprised to see how late it was. I briefly toyed with the idea of skipping dinner for another pot of hot cocoa. I was fretting over Laila, and in typical Josie fashion, I was trying to fill the idle space with sweets. Deciding that I'd exceeded my treat-therapy for the day, I begrudgingly reheated some baked beans, slathered some day-old cornbread in butter, and rounded out the meal with some sauteed okra.

Plate in hand, I briefly thought about being responsible and eating at the table. Though my couch and any dribbles of baked bean sauce would not be friends, I was feeling mopey and decided to throw caution to the wind. I figured I'd already paid my blop-price for the day with the ice cream, and I needed the cozy comfort of the couch.

I managed to keep the plate balanced as I pulled the blanket back over my legs. I poked at the food. Unable to shake the uneasiness, I put my half-eaten plate on the coffee table and texted Laila.

How are things?

She responded immediately.

My parents are mercifully sleeping.

I barked a laugh.

Did they give you any more crap?

Oh yeah. My dad is very angry.

Her not-answer made my stomach clench, and my worry clicked up a notch.

Want to call?

Sure. Give me a sec to hide so I don't wake them up.

Less than a minute later, my phone rang.

"Hey," I answered.

"It's been absolutely awful," she half-whispered, jumping right in.

I felt a surge of protectiveness. "Want me to come over?" I offered, trying to lower my hackles.

"No. I don't want to wake them up," she said.

"Want to come over here?"

"No. Thanks, though," she deflected again.

"What happened after I left?" I asked.

She sighed. "My mother pointed out every single, itty-bitty thing wrong with my house. My father gave me the silent treatment, which was almost worse. He has this way of judging me without saying anything."

Even though she couldn't see me, I shook my head sadly. "Dang," I sympathized. "I don't know. I guess I thought since they hadn't seen you in forever that they'd be a bit nicer."

I didn't have much of a family, but I knew that no matter what I'd done, Aunty would've bundled me into a hug and fed me until I burst if she hadn't seen me in five years. The situation with Laila's folks felt more like a storyline from *Game of Thrones*.

"It'll be like this until I'm married," Laila huffed. "Actually, I take that back. It'll be like this until I'm married *and* have kids. Then, they'll torture my children with their expectations."

"Did they bring up marriage again after I left?" I asked.

I could practically hear Laila's eyes roll.

"Oh, you bet they did—well, my mother did, at least." She was still whispering, but it was loud and agitated. "You'd barely left before she had her phone out to show me potential husbands."

I snorted.

"Yeah, I know," she replied. "When she was done with that, she went around the house, giving me a verbal list of things to do to prepare for children. Pointing out the ways that I would need to improve the place to be a good wife and mother."

"Geez," I murmured.

"That's not even the worst of it," she said dejectedly. "Get this. She then starts nagging me about how I need to do all of these things now so that I can even catch a husband. To show how I can be a good wife and a good mother."

I was speechless.

Yersi must've sensed the drama because he moved onto my lap and started making biscuits. Petting his soft black fur and hearing the rattling of his throaty purr lowered my blood pressure infinitesimally.

"Then, like the cherry on top, my mother said my husband would have to buy a new house anyway because mine wasn't good enough for her grandchildren," she added.

"Dude. Laila. What the hell?" I said, unable to keep the dismay from my hushed voice.

"I know, right?" Her volume had dropped again, and now she sounded defeated. "That's what I've been saying. It's going to be terrible." After a long, resigned sigh, she continued, "I'm constantly tiptoeing around them, just waiting for something really awful to happen. It's like a bear trap, hidden beneath the leaves, until—surprise!—it snaps closed on my ankle, crushing it."

My eyebrows furrowed. It wasn't like Laila to drop a metaphor like that, especially one so graphic. The thread of worry started to grow, and my thoughts raced.

"You don't want to get married, right?" I asked.

It was a rhetorical question, and her responding silence came off as slightly incredulous.

"And you don't want your parents pressuring you into it either, right?" I pressed.

"Absolutely not," she replied firmly.

"But you can't tell them to just go away," I continued, again stating the obvious.

"Uh. That's a hard no." There was a faint laugh in her response.

"So, we hold strong," I said. "Maintain the front. Don't concede any ground. You're the smartest person I know. We just gotta figure out the best way to convince your folks that there's nothing they can do to change your mind. That way, they just pack up and leave."

She responded with a doubtful *hmm*.

"You know your folks better than I do. But I think we can figure this out. I *know* we can figure this out. And, once we send them packing, we'll throw the best ice-cream-scary-movie-game party ever. You owe me. We have to watch *They Live*. Remember?"

Her responding chuckle was all I needed.

"Go get some sleep," I said, not unkindly. "Maybe you can make an excuse to go to work tomorrow before they wake up. If not, call me, and I'll show up with coffee and donuts and talk about the weather to keep them off your back."

She replied with another laugh, this one stronger. "You know I can't turn down a maple bar."

Though I'd gotten her to laugh and quip, I knew in my heart that she still wasn't in a good place. The family pressure was just too much.

Knowing I wouldn't be able to convince her to let me swing by in the morning, I tried another tack. "I know the roads are still awful, but want to grab lunch tomorrow?"

"Yes, please," she said, sounding relieved. "It'll give me something to look forward to."

"Where do you want to go?" I asked.

"Red Rock?" she proposed.

"Sounds good," I replied. "I'm on duty, but it should be slow. Noon work?"

"Sure. Sounds good."

After plans were made, we said our goodbyes. I sent her a quick text.

> Keep your chin up! You got this.

I added a gif of Wonder Woman deflecting bullets with her wristbands.

She added a laughing tag.

> More like...

Then, she sent me a gif of Ripley holding that blowtorch gun-thingy she used on aliens.

> Hell yeah!

With that, I felt a bit better leaving Laila overnight with her parents.

CHAPTER
THREE

On Monday morning, I was feeling bright-eyed and bushy-tailed, ready to face the world. Necropsy duty was going to be light this week, and I was looking forward to hanging out with the crew during the downtime.

First things first. I grabbed my phone to check in on Laila.

Yersi let out a dismayed *merf* when he realized that I wouldn't be immediately popping open a can of cat food for him. He huffed at the bedroom door, tail twitching, and let out a plaintive yowl. Despite several thousand years of evolution to the contrary, I did my best to ignore his baby-like cries and texted Laila.

> How are things?

She must've had her phone handy because the ellipses started bobbing before my phone could lock.

> My mother was awake when I got up. She started in on me before I even had a chance to have my coffee.

She added a sobbing face emoji.

I wasn't sure if that was a sarcastic "this sucks" emoji bemoaning the fact that an ass-chewing had come before caffeine or if she was really crying. Either way, I knew she needed some cheering up, so I texted back.

> Doesn't she know better than to get between someone and their coffee?

I added a gif of Stephen Colbert holding his hand out with the caption, "Give it to me now." To my relief, she responded with a laughing tag.

> I'm going to work as soon as possible.

I pursed my lips, thinking. Something was definitely up if she was getting out of dodge before the sun was even out.

> Did you at least get your coffee? Anything I can do to help?

> Yes. I'm currently hiding in my room finishing my third cup. I think I'll survive...maybe...

Again, I wasn't sure if there was a hidden meaning behind her response. Despite her playfulness, I couldn't help but read an edge of panic into her texts.

> K. Call me if you need anything. See you at lunch.

She sent a thumbs up.

To Yersi's immense relief, I put my phone away and finally fed him. He replied with a half-meow around a mouthful of food that was both relieved and judgy. With my main man satiated, I buzzed around the kitchen, getting ready for work. I made a quick spinach and mushroom omelet as the kettle warmed up, humming to myself.

After enjoying my meal, I slipped into a pair of jeans and a warm sweater. I quickly scraped my hair back in a ponytail and skipped any jewelry. With a quick scratch for Yersi, I headed out the door, feeling confident and ready to face whatever fate decided to drop in my lap. Even with the cold kissing my cheeks, my coat kept me warm, and I felt like nothing could dampen my good mood.

About ten minutes later, I pulled into work, bass stretching the Prius' speakers as far as the little buggers could go without scratching. Vibing to the song, I left it to play to the end with the engine turned off. Within seconds, the cold started to seep through the closed windows, but the chill didn't phase me. This was my power song, and I was going to blast it at full volume, even if I froze to death.

After the last note, I took an empowered breath. The next two weeks were going to be super easy. The students were gone, half the lab was on vacation, and dead bodies didn't often roll in this time of year.

Plus, the lab is finally starting to feel right *again*, I reassured myself.

A few months ago, some valuable items had gone missing from the lab, turning everything on its head. All the political infighting that typically stayed below the surface had exploded everywhere. Things still weren't back to normal, but they were getting there. People were now able to muster the typical "Oklahoma-polite" and be half-decent to each other. It also helped that most of the problem children were on vacation this week.

Not Gerald. That troll never takes time off.

I shook off the thought. I was feeling pumped, and damned if Gerald was going to take that away from me. Collecting my purse, I stepped out of my car, humming the song and hitting the key fob to lock the doors.

As if the simple act of thinking his name had been a demon-summoning spell, Gerald popped into my peripheral vision about twenty feet away. He was making his way across the parking lot and up the few steps into the lab.

Dang it, Kip Dynamite's nasally voice whined in my head. The last thing I wanted was a run-in with the douchebag this morning.

As if alerted to the scent of prey on the wind, he turned to face me. He paused his climb up the stairs, eyes locked on target.

Aaaand he saw me. Great.

Resigned to my fate, I decided to put on a strong front. Turning to fully face him across the parking lot, I hoisted my purse over my shoulder, straightened my back, and put on my best fuck-off face.

I must've successfully channeled my inner Deebo because Gerald's face grew clouded and hurt. He shifted his gaze away and hunched his shoulders. Taking the steps two at a time, he sped up the stairs and through the front doors.

My initial shock at his speedy retreat was slowly replaced by a novel and somewhat confusing emotion: guilt. My normal feelings toward Gerald were a soupy mess of anger, frustration, and disgust with a dash of fear. The way he treated people made it difficult to feel any other way.

He didn't pound on the roof of your car today, and he totally could have, the self-flagellating part of me whispered. *And you were still mean to him.*

I frowned. All the crap with the tiger had completely shifted the playing field. Since that hot mess, Gerald's behavior had started to change for the better. Granted, it was at a glacial pace and somewhat cringe-worthy, but still, I could tell he was trying. And thus, my feelings of guilt for kicking the guy in the preverbal dick. It didn't do any good to punish a puppy for piddling *near* the pee pad, even if he still missed it.

He hasn't called you Pocahontas in forever, either, the voice continued.

I tried to shake off the inner monologue. It wasn't helping, and I was starting to feel gross that the little voice inside of me was actually defending him.

Gerald has done some seriously evil shit, I reminded myself.

There was no coming back from some of that. It would take a lot more than him cutting it out with the racial slurs and not pounding on my car to make up for all of the crappy things he'd done to people in the lab. I'd stood up for him with the tiger mess because it was the right thing to do, not because he was a good person.

I slowly crossed the parking lot and headed inside, hoping to put enough space between Gerald and me so that I wouldn't run into him in the hallway. The artificial warmth hit me as soon as I crossed the threshold, and I pulled off my winter coat, hanging it over my arm.

Lost in turbulent thoughts, it took me a moment to realize Zoe's office was open and her light was on. Surprised, I backtracked to peek in.

"Morning," I said, eyebrows furrowed in confusion. "What're you doing in today? I thought you had this week off."

She looked up from her microscope. "Howdy, Josie." She waved me in.

I loved Zoe's office; it was the epitome of ordered chaos. Despite all of the flare, it was exceptionally tidy. A dust bunny didn't dare make an appearance. Splashes of color were everywhere, creating a cheery space. Between the pride flag, brightly painted pots overflowing with plants, and her anime bling, there was always something cool to admire.

I took a seat across from her, lumping my coat and purse in my lap. My eyes traced over her, taking stock.

She definitely did not look like her usual, immaculately groomed self. Her long blonde hair was tied up in a messy bun. Instead of her usual business-casual blouse and slacks, she sported a t-shirt and jeans.

She flashed a weak smile, but it didn't fully reach her blue eyes.

"I thought you were headed to Oregon," I probed.

"Yeah, we are," she said, flustered, and waved a hand at the stacks of slides on her desk. "I just have so much to do."

She'd been the pathologist on duty last week and had been slammed despite the impending storm. Instead of the usual one to three cases per day that would trickle into the lab, she'd received a whopping nineteen cases last week. Granted, some of them had been cut-and-dry, with a quick gross diagnosis. But several had required histology, and she'd be looking at the tissues from those cases under the microscope for a couple of weeks as she made her way through a mountain of glass slides.

She fiddled with some of the cardboard flats on her desk. "I'm triaging and trying to get the herd health stuff out before I go. The one-off cases can wait until after the holidays."

"Makes sense," I conceded.

At the diagnostic lab, we could get anything from cancer cases from the vet school to complex toxicology cases that were wiping out entire populations. The Shadowhawk case from the summer had fallen solidly in the latter category. I shuddered thinking about that case; they'd lost quite a few horses before we'd figured that one out. Cases like those couldn't wait through the holidays.

Though I admired her willingness to push the herd health stuff out before she dipped for the holidays, I still worried about her overworking.

She shuffled a flat of slides to the top of the stack. "I've got what I think is a Johne's case. That one should be pretty easy. I've got a neuro goat. That one's gonna suck. And a dog that was found dead at a boarding facility."

She flipped a few of the cardboard flats open to check the slides inside. "Oh, yeah, and the rabbits."

"Rabbits?" I asked, curious. We didn't get rabbits very often. The cost of a single necropsy was typically more than buying several new animals, and it just wasn't worth the money to figure out why one died.

She looked up and waved a hand, frowning. "Outbreak of diarrhea in some meat rabbits. I'm sure it'll be coccidia or something. But I had six of the little buggers. So, I gotta sift through everything."

"The parasitology isn't back yet?" I asked.

"It's back. It was negative," she said dispiritedly.

"Bummer," I empathized.

A negative fecal didn't mean squat, though. Rabbits could be loaded with parasites, and the fecal tests could still be negative. The "bummer" part was that Zoe was going to have to read all of those slides to get a diagnosis. And six rabbits meant a heck of a lot of slides.

After picking the relevant flats, Zoe set a bundle of them to the side. That stack represented oodles of work. If every slot was full, that was a hundred and twenty pieces of glass with who knows how many sections of tissue stuffed on them. I sympathized. I also didn't like the idea of chillaxing in my office while Zoe was frantically trying to plow through cases a few doors down.

"Anything I can do to help?" I offered. "It's gonna be slow this week. I'll have time."

She leaned back in her chair, rocking a bit. "Nah, I'm good. I think I should be able to get them done before we fly out on Wednesday."

Despite her attempt to reassure me, her eyebrows were still creased. I felt a thread of worry.

"Well, if you change your mind, I'm around. I'll probably die of boredom these two weeks. It's gonna be so slow I bet I can get Dustin to play cards with me," I teased.

Dustin was our one and only necropsy technician, and saying he disliked games would be an understatement. Though I was certain the lab would be a ghost town this week, there was a snowball's chance in hell that Dustin would ever be bored enough to play cards.

By cracking the joke, I'd hoped to get a laugh or even a smile from Zoe, but the comment seemed to bounce right off her. She kept her eyes locked on the flats of slides, a frown pulling at the edges of her lips. A small squeak repeated on an endless loop as she rocked restlessly in her chair.

"Sure you're okay?" I asked, unable to help myself.

Something else was going on, and it was more than the slides waiting on her desk. Since I'd been on Gerald's heels coming into the lab, I was pretty sure he hadn't had a chance to mess with her yet today. But there was serious bad blood between them, and it could be residual drama from a previous altercation.

I decided to hazard a guess. "Is it Gerald?"

She snorted softly. "Believe it or not, no. It's not Gerald this time." She shifted in her chair and sighed heavily. She looked down at her hands, playing with her manicured nails.

I waited as long as I could for her to fill in the blanks. When the silence started to feel awkward, I backpedaled a bit, worried I'd pushed it too far.

"We don't have to go into it if you don't want to," I said, holding up a hand in surrender.

My mind whirled with all of the things that could be going on. She and Jayden seemed to be in an amazing place. I didn't think anything was wrong with her dog, Nita. And even though everyone could get a little anxious about seeing their family over the holidays, I knew Zoe had a good relationship with Jayden's folks.

Maybe it is *something with work.*

Things had gotten pretty ugly between Zoe and Gerald when the tiger parts had gone missing. I hadn't heard anything about her getting reprimanded over it, but she did have her tenure review looming in the future. Maybe it was that. Or Fran. Our boss had a tendency to pick on Zoe, too.

"I'm here if you need me," I said, unsure of the best way to support her. I pulled my purse over my shoulder and moved to leave her office.

She rubbed her forehead and sighed heavily. "Sorry, Josie. I'm just not ready to talk about it yet." Her expression begged for forgiveness.

My face softened with concern, but I decided to give her the space she needed. "It's all good. I'm right there if you want to talk." I pointed in the direction of my office.

She nodded, avoiding eye contact and fighting tears.

I rose and smiled softly. "Hug to start your morning?"

She looked up at me, nodded again, and rose to fold me into a big hug.

"Will you be sticking around for the whole day?" I asked.

She shrugged. "Maybe. Jayden packed me lunch, just in case. But I still have to clean the house for Nita's pet sitter. We'll see how far I get."

"Again, let me know if you need me to finish any cases for you," I said. "I'm happy to help. It'll be no sweat."

She tossed me an appreciative smile that still looked sad around the edges. With a supportive wave, I left her office, the niggling thread of worry following me.

***

I thought about diving straight into emails, but the short conversation with Zoe had dampened my mood.

Instead, I dropped my purse next to my desk, hung my winter coat over the back of my chair, and made my way to Dustin's little cubby of an office next to the necropsy floor. Dustin was the best necropsy technician I'd ever had the pleasure of working with and was also an all-around amazing dude. I figured a quick chat with him would get my mental train back on the happy tracks.

I found him perched at his desk, nursing a steaming cup of coffee. His tall, wiry frame was folded into his well-loved chair, and a necropsy supply catalog was splayed open in front of him. With a quick knock on the door frame, I made my way in.

He looked up, and his mustache and bushy beard tilted up with a big smile. "Mornin', Doc," he said in a thick Oklahoman accent.

"Morning, Dustin." I grinned back.

I took the only other chair in his tiny office and asked, "Anything come in?"

He shook his head. "No, ma'am."

Though I knew it was going to be mellow this week, it was always a treat to come in Monday morning to find an empty cooler and no dead bodies.

As if reading my thoughts, he mused, "Should be nice 'n slow. Not expectin' much to come in."

"Yeah." I nodded. "It's always dead this time of year. That's why I jump to cover these two weeks."

He huffed a laugh. "Yes, ma'am."

Our conversation shifted to the storm, the rising electrical costs, and what we had planned for the holidays. I was even able to get him to bark a couple of loud belly laughs.

It was good to see him smiling and laughing again. When the tiger parts had been stolen back in September, it had been a rough go. Some people in the lab had painted Dustin the villain, calling him a thief, and Gerald had led the charge. The whole thing had really shaken him. Every once in a while, I'd see a thread of hurt and get a peek at the scar that would be with him forever.

Lately, he smiled more than he frowned, and I took that as a win.

After a bit, I said, "Welp, I better go pretend to do some work. Let me know if anything comes in."

He tossed me a friendly salute. "Will do."

As I left his office, I said cheekily over my shoulder, "Don't be a stranger. You know you can still come by and say hi even if we don't have any bodies coming in. Maybe even play a game of kings-in-the-corner."

He barked another laugh before turning back to his catalog.

CHAPTER

FOUR

As Dustin had prophesied, Monday morning was slow when it came to all things dead.

I spent the first part of the morning plowing through the revisions of an article I'd submitted. It was publish or perish in my world, and I had to keep popping out journal articles and growing my *curriculum vitae* or else I'd forever be in the role of assistant professor.

It was agony.

The peer-review process had a predictable trifecta. Two reviewers would say they loved the article and have minor changes, if any at all. But there was always that third reviewer. Anyone who's ever published scientific articles would know exactly who I was talking about: that one person who wailed and gnashed their teeth about how god-awful the paper was. This would usually be accompanied by erroneous corrections of scientific facts, grammar, and punctuation. Typically, it was someone straight out of their residency or PhD, thrilled to be asked to critique another person's work but often coming from a position of knowing fuck-all.

I turned the music up and snacked on some dried apple slices, trying to get into the groove. Even then, it was difficult. I absolutely hated revising research papers. It was my least favorite part of my job, and I couldn't help but feel like bits of my soul were being sucked away.

I continued reading through the reviewers' comments. The sound of Flo Rida's "My House" thrummed in my earbuds. I snarfed down two more apple slices, and the cinnamon flavor lowered my blood pressure a tad.

Thankfully, the third bugger hadn't been as critical of this manuscript as usual, but it was still annoying. I'd have to answer every single comment, even if it was to tell them I wasn't going to make the changes. It wasn't my first rodeo, and I knew exactly how much I could push back without having the paper rejected. I ate three more apple slices to try to soothe my soul.

When my desktop phone rang, I almost didn't hear it over the music. Startled, I yanked my earbuds out and picked up the phone.

"Dr. Harjo," I answered.

"Hello, Dr. Harjo," Anna began.

"Hey, Anna. What's up?" I replied, a bit too eager to get away from responding to reviewer comments.

"I've got an owner up front who brought a pig in. Wanna interview them?" she asked.

My heart sank slightly. Pigs were not my forte. But cutting up a dead pig was dramatically more pleasant than explaining to the reviewer why "defuse" was not how one spelled "diffuse."

"Sure," I answered, relieved to get away from corrections. "I'll be there in just a sec. Thanks."

"You're welcome," she replied neutrally.

We said quick goodbyes before hanging up.

A pig, I whined to myself.

I didn't know much about pigs, and I already felt out of my element simply interviewing the submitter. Sure, I'd had to learn about them during my residency, but after the board exam, all those gagillion factoids had been flushed. I could count on one hand how many times I'd done a pig necropsy since then, and I'd been working at the lab for six years. It wasn't like I was in Iowa, where they lived and breathed pigs.

An audible sigh escaped. Feeling fidgety, I grabbed a pen off my desk and twirled it at my side as I made my way to the little interview room off the receiving department. Hopefully, it would be easy: a nice pneumonia or something. It was certainly the time of year for respiratory diseases.

The receiving area had a separate entrance for customers that led to a short vestibule. To the right of the door, there was a large, square opening in the wall. Anna sat on the other side, facing the vestibule. During open hours, this was where customers would fill out their paperwork and drop off their samples.

Opposite the receiving desk was a large glass window that looked out onto the necropsy floor. It was there that I found a woman looking out, arms crossed over her chest. A deep frown tugged at her mouth.

It was quiet as a graveyard out on the floor, and I wondered what had captured her attention. I tossed Anna a questioning look.

She shrugged. Normally, Anna would ask the submitter to have a seat in the interview room. I could only assume the woman had declined.

I took the submittal form for the case and scanned it. Rachel Hoskins was listed as the owner, and the pig was from Rising Sun Farms in Watonga. This person had driven almost two hours in sketchy weather conditions to bring the dead body in.

My gut clenched. Most people wouldn't make that drive unless it was something serious.

Just suck it up and get it over with.

I approached the woman. "Mrs. Hoskins?" I hazarded.

The woman turned to me, and her frown deepened.

"Ms.," she corrected me. "I ain't owned by no man. That 'r' stuffed in that M-R-S is an 'r' of ownership. Don't be calling me no 'Mrs.' if you please."

My eyes shot up from the form to meet hers. I'd never been greeted that way and was a bit gobsmacked.

"Apologies," I stammered. I glanced at her left hand, wondering if I'd made one too many assumptions.

She caught the look. "Yes, I'm married," she said curtly.

"Oh," was all I could squeak out. I'd inadvertently perpetuated the same societal expectations that irked me so much, and I was mortified.

My cheeks flushed. I'd had interviews veer onto a lot of tangents before. But I'd never had it go this direction.

She considered me. "Men don't change their titles when they get married. Women shouldn't have to either," she added as a way of explanation.

"Huh." I tilted my head, respect building for the gruff woman. "I never thought about it like that."

She gave a slight nod.

I reached out my hand and tried again. "*Ms.* Hoskins, I'm Dr. Josie Harjo."

She clasped mine with a solid, calloused grip, and we shook.

"If you have a couple of minutes, I'd like to ask you a few questions," I said.

"Sure," she answered curtly.

I held my hand out to the small, depressing room that squatted to the side of the receiving department. "This way."

She took the lead, and I followed her in.

The room was tiny and had just enough space for a single table and a few chairs. The buzzing fluorescent lights drained the life out of everything. The walls were covered in scuffed, bland, off-white paint typical of government buildings. The only decoration in the room was a wall hanger with limp cremation and grief counseling pamphlets. They'd been there since before I'd started and were looking pretty sad.

I studied Rachel as she took one of the chairs. She was built like Brienne of Tarth: tall and broad-shouldered. I figured she could hand me my ass in about two seconds.

She wore a thick, dark brown Carhart jacket and jeans with low-heeled cowboy boots pulled up over the cuffs. Her skin was light brown, and her straight, black hair was pulled into a tight braid.

She crossed her arms and stared at me, expectantly.

I sat opposite her, twirling my pen as I read through the submittal form again. The provided information was fairly sparse. Other than the usual name-and-address details, all that was written was "dead piglet."

The lack of information wasn't surprising. Threadbare histories were pretty typical regardless of whether it was provided by an owner, a veterinary clinic, or a government employee. That was why interviews like this one were so important.

Part of my job as a pathologist was to tease the critical bits out of a submitter during an interview. Last summer, the Shadowhawk situation had pivoted quickly when I'd learned that they'd had more horses die than the one they'd brought in. That little nugget of info had been a game-changer in how I approached the case.

I kicked myself for thinking about the Shadowhawk case. The last thing I needed was a cluster-fuck like that over the holidays. Waving away the bad juju, I tried to focus on gathering more intel. I looked up at Ms. Hoskins, who was still watching me intently.

Normally, this was when I'd offer condolences and, if necessary, provide a bit of grief counseling. I could tell by the set of her jaw and no-nonsense attitude that an "I'm sorry for your loss" was not required.

I decided to cut to the chase. "Can you tell me a bit more about the piglet? How old was it?"

"It's a fetus," she replied curtly. "'Bout three months along."

"So, the sow aborted?" I tried to clarify.

Though "abortion" was a trigger word no matter what side of the political fence someone sat on, it was a commonly used term for natural fetal death in animals. Though I'd be cautious using the word in a restaurant in Stillwater, Oklahoma, I wasn't worried about using it with a pig farmer.

She didn't flinch and said, "Yes, ma'am." Anticipating my next question, she continued, "The sow ate her placenta and most of the piglets. I brought the only intact one." Her tone was matter-of-fact, and she seemed almost apologetic.

This woman knew her stuff, and I was impressed. She was also completely unphased by the brutality of natural behaviors.

"Thanks for checking for placenta," I said, disappointed that a critical piece of the puzzle was missing.

She grunted in reply.

"Any other issues in the herd?" I asked, leaving the question vague to see where it would take me.

She shook her head. "Nu-uh."

Well, that didn't work.

"Any recent abortions, stillbirths, or neonatal deaths with any of the other sows?" I asked.

An annoyed look crossed her face. "No."

"Bear with me here," I half-pleaded, sensing her frustration. "Just to confirm, the adults aren't exhibiting any signs of sickness, right? Like diarrhea, coughing, weight loss, anything like that?"

"I said there weren't nothin' else goin' on," she said brusquely, now looking downright pissed.

I cleared my throat uncomfortably as I tried to puzzle her out. With a start, I realized that she probably thought I was talking down to her. I wondered how much flack she got for being a female pig farmer and if that was part of what was driving the gruff exterior. She probably had to be tough to survive in that industry.

With the placenta comment, I was getting the impression she knew her way around animal husbandry. I wondered if maybe she thought I was questioning her ability in some way. If someone had done that to me, I'd be pretty pissed, too.

Needing to get on a better foot with her, I tried again, "Apologies. Most farmers wait until there's a trainwreck before they bring an animal in. You know how expensive testing can be. And many of them don't think to mention that the animals are coughing or something. It's great that you brought the piglet in with just the one sow aborting."

With my apology, her frown softened ever so slightly. We were still feeling each other out, but I thought she realized I wasn't judging her.

"Better safe than sorry," she said. "I know you ain't likely to find nothin', but it's worth a check."

Once again, she was spot-on. Most cases of fetal loss went undiagnosed. My job was to rule out anything infectious or toxic, the type of things that might affect the rest of the herd. It was refreshing working with a practical, proactive farmer.

Smiling, I said, "Agreed. We'll do an abortion panel to rule out the infectious stuff, but as you said, most times, everything comes up negative. Sometimes ruling stuff out is just as important as finding the actual cause."

She gave a slight nod.

"It sounds like you run a tight ship, but I'd like to ask a few more questions," I continued cautiously. I was walking a fine line. "Can you tell me a bit about the facilities, how many head you have, the feed, the water supply, things like that?"

I didn't think I'd ever use this information, especially with only one litter lost, but I wanted to do my due diligence.

She seemed to get what I was putting down and rattled off the information. "We have around fifteen hundred animals at any given time and use an all-in, all-out system. We have twenty temp-controlled buildings. 'Cept for the farrowin' barn and the nursery, we have 'bout one hundred pigs to a building. They're on county water. We mix our own rations dependin' on the stage. We got twelve employees doin' the regular feedin' and cleanin'. Chuck and me spend most our time in the farrowin' barn."

Despite the numbers she was rattling off, it was a relatively small business as far as pig farms went. I didn't know much about pig farming, but it *sounded* like she was running things well. I wouldn't be certain unless I got eyes on the facility.

I quickly nipped that line of thought in the bud.

This is going to be an easy case, I tried to tell myself, unable to ignore the tingle of dread. *I won't need to visit the farm. Why did I even* think *that?*

I figured the apprehension over the drama with Laila and her folks had me blowing everything else out of proportion. This was going to be a simple case. I'd go through the motions, collect the usual samples for infectious diseases, and move on. I was already dragging things out way too long.

I rounded the interview off with one last question. "What's included in your vaccination program?"

"The usual," she answered and rattled off a few vaccine brands.

I didn't know squat about pig vaccines; that information had been dumped long ago to make room for other random bits of knowledge I'd needed to pass boards. If she'd asked me the function of bradykinin, I could've aced that one. But pig vaccines? That was a big, fat nope.

I nodded as she listed them off and wrote the brand names down on the form; if it became necessary, I'd look up what diseases were covered later.

"Thank you. That's all I need, I think," I said.

I rested my pen down and stood to walk her out. "I'll get started right now and issue a report today. I'll collect samples for infectious disease testing. That'll take a bit longer, especially with the holiday. But you'll get the results as soon as they become available." I looked down at the form to catch the vet's name and added, "We'll make sure Dr. Hughes gets a copy of the results, too."

"Alrighty then," she said, all business-like, slapping her hands lightly on her legs before standing.

"If anything else comes up or you have any questions, just call the lab and ask for me: Dr. Harjo." I reached out my hand to shake.

She took it and gave a slight nod of thanks. With a grunt, she saw herself out of the room.

On her way out of the building, she paused in front of the window that looked onto the necropsy floor. The lights were now on, and the piglet was laid out on one of the small animal tables. Dustin was busy labeling sample collection containers, knowing exactly what I'd need once I got out there.

After taking in the scene, her eyebrows crinkled, and her frown deepened. With a huff, she fished her keys out of her pocket and headed out.

With that one look, a sliver of worry started to build.

CHAPTER
FIVE

Since the little piggy was just that, I figured I might as well get 'er done before meeting Laila for lunch. Between Dustin and me, a simple necropsy shouldn't take more than half an hour.

When I stepped out onto the necropsy floor, it felt like I was putting on a comfortable pair of shoes. Between the familiar, soft crooning of Hank Williams and the fresh scent of sanitizer in the foamy footbath, this was my happy place.

The necropsy floor was huge. The ceilings were high and laced with the tracks for the large animal hoist. The hydraulic large-animal table crouched near the far wall. To the left, there were three smaller, stainless steel tables for small animals. The piglet was lying stiffly on the nearest one, left-side-down.

I finished buttoning up my lab coat and stood opposite Dustin at the table. He'd already labeled all the containers and was laying out a scalpel, scissors, and rongeurs.

"Howdy, Doc," Dustin greeted me.

"So much for a quiet week." I nodded my chin to the piglet.

He snorted playfully. "This ain't nothin'. It'll be done before lunch, and then it's smooth sailin' the rest of the week."

I snapped on a pair of gloves. My retained knowledge of porcine medicine was limited, but the procedure for a fetal necropsy was more or less the same for any mammal, and I knew that like the back of my hand. I could practically do it with my eyes closed.

I flexed my hands in the gloves to get the rubbery fit just right and looked down at the piglet. The fetus was about ten inches long, slightly red-tinged, and lacked hair. It was otherwise in fairly good shape, nice and fresh. The carcass was also remarkably intact. After what Ms. Hoskins had said about the sow scarfing down the placenta and parts of the other piglets, I hadn't been sure what to expect. Having an entire piglet was a blessing, all things considered.

I picked the piglet up to check for external deformities, inspecting the outside of the body and the oral cavity. Thankfully, the fetus looked normal from the outside, with no evidence of a domed skull, twisted legs, or a cleft palate. It also wasn't swollen or puffy, so there was no evidence of anasarca. I wasn't expecting to find anything, but I always had to check.

"Fetuses are boring," I lamented, stating the obvious. Pathologists lived for cool lesions, and fetuses were often stingy in that regard. This necropsy would be all about sample collection and not much else. A total snooze.

"Want me to do it?" Dustin offered.

If I'd been in a rush or had other animals waiting for me, I'd totally take him up on the offer and just glance over everything as he worked. But things were slow, and a fetal necropsy was better than article revisions. *Anything* was better than article revisions.

"Meh, I got nothing better to do. Thank you, though," I answered. "Let's just knock this out together."

"Yes, ma'am," he said casually.

A companionable silence settled between us as Hank Williams continued on an endless loop, and I was soon lost in the rhythm of dissection.

The thoracic and abdominal cavities were open in less than five minutes, and I paused again to assess the carcass. The fetal tissues had the juicy, dark-red appearance typical of underdeveloped organs. Other than that, everything looked peachy keen.

I collected stomach contents with a needle and injected the fluid into a red-top tube for culture. Because fetuses swallowed amniotic fluid, we could sometimes pick up microorganisms in stomach contents that we might not be able to culture from the other tissues. I didn't expect anything in this little bugger, but it was all part of the procedure.

"Dr. Smith is in today," I said, making small talk. "She's trying to pound through a hefty stack of glass before she leaves for Portland. Seems like y'all were pretty busy last week."

He pursed his lips and nodded. "Almost twenty of 'em, one of which was a neuro goat. At least the rabies came back negative."

I *hmmed* in sympathy. I still had a nagging worry about Zoe and couldn't help but feel like there was more behind her stress than a crap-ton of cases to finalize.

"On the upside, looks like the universe cleaned out the chute for us," Dustin said. "Should be nice 'n slow this week."

I gestured down to the piglet and arched an eyebrow playfully. "Don't go tempting fate."

Dustin huffed a laugh. "It's a short week, and there's still ice on the ground. I'm bettin' this is our last case before Christmas."

"Oookay," I drawled, lifting both eyebrows in mock doubt.

I plunked a cube of liver into the Petri dish he held out for me and plopped another section in formalin. I did the same with the kidney.

"You going to be able to get outside at all this week?" I asked.

I figured Dustin must be a bit stir-crazy after two whole days trapped in the house. He loved being outside. If it wasn't hunting or fishing season, he'd be out on a hike or in a folding chair by the fire pit with Dolores and his dog. The terrible weather had been too rough for anything but hiding in a cave last weekend.

He shrugged noncommittally. "Gonna try."

I shifted my attention to the pluck, removing it in a small clump. I examined the tiny heart and opened the chambers, looking for any defects.

"Didn't ya pick up Laila's folks this weekend?" Dustin asked. "How'd that go?"

It was a casual small-talk question, but the answer caught in my throat. I didn't even know where to start.

Side-stepping the meat-and-potatoes part of the answer, I said, "The drive was a little sketch. Cars had spun off of Highway 35 and were sitting on the side of the road like dead flies. We made it there and back, but I was a bit nervous at some points along the way."

"You took the Prius?" he asked, eyes widening slightly.

"Hell no. We took Laila's car. It's a Subaru," I answered with a laugh.

"How'd it go with her folks and all?" he asked. Again, it was an innocent question, but I couldn't help feeling a bit pinned down.

"Um," I started.

I didn't want to air Laila's business. It felt gossipy talking about her, even though Dustin had only crossed paths with her once or twice. As I was noodling over how to summarize the experience, I finished up the pluck, collecting sections for the formalin bucket and ancillary testing.

I cleared my throat before settling on, "It was very awkward." As I disarticulated the head to get the brain out, I said, "Her mom is nice enough. But she is very judgmental. I wasn't even the target, but I still felt like I was disappointing her by osmosis. And her dad...."

I shook my head slightly and paused my sample collection.

"He's interesting," I continued. "He spent most of his time snapping at Laila in Hindi, so I didn't catch most of it. But based on how she responded, I'm pretty sure he was saying some nasty stuff. I felt bad leaving her alone with them."

Dustin grunted in sympathy.

I didn't know the details behind Dustin's upbringing. But whenever his dad came up, even peripherally, his eyes would cloud over, and he'd go someplace else. I figured the wolf he'd grown up with was about ten times worse than Laila's dad.

Using the pointed jaws of the metal rongeurs, I snipped through the fetal skull. "I'm gonna try to weasel my way over there as much as possible to check in on her," I said, trying to get past the subject.

He nodded. "You're doin' right by her."

I pulled the calvarium off and snipped away the dura with the scissors. Being that it was a fetus, the brain was super mushy, and it pooled in the base of the cranial vault.

"Does that cerebellum look normal to you?" I asked, tilting the opened skull toward him.

"As normal as a half-baked fetus' cerebellum can look, I guess," he answered, shrugging.

Some viruses could cause the cerebellum to be underdeveloped, including reportable diseases that would raise alarm bells. I wasn't expecting any cerebellar hypoplasia, but it felt good to stretch my brain and remember some of the things I'd had to learn for my board exam.

Because the brain was so mushy, I tipped the skull over the formalin bucket and carefully snipped away the remaining attachments. The brain plopped into the bucket like a cracked egg dropping into a pot of water. Even with fixation, it was going to be soft as butter and challenging to place neatly into a cassette for histology.

All told, the necropsy took about twenty minutes. As expected, I hadn't found anything. And even though I'd collected tissues for histology, I probably wouldn't find anything under the microscope either. The samples would be sent off to the various labs for infectious disease testing, and I'd be satisfied when everything came back squeaky clean. It was a fetus, after all.

Nice and easy.

I started cleaning the station, and Dustin headed over to the cooler to grab an offal bin. He rolled it out, the wheels rattling across the epoxied floor.

"This is going into the digester, right?" I asked, more out of curiosity than concern.

"Yes, ma'am," he answered.

The renderer had stopped picking up animals about a month ago. When an owner didn't want the body back or didn't want it cremated, we'd been forced to send the parts to the landfill. The whole thing was shady and made me super uncomfortable. I knew food scraps went to the landfill, and the bits and bobs from a necropsy weren't much different. But there was something about sending potentially infectious parts to the dump that made me squeamish. Thankfully, the digestor had been installed a few weeks ago.

"How's the digester working for you?" I asked.

He held his hand up, rocking it back and forth in a so-so gesture. "I ain't sure it's gonna be able to handle a lot all at once. I'm gonna have to part out the large animals. They gotta fit in somethin' yea big." He circled a gloved finger about an inch off the rim of the offal bin.

"Oh, that is all sorts of lame," I said with sympathy. Getting something like a horse or a bull into parts small enough to fit through the mouth of a fifty-gallon trash can was a Herculean feat.

"Yes, ma'am. It sure is," he said and sucked on his mustache. "I ain't sure about all of the fat, neither. Don't know why, but everythin's still pretty darn greasy despite all the acid."

I harrumphed.

After the professional installation, our boss, Fran, had just left Dustin to figure everything out on his own. For something that important, she should have sent him to another facility to learn how to use it and provided some training.

But it's Fran, I sighed to myself.

"Let me know if I can help at all," I offered.

"Thanks, Doc," he replied. "I figure it'll take some time to suss it all out."

With the table cleaned up and the smell of disinfectant in the air, I gave Dustin a wave. "Thanks for the help."

"Anytime, Doc." He brought his gloved hand less than an inch from his brow in a friendly salute.

"No more bodies this week. Promise?" I teased.

He grinned as the door swished closed behind me.

CHAPTER

SIX

Less than an hour later, the piglet was in my rearview mirror, and I was getting ready to face the icy cold to meet Laila for lunch.

Usually, I'd be joining the crew in the breakroom and supplementing my meal with one—or two, or five—of Carol's baked goods. Today, I needed to get my eyes on Laila and figure out how serious things were. I didn't like how her folks were bullying her, and I was just about ready to grab the brass knuckles and hightail it over there.

The drive to Red Rock was creepy. Low, gray clouds hung threateningly in the sky, and the normally busy roads were deserted. With all of the students gone for winter break, the little town of Stillwater had a very post-apocalyptic feel, and I was eager to get into the warmth of the restaurant.

I managed to avoid any black ice on the way over, and I had my choice of parking spaces in the empty lot. The tiny restaurant beckoned, a cheery neon "open" sign greeting me from the window.

I patted myself on the back for making it from the car to the building without falling on my ass or freezing to death. When I opened the door, a rush of warm air and the smell of fresh bread kissed my cheeks. I took a deep breath, feeling my shoulders relax.

A quick scan of the place confirmed that I was the only customer. Since it was a casual joint, I figured I'd place my order and grab a table to wait for Laila. My stomach grumbled in agreement.

The cashier greeted me with a friendly smile and took my order of tomato soup and grilled cheese. Grabbing my number and a hot tea, I wove to the far corner near the windows. I threw my coat over the back of the chair, took a seat, and cradled the steaming cup.

As unpredictable as our schedules were, it wasn't a huge deal when one of us arrived at a place five to ten minutes before the other. But I couldn't help but fidget while I waited, and when my order came before Laila did, I felt a prickle of unease.

The smell of buttery grilled cheese hit my nose, and my stomach grumbled again. I debated starting before everything got cold; grilled cheese could get a bit manky with time. But a knot of worry sat between me and sustenance. With my anxiety building, I decided to text her.

> You okay? Are we still on for lunch?

I waited a hot second for a reply, tapping the screen to keep my phone from locking. When I didn't receive one, I placed my phone on the table and bounced my leg. I wasn't used to worrying about Laila; she was normally the one who was dialed in. She was the one who was always there for me when things were rough.

Since her parents had called a couple of months ago to announce their visit, Laila had been distracted. In the days leading up to their arrival, she'd been a downright trainwreck. On Saturday, I'd finally had to have an intervention when I found her cleaning her grout with a toothbrush for the fifteenth time.

Just as I was about to call her, I saw her Subaru pull into the parking lot, and I relaxed slightly. I was happy she'd made it in one piece, but she still looked like shit, and I couldn't fully chase away the worry.

Hunched in her coat, beanie pulled tight over her hair, she hustled into the building. I caught her eye as she was wiping her feet and waved. Normally, her face would light up, and she'd grin in greeting. Today, a small smile barely broke through her harried expression. She made her way over, pulling the beanie off her hair, the static creating a frizzy halo.

"Sorry I'm late," she said, flustered. She took her coat off and threw it over the chair across from me.

We exchanged a quick hug.

"I was worried you'd hit some ice. I was about ready to send out a rescue team," I said with a smile, half teasing, trying to lighten the mood.

"You don't even know, Josie," she said ominously. "Go ahead and start. I'm going to order. I'll be right back."

With a swish, she whisked herself away to the counter to place her order.

My stomach grumbled for the millionth time, and I looked down at my meal. The cheese in my sandwich had started to congeal, and there was a thin film over my soup. I suddenly wasn't very hungry anymore.

Laila returned a few minutes later with her order number in hand and slumped into her seat with a huff. She looked terrible. Her eyes were sunken and cheeks hallowed. Deep wrinkles formed canyons between her eyebrows. Even her clothes dared to look a bit rumpled.

I raised my eyebrows. I wasn't sure if I should dive right in and ask how things were going or if she needed to talk about some fluff as a distraction.

"Weather sucks out there, doesn't it?" I started a bit lamely.

She snorted. "Pretty much. If my parents weren't in my house, I would've worked from home today. It's like the Ice Queen went on a bender out there. I'm surprised I didn't die on my way in."

There's my Laila.

A smile danced around the edges of my lips.

"Another storm is coming in on Wednesday." She shook her head. "If the roads close, I'm gonna lose it. I can't be trapped inside with them."

"You should come to my place right before," I offered, half-jesting. "Say I need help with something, and then—oops! Sorry! You're stuck at my place. You can shelter with me and Yersi."

She huffed a laugh. "If only."

"Was anyone else in the lab today?" I asked and then took a bite of my grilled cheese.

Yep, it's started to congeal.

I switched to my soup.

She shook her head. "All my grad students are off for the holidays. The weather probably kept everyone else at home. The building is empty. Kinda spooky but also lets me get a lot of stuff done. How about you?"

"Same here. Just a skeleton crew. But I like it that way. It's nice to get a break from some people."

"I feel you there," she said. "Bet you like not having to worry about being ambushed by Gerald."

"Oh, no. I still have to deal with that shitass. He never takes a day off," I snarked. "But some of the other folks are out, including the ones who gave Dustin so much grief. It's nice having space from them. Things are still a bit awkward with some of the techs, but it's getting better."

If I was honest, things were also getting better with Gerald. I just couldn't bring myself to say it.

"Any cool cases lately?" Laila asked. There was a heaviness to her voice, and I could tell she was trying to keep her mind off of other things.

"Zoe was on duty last week and got slammed. Storms have a tendency to push the sick ones over the edge. Anything that was gonna go already did on her watch," I said with a shrug. "I've only had one case so far, and it was super boring. Just a fetus. I expect it'll be slow the rest of the week."

As soon as the words were out of my mouth, I felt a tingle of apprehension, like I'd poked a sleeping bear.

Laila's food arrived, interrupting the line of conversation. She leaned back as the server placed the plate in front of her and took her number. With her hands in her lap, she stared down at her sandwich, and her throat bobbed.

"I'm not sure I can eat," she said glumly.

A wave of empathy washed over me. "That bad, huh?" I probed.

She responded with a slow nod. "Yeah, it's pretty bad."

"Want to talk about it?" I offered.

She sighed. "Sure. I should probably exorcize my demons so I don't go supernova with my parents."

She leaned forward, resting an elbow on the table and running her fingers across the creases on her forehead. "My mother was up at like two or three this morning, clanging around the house. When I went into the kitchen, she started telling me how a good woman should be up early to cook for her family and asked why I wasn't up already to take care of them. And the way she does it. She doesn't yell. She just says it matter-of-factly, and I can feel the disappointment radiating off her."

"And she got between you and your coffee," I added, lamely trying to keep things light. Seeing Laila's expression unchanged made me realize I'd rolled a critical fail. We were headed to a dark place, and it wasn't the time to joke.

"Yeah, and that," she replied flatly. She picked up half of her sandwich, looked like she was going to yack, and put it back down again. Shaking her head slowly, she continued, "My father's worse than my mother. He just glares at me, resentful and disappointed. He talks about me to my mother. Right in front of me. Saying how I've let the family down. How I'm not good enough. That kind of stuff."

"What a dick," I blurted before I could bite back the snark.

It was hard not to feel triggered. Gerald played games like that, and it was nine circles of messed-up. I didn't like the idea of *anyone* doing that to Laila. The momma-bear in me was starting to wake up, and she was angry. I had a burgeoning desire to jump in the ring with Pops and lay a beat-down.

Laila sighed heavily, shaking me out of my thoughts, and continued, "He says stuff like 'this is why she needs to marry' and 'talk to your daughter; she needs to be a good wife and have children.'" The corners of her mouth turned down. "Then, he started blaming my mother for me not being married. That it was her fault for putting ideas in my head. That I'm a disappointment because of her. That kinda stuff."

My lips folded into a frown, and I shook my head. I pulled my hands beneath the table so Laila couldn't see me clench my fists.

"Yeah. I know," she said, catching my response despite my best effort to hide it. "He always does that. My mother will also do it sometimes. Talk trash about me when I'm standing right there. Like when she's talking to my aunts or cousins or whatever."

"That's horrible," I murmured in sympathy.

"Yes, it is," she agreed. She finally picked up her sandwich and took a bite, chewing slowly before putting it back down.

I felt my hands relax a bit. Needing to do something with them, I scraped the last bit of soup out of my bowl in the silence, the tomatoey taste souring in my mouth.

After a bit, I asked, "Have they decided how long they're staying?"

"No," she replied. "But their visa is good for a hundred and eighty days."

"A hundred and eighty days?!" I blurted, incredulous. "No way they're staying for six months!"

"Clearly, you haven't spent enough time with my parents," she replied bitterly.

"Can you make them go stay in a hotel or something?" I said, still trying to wrap my brain around having house guests for six months.

She huffed a laugh. "I wish. But, no, that's not the way we do things."

Frowning, I asked, "So, what's the plan then? How can we get them to get off your back about this? How can we convince them that you don't need to get married and pop out fifteen babies?"

She shook her head. "No clue."

"How did you make that guy they tried to push on you last year go away? What was his name again?"

"Oh, God," she said, rolling her eyes dramatically. "Arjun."

"Yeah, that guy," I said, twirling my hand in a keep-going motion. "How did you make him go away?"

She sighed and picked at the edge of her sandwich. "I just kept looking for reasons why he wasn't good enough. But that totally backfired."

"How so?" I asked.

"At first, I'd thought I'd worn them down with pickiness and that they'd finally given up. But they just took that as a challenge to find someone who met all of the ridiculous criteria I had neatly laid out for them."

"So, you inherited that competitive shit from your parents?" I teased.

She laughed. It didn't quite reach her eyes, but I hadn't expected it to. "More like stubbornness," she replied.

"There has to be a way to make them stop," I mused and nibbled at the edge of my grilled cheese as I let the thought settle.

"Family is just.... It's different," she said and then took a small bite of her sandwich.

I knew what she was trying to say. At work, Laila had a charisma of twenty. She was confident but friendly and just had this way of navigating difficult personalities. Around her folks, all that family baggage weighed her down, squashing that bright light that was my best friend. It was killing me to see her this way.

I reached across the table and squeezed her hand. "I get it."

She looked up from her plate. The stress was etched in every wrinkle of the skin between her eyebrows and around the edges of her eyes.

"It's hard, Josie," she said, tears threatening. "I think they're going to break me, and it scares the hell out of me."

Straightening my back, I said, "I got you. There's no way I'm letting them force you to do a damn thing you don't want to do. Even if we have to Thelma-and-Louise that shit. We'll find a way to get them to back off and go home."

A smile twitched at the corner of her mouth, and for the first time since she'd gotten that dreaded phone call, I saw a glimmer of hope.

CHAPTER
SEVEN

Back at the lab, the building felt deserted. The hall lights blinked on as I navigated the corridors. The squeak of my shoes on the linoleum splashed against the low background hum of the ventilation and laboratory equipment.

The door to Zoe's office was open, and the lights were on. Peeking in, I found her still perched at her scope, back straight and eyes glued to the oculars. A half-eaten sandwich sat on her desk.

Stopping, I knocked on the door frame. "What're you still doin' here?"

She leaned back in her chair, looking exhausted. "I didn't get as far as I wanted to. I'll probably have to come back tomorrow." She flapped her hand dejectedly at the stack of cardboard flats next to her desk. "I still have the rabbits."

"The offer's still there," I said, leaning against the door frame. "I can totally take a couple of cases. Just let me know."

"Nah," she said, not unkindly. "I'll be okay. Thanks, anyway." After a beat, she added, "And you never know. You could get something this afternoon. Dustin said y'all had a pig this morning."

"Meh," I said, brushing it off. "It was a fetus. Super easy."

"Yeah, but a *pig*." She fake-gagged. "I've done like two pigs in my career. All I remember is the gestational length because 'three, three, and three' is just a tad hard to forget. And yet it's the most useless piece of information to remember *ever*."

I huffed a laugh. "Yeah, I'm just hoping everything comes back negative, and I don't find anything on histo. If there's a lesion, I'll be cracking open the books." After a beat, I added with a shrug, "It's a fetus, though. It'll be boring. I'm sure."

I felt a small ripple of gooseflesh and tried to shake it off.

"Yeah, probably," Zoe answered, sounding unconvinced. "Still. A *pig*." She shook her head.

Despite the idle chit-chat, Zoe's expression was tight with tension, and I was certain something else was hanging over her. Knowing she'd share when she was ready to, I let it slide.

Instead, I nodded my chin at the flats at her desk. "Last chance. Sure you don't want me to take some of those off your hands?"

"I'm good. Thanks, though," Zoe said with a tired smile.

"Well, I'll leave you to it," I said. "Don't stay too late. Promise?"

"Promise," she answered.

With a wave, I left her to her cases. I passed right by my office and down the hall to check in with Dustin. He was at his desk, leaning back in his chair, his legs extended and crossed at the ankles. To my surprise, he was scrolling on his phone.

Work had to slow if Dustin was on his phone. He never did that.

With a knock on the door frame, he looked up. "Howdy, Doc." He put his phone down but stayed reclined, hands clasped on his stomach. "What's up?"

"Nothing much," I answered, sitting across from him. "Assume nothing came in over lunch?"

"No, ma'am. All's quiet."

"Cool," I said, surprised by the thread of relief I felt. "I'm gonna go type up the report from this morning and then probably bug out early. Just text me if anything urgent comes in."

"Will do," he said with a slight nod. "Before you go, 'bout that piglet. I dropped off the samples this mornin'. Everyone in the microbiology lab is either on vacation or called out 'cause of the ice. Dr. Richter was in a tizzy. My guess is he'll plate the samples, but there's a chance he'll just toss them in the fridge for tomorrow."

I bit back a laugh. It was easy to imagine Gerald all a-fluster with his entire staff gone. Granted, the number of samples coming in was minimal this time of year, but he would begrudge every single one he had to process himself.

My heart went out to the microbiology technicians. Hell hath no fury like a Gerald scorned.

"Most of the PCR or serology techs are also out 'cause of the ice," he added.

"Damn," I said sympathetically. "I knew it felt quiet today. But I didn't realize how many people couldn't make it in."

He sucked his mustache. "Yup. Anyone livin' outside o' town is pretty much outta luck unless they gotta truck," he drawled.

Though the city of Stillwater didn't have the best winter-weather procedures, the crew had tossed enough sand on the roads that my little Prius could make the slow crawl into work from the south side of town. I couldn't imagine having to make that trek on the rural roads. If I'd lived just a tad further out, I probably would've had to stay home, too.

"When I swung by, Dr. Rodriguez and Beth were busy working on a ton 'o EVA samples for some horses that are supposed to ship out soon," he continued. "He asked if your case could wait. I figured that wouldn't be a problem since it's just the one."

He lifted an eyebrow at me to confirm.

I nodded. "Yeah. The EVAs are more important." There was a tight window for equine viral arteritis testing prior to interstate travel, and horse owners could get mighty antsy.

"Jess and Dan are out for the week on vacation," he continued. "Austin couldn't get outta his driveway this mornin'. Dr. Rodriguez thinks he'll be back tomorrow. He's hopin' to get your testing done in the next day or two if the incoming storm doesn't shut things down."

"Yeah, I heard another one is coming in this week," I mused.

"Yes, ma'am. Though, it sounds like it'll be snow and not ice. Still, it'll keep things nice and slow for us." He bent his legs under his chair and started rocking a bit. "But it also means that more'n half the lab'll be out."

"Maybe Fran'll close the lab for a day or two," I said.

He lifted an eyebrow, and his mustache tipped down in a frown.

His doubt wasn't misplaced. Fran had fled to some sunny island in the Caribbean for these two weeks. It was easy enough for a neglectful boss to insist that everyone risk life and limb to get to the lab in the middle of a snowstorm when said boss was sitting on the beach enjoying a Mai Tai.

"Well, what she doesn't know won't hurt her," I said. "If things get nasty, I'll talk to Sandy, Manuel, and Gerald about closing early."

His expression was skeptical, but he didn't say anything.

I knew Sandy and Manuel would go for it. Gerald was another matter. He had a work ethic that was borderline obsessive. I'd just have to wait and see how bad things got.

I stood and said, "Welp. I'm gonna get trucking on that report. Drive safe, and see you tomorrow."

He tossed me a salute and a smile as I headed out the door.

Back in my office, I typed the gross report on the piglet, fingers speeding across the keyboard. The whole kit and caboodle took me less than fifteen minutes; there just wasn't much to say. I padded the wording with the pig's signalment, weight, and length. In the comment section, I noted the lack of any fetal mummification or developmental deformities. Then, I listed the pending tests. It was a fairly blah report, and I knew the vet would be underwhelmed. I hoped they were used to working up abortion cases and knew that blah was par for the course.

I finalized the report, sending it through the ether to Rachel and her vet. Not thinking much of it, I didn't bother calling her to give her verbal results.

I should've known better.

***

No more bodies rolled in that afternoon, and I skipped out of work early, keeping my phone handy on the off chance that an urgent case came in.

I tried to enjoy the bit of winter sunshine that was peeking through the clouds. It was still cold, but enough of the sun's rays had hit the roads to chase away the sheets of ice that had peppered the surfaces.

When I pulled into the driveway, a gray fluff bounded from the porch and sped across the street. Yersi was stationed at the window, watching intently. When he noticed me exit the car, he leaped from the windowsill, and the muffled sound of his meows came from the other side of the front door.

As soon as I was inside, Yersi swirled around my legs, continuing his kitty monologue. He acted like sleeping all day in the warm house had been downright awful, and he'd waste away into nothing unless I fed him immediately.

"I know, I know," I said, smiling down at him. "Your life is just so hard."

He made a *merf* sound in agreement and trotted to the kitchen to sit by his food bowl. He waited for me expectantly, tail swishing.

I put my stuff down on the entryway table and went through the motions. If I didn't tend to his needs first, even if I was home an hour earlier than usual, he'd be underfoot until I fed him. He acted all tough with the neighbor's cat, but the only title he could boast was the Great Slayer of Canned Food.

While Yersi snarfed down his wet food, I pulled my coat on and braved the outdoor temps one last time to make sure the chickens were settled.

The backyard was glum. Because it sat in the shade most of the day, bits of remnant ice still coated the brown, leafless plants and trees. Some people thought winter landscapes were beautiful. In a sterile monochromatic way, maybe they were. I preferred the colorful chaos of a spring garden, with bees bobbing around and squirrels chirping from the trees.

Distracted, I failed to notice a patch of ice coating the patio, and I felt my weight shift awkwardly. I flailed and eventually managed to grab onto one of the pergola's posts, somehow saving myself from a face-plant. With my heart thudding and my breath puffing out in front of me, I got my feet back underneath me and cautiously stepped away from the malicious ice patch.

Unable to shake the feeling that my winter garden was out to get me, I hustled to the Eglu. The chickens clucked softly in greeting but stayed huddled near their heat lamp. I broke the ice on their water and nudged it closer to the lamp. I fed them extra, knowing they'd be burning a massive number of calories to stay warm. At the sight of the food, they hopped down excitedly to peck at the ground.

I pursed my lips, debating whether to move them indoors. Chickens tended to paint with their feces, so I wasn't too keen on bringing them into a room with four blank canvases unless I absolutely had to. Sure, there was a lot of blood and guts at my work, but the epoxied floors, hoses, and oodles of pleasant-smelling disinfectant made it less of an onerous task. Cleaning up chicken poop in my garage? Not so much.

I decided they'd be fine outside for tonight and said, "Stay warm, ladies."

The girls ignored me as they pecked and scratched at the ground, clucking softly to each other.

I headed back inside. Yersi was seated on a chair at the kitchen counter, taking a post-meal bath, swiping his black paw across his ear with closed eyes.

Time to feed myself.

My fridge was as barren as my yard, and the fresh options were limited. I opened the freezer, and the pint of mocha almond fudge sang to me.

Surely, I could eat ice cream for dinner. Right?

I stared at the container for a solid minute. The cold fog rolled out of the freezer and caused goosebumps to break out on my arms. I changed my mind. It was just too damn cold out to eat ice cream, if that was even possible. I closed the freezer door, feeling frustrated.

Eating dinner out of a can didn't sound appetizing, but I had some soup in the cabinet that would do. I grabbed some hearty chicken and rice, poured it into a bowl with a *glop*, and zapped it in the microwave. With the steaming bowl in hand, I settled down at the kitchen counter to eat. As I blew on a spoonful, I pulled out my phone to check in with everyone.

Aunty was the first on the list. I'd had to miss our standing brunch yesterday to join Laila, and I was missing her.

> Just checking in. How are things?

She replied back right away.

> Hey sweety! All's good here. Missed you yester-day.

> Missed you too. Did Tessa make it?

> No, she didn't come.

> She tried but her car kept sliding and she turned around.

I wasn't too surprised. Tessa's beater was only operational because of several layers of duct tape, a hope, and a prayer. Plus, I wasn't sure she even had enough cash to cover the gas for the two-hour drive to Ada and back.

> Bummer

> I'll check in with her. Maybe I can get her to come over for dinner sometime this week.

> She's coming Friday, right?

After Tessa had gotten into a serious legal entanglement back in September, we'd grown tight, and Aunty had practically adopted her. Tessa wasn't blood-kin, but she was part of our family, nonetheless. I'd been delighted when she'd taken us up on the offer to join us for the holiday.

> Yep, she's coming to my place at around 9. We'll drive together.

Aunty hearted my text.

> Drive safe. This next storm is supposed to be a nasty one.

> Will do.

> Stay warm! Love you

I texted her three hearts in a row.

After hearing that Tessa hadn't been able to get to Aunty's, I knew I needed to check in on her. Missing a brunch because she was busy with rotations was one thing. Missing brunch to sit alone at home was another. Depression always crouched on the periphery, its long nails scratching on the door to come in.

My thumbs sped across the phone screen as I texted Tessa.

> Thinking of you. How are things?

I'd eaten about half my bowl of soup before she texted back.

Hey! Things are good. Missed Sunday brunch tho.

She added a sad face emoji.

I'm sure Aunty will make up for it by feeding us twice as much on Friday.

She responded with a laughing emoji.

My heart warmed a little. I was looking forward to seeing Aunty and Tessa on Friday. I hadn't realized how much missing our weekly brunch together had messed with *my* mental health.

How's working with Charlie?

Dr. Anderson is great. I love working there. Thank you for connecting us.

Exxxcellent, Mr. Burns whispered in my head.

I smiled inwardly.

In her heart of hearts, Tessa wanted to do a residency in Behavior. But with all of her student loans, she needed to work in rural practice to get some of that debt forgiven and get her money situation in order. Charlie was a good egg, and the people working at Willow Park Mobile Vet were wonderful. Since Charlie was well past retirement age, I was hoping he'd pass the baton off to Tessa when she graduated. So far, my master plan seemed to be playing out just right.

I added a thumbs-up to her text.

> Stay warm. It's supposed to be a doozy later this week.

She thumbs-upped my text.

> Dr. Anderson said he'll probably close Thursday.

> I'm not sure if the lab will close. If it does you should come over. We can play games and have a pre-holiday party!

She hearted my text.

Feeling better that Tessa was in an okay spot, I finished up my soup and put my bowl in the dishwasher. I nestled into my favorite spot on the couch and pulled a blanket over my legs.

My phone stared at me from where I'd set it down on the coffee table.

I toyed with the idea of texting Laila. I wanted to be there for her, but I didn't want to be in her face either. It was a weird situation to navigate, and I didn't know how much was too much. Even though it was agony to do nothing, I decided to let it lie. She knew I was there if she needed me.

I realized what I *really* wanted was to call Armand and hear his soft, accented voice. But it was one or two in the morning over in Romania. *Sigh.*

He'd been gone about a month, and my heart was still ragged. I was counting down the days until he returned in January. Video calls weren't cutting it. I longed to hang out on the couch together and see his smile in person. I ached to smell his aftershave, run my fingers through his soft, curly hair, and have his arms around me.

Feeling a tug, I sent him a message. I knew he was likely asleep. But I was hoping he'd answer as soon as he woke up.

Miss you.

Any chance you can video call? 1 PM your time?

He was eight hours ahead of me, so 1:00 PM in Romania would be damn early for me in Oklahoma. But I wanted to catch him around his lunch. Plus, he was worth waking up that early for.

I added a kissy-face emoji.

I set my alarm for 4:45 AM, come what may. If he couldn't meet, I'd swallow my misery in frozen waffles with whipping cream and strawberry compote or something.

Yersi jumped in my lap and started to purr. With some chin scratches, his purr deepened, and he started drooling. A smile tickled across my lips, and my shoulders relaxed. I figured an hour or two of reading before bed with Yersi on my lap, and I'd be right as rain.

As much as I loved Armand—and yeah, I was sure it was love at that point—Yersi would always be my main man.

CHAPTER
EIGHT

My phone alarm jerked me awake in the pitch black of the early morning. Yersi's claws clamped into the meat of my back before he skittered out of the room.

I fumbled for my phone, squinting at the screen to hush the screaming banshee. A notification waited for me. Armand had responded and was available to connect this morning.

In fifteen minutes.

Heart thudding, I scrambled out of bed.

Yersi had disappeared into that place outside of time and space where all cats go when someone has scared the ever-loving crap out of them. I had about five minutes until his kitty-brain-fog cleared enough to realize I should be feeding him.

I quickly peed, changed into a video-call-worthy top, and combed my hair into a braid. By that time, Yersi had magically reappeared and taken up his station by his food bowl, plaintively meowing. I clicked the kettle on and plopped food in his dish. He replied with a *merf* of excitement, burying his face in his food.

With less than a minute to spare, I plunked a tea steeper into the steaming mug, flopped on the couch, and pulled my laptop on my lap. I rubbed my dry eyes, trying to wake up. Yersi hopped up next to me to take his post-meal bath, lulled into cute-kitty mode by postprandial hormones.

Even though the caffeine hadn't kicked in yet, I was buzzing with happiness at the idea of seeing Armand. It had been a couple of days since our last video call. Screen time wasn't as good as having him next to me, but it was better than nothing.

Sixteen more days, and he'll be here. In person.

I couldn't wait.

I took a cautious sip of tea just as a ringing chimed from my computer, and I clicked to answer.

A tightness had been building in my chest. I'd been working hard to keep my feelings stuffed in a box, tucked away in a dark corner as I busied myself with work. When Armand's face filled the screen, all I could see were his soft brown eyes, crinkled a bit around the edges with a smile, and all of those feelings bubbled up again.

Yeah, I've definitely fallen for him.

"Good morning, *iubita mea*," he said with a soft Romanian accent.

Those few words made my heart melt. He tilted his chin down, and a curl of dark hair tumbled across his forehead.

My toes curled. *Sixteen more days.*

"Morning," I replied, unable to keep a mischievous grin from tugging at my lips.

"I miss you," he said. "I wish I could hold you."

I imagined him reaching through the screen to place a hand on my cheek and then kissing me. I could practically smell his aftershave. From there, my mind drifted.

"I miss you, too." *So much that it hurts*, I added in my head.

He gave me a knowing smile. After a beat, he coughed lightly and leaned forward, resting his laptop on the coffee table.

"What have you been up to?" he asked, pulling me back to reality.

"Not much," I answered as my mind switched gears. "I went with Laila to pick her folks up on Sunday. Work has been chill. Just one case yesterday."

"And how is Yersi?"

At the sound of his name, Yersi stopped his post-meal bath and insisted that I make space for him on my lap. I lifted my laptop, shifting it to the armrest. His tail arced across the screen as he got settled.

"Yersi is as all glorious rulers should be," I teased. "I have bowed down and made my morning offering of food. He is satisfied."

Armand laughed.

Forced to worship said ruler, I ran my hands along his midnight-colored fur to get him settled on my lap, one hand holding the laptop steady. His purr rattled loudly.

"How are things with you?" I asked. Noticing his background, I added, "Working from home today?"

He ran his hands through his hair, and that frustratingly gorgeous loose curl fell back across his brow. "Yes. I'm trying to finish everything before I leave."

"Think Ileana's figured it out yet?" I asked.

The first time he'd come to Oklahoma, his dog, Ileana, had stayed behind with his brother. Three months had been a long time without his buddy, and he'd missed her. There was no way he was leaving her again; she'd be coming along this time. I still wasn't sure she'd gotten the memo that she was joining him, though, and I suspected all the packing was probably stressing her out.

"She keeps leaving toys in my work bag," he said in way of an answer.

"Awww," I said. "That's super cute. She doesn't want you to leave without her."

He smiled. "That would be impossible."

I loved how much he cared about her. *One more point in the "awesome" column...or two, or three....* My heart skittered in my chest.

"How's the crate training going?" I asked.

The one hiccup in the whole plan was that Ileana needed to be in a crate for the flight. Armand had ordered one as soon as his return visa had been approved. Since then, he'd been trying hard to get her comfortable. She'd never seen a crate before, and the training had been a bit dicey.

"Not good," he answered with a slight frown.

"I take it the KONG with peanut butter didn't work?" I asked.

"It works for about ten minutes," he huffed. "Then, she realizes the crate door is closed and starts drooling and shaking."

"Poor baby," I sympathized.

I knew how hard it was to see your buddy freaking out. Unwilling to treat anything alive, especially my own cat, I'd take Yersi to the vet down the road for his annual checkups. He would sulk in his carrier and growl. Anyone who dared open the crate regretted it instantly as Yersi morphed into a fur-demon, all claws and teeth. I quickly learned that gabapentin was my BFF on such excursions; it kept him gorked enough to not slay the vet staff.

Gabapentin wouldn't be an option for Ileana on an international flight.

"Don't feel too sorry for her," he said. "I've bought her several new things because I feel bad."

He turned his laptop around to point the camera at Ileana. She was looking at him adoringly from a new, cushy bed. Several toys were arranged around her.

As if sensing an audience, she picked up her head and wagged her tail with a soft *thump, thump, thump* on the floor. Her blonde ears flopped forward and looked soft as velvet.

"Oh, my gosh," I cooed. "She's so friggin' cute. I can't wait to meet her."

"She is spoiled," he said affectionately as he turned the laptop back around. Shifting gears, he asked, "How did it go with Laila and her parents?"

"It was...interesting," I answered, struggling to find the right words. It wasn't my place to air Laila's dirty laundry to one of her colleagues.

His eyebrows rose questioningly. "What does that mean?"

I fumbled for a way to explain without sharing too much private stuff. "Her mom deals out some serious judgment. Her dad's kinda mean to her. But it's a cold, silent kind of mean. It's hard watching people treat her that way."

I pressed my lips together, feeling like I'd said too much.

"Hmm," he answered.

I trusted Armand, but he'd be working in Laila's lab during his six-month stint on campus. No matter how much I wanted to share the nitty gritty details with him and get everything off my chest, doing so didn't feel right.

"I'm just trying to be there for her." I shrugged. Feeling uncomfortable, I changed the subject. "You're going to your brother's for the holidays, right?"

Armand rolled with it, and I relaxed as the conversation drifted to holiday plans.

It was nice to hear his voice and see the curve of his smile. I wanted to have this same conversation but curled up next to him. I felt a deep swell of affection build in my stomach and then flutter up to my chest.

It must've shown on my face because he asked, "What?"

I knew I looked goofy and love-drunk, but I couldn't help myself. "I just love hearing your voice."

He smiled shyly, and it was the cutest damn thing I'd ever seen.

Throwing caution to the wind, I pleaded in a hushed voice, "Come back. Come back, and don't ever leave."

His smile grew. "I'm trying, *iubita mea*. I'm trying."

***

After the call with Armand, my feelings were a swirling smoothie in a blender. The strawberries and banana were all the warm fuzzies I got when I was around him: how he made me laugh, how I was always comfortable around him, how much Yersi liked him, and, and, and. But there were hidden, bitter veggies in there, too, the stuff that kept popping into view as everything whirled around. All sorts of things snuck their way in, like the fact that I was more than happy on my own, how long-term relationships were scary, how I'd always been disappointed in the end, and, and, and.

I was pretty sure I'd fallen head-over-heels for the guy. I felt giddy, nervous, and excited. But I also felt apprehensive and scared. It was all a bit messy.

Trying to distract myself, I packed a lunch and a thermos of tea for work. It took me less than a half hour, and by the time I was ready, the sun still hadn't come up.

73

Figuring Laila was also likely awake, I snuggled back on the couch to check in.

> How are things?

Within a millisecond, she replied with an eye-roll emoji.
Her next text said everything.

> I'm at work already.

My eyes jumped to the time on my phone. It wasn't even seven yet. Laila woke up pretty early, but she wasn't one to run into work when it was still dark out.

> That bad, huh?

> My parents are driving me nuts.

> Want to call?

My phone instantly started ringing.

"What happened?" I asked in greeting.

She started with a heavy sigh, and I could practically see her shaking her head.

"I barely got in the door after work yesterday before they ambushed me. I'd half hoped they'd be asleep, jet lag and all. But *nope*." She let out a curt, bitter laugh. "My mother was wide awake and kept shoving her phone in my face with pics of potential suitors."

I sighed, frustrated on her behalf, but didn't interrupt.

"I tried to deflect, saying I was tired from work," she continued. "That was definitely the wrong thing to say because she started laying in on me about how work interfered with my ability to find a husband."

"Dang," I said softly, my heart filling with sympathy for my friend.

"Yeah, I know." She sighed again. "Then she spent an hour trying to convince me that I needed to resign from the Chair position so I'd have more time to focus on what was important."

I felt a flash of defensive anger. "Over my dead body. No way am I letting you give up on your dreams. I don't care what your folks say."

"Yeah, but you don't have to live with them," she said, resigned.

Neither do you! I thankfully didn't quip.

In my heart, I knew it would be almost impossible for Laila to kick her parents out, regardless of how awful they were treating her. It wouldn't help if I kept pushing her to do it.

Family pressure was a bitch.

"You could make an excuse and come over to my place, even if just for tonight," I offered, knowing it was a stupid idea as soon as I said it. Running away wasn't going to solve this problem.

"Nah," she answered like I knew she would. "If I don't go home, it'll only make it worse."

"Want me to come over there? Be your backup?" I asked, not wanting her to have to face her parents alone. "I could help redirect the conversation."

At least, I thought I could guide the conversation. Her mom was one thing. Her dad's silent condescension was entirely different. I didn't even know where to start when handling someone like that.

"Ummm...maybe.... Want to come over for dinner tonight?" she said and then quickly added, "Wait. Aren't you on call this week?"

"Psht," I said, waving my hand in the air. "I never get called in during the week. If anything comes in—which I doubt it will—the on-call student can receive it and put it in the cooler. It'll be fine."

"You sure?" she hesitated.

"Absolutely," I said. It felt good to be able to do something to help her. "What time?"

"Six, I guess?" she answered. "I'll call my mother and let her know. She'll want to make something for you."

"What can I bring?" I asked.

Laila and I were such good friends that host gifts were no longer required. But it wouldn't be one of our usual visits tonight.

"Flowers, maybe?" she said with a sliver of doubt.

"I can do that," I said with more certainty than I felt. It was the middle of winter in an empty college town, and finding a half-decent bouquet would be a bitch. I was pretty sure Laila had bought the last one in Stillwater to bring to the airport on Sunday, but I'd still try my darndest to find something.

"I'll be there at six with bells and whistles," I said cheerfully.

"Thanks again, Josie. Seriously. I'm not sure what I'd do without you."

"Anytime, Laila. I got you."

CHAPTER

NINE

Less than an hour later, I was sitting in the car with my heater running, listening to the last few bars of Pitbull's "Timber." Gen Alpha might call it an oldie, but it was still a goodie and always pumped me up. I figured it would be a pretty chill day, but after waking up so early, I needed to put a little get-up in my step.

As soon as I cut the engine, a large, gray pickup truck pulled into the space on my right, blocking the view from the passenger window. The truck was immaculate, seeming to laugh in the face of the melting ice and sand on the roads that made everyone else's vehicles look like car-zombies.

Gerald's truck always made a statement.

My heart sank. No matter when I rolled into work, Gerald always seemed to be right there, ready to pounce. It was like he had a tracker on my car.

I thought about grabbing my stuff and dashing to the front door to avoid him, but my ass was welded in place. I involuntarily ducked to look out the passenger-side window, clutching my purse and coat to my chest.

He was sitting stiffly in the driver's seat of his truck with his hands still on the wheel. And he was looking straight at me.

A thread of something traced up my spine. I couldn't tell if it was fear or some other feeling. My adrenals squeezed out some juice, but my body didn't quite know how to respond.

Stupidly, I stayed frozen, staring back at him with my mouth in a firm line.

If anyone else from the lab had pulled in next to me and looked over, I probably would've plastered on a polite smile and shared a wave. Even if it had been one of the turds who had placed a bet against Dustin, I still could've managed to be fake-nice.

But this was Gerald.

Ever since the tiger pelt had been stolen, he'd become unpredictable. Before that pivotal event, he'd just pound on my roof, say something mean, and walk into the lab with a leer. Since then, he'd either avoid me, or we'd share an odd, stilted conversation.

The fact that today, he was just sitting in his car, staring at me like Jeffrey Dahmer, was almost more off-putting than if he'd shouted a racial slur.

We stared at each other for a few awkward seconds before I finally gave him my best fighting face and challenged him with a sharp "What?" through the window.

I knew he couldn't hear me, but the combination of my body language and my lips forming the word must've been enough.

He flinched ever so slightly, and a frown tugged at his mouth. He looked away.

The tension popped like a balloon. I climbed out of the car and headed into the lab, doing my best not to look over my shoulder. Despite my racing heart, I kept my pace even, trying not to look scared. Prey behavior tended to bring out the worst in the resident work troll.

Even though I hadn't heard him leave his truck, the back of my neck tingled like he was watching me through his mirrors.

As I passed through the doors to the lab, I found myself wishing for the old Gerald back. At least I had a pretty good idea of what that guy would do. This new version was incredibly creepy.

***

Once I was in my office, it took a hot second before I could chase away the heebie-jeebies. Trying to calm my shaking hands, I went through the motions of hanging my coat over my chair and tucking my purse under my desk.

I hated that Gerald could rattle me with just a look.

After a few deep breaths, I felt a bit better and ventured forth to check in with Dustin. He was as I'd found him yesterday: perched at his desk. A line of steam swirled up from his coffee mug.

I knocked on the doorjamb and said, "Good morning."

He turned from the computer and replied, "Mornin', Doc."

"Anything yet?" I asked.

"No, ma'am. Nice 'n quiet."

"No bodies is good bodies," I said.

His mustache twitched up with a smile.

"I'll either be trimming tissues or in my office if you need me," I said. "See ya at lunch."

He tossed me a friendly salute.

On the way back, I found Zoe's door open. I knocked on the frame with a smile and leaned in. "Good morning. Still working your way through all that glass?"

She slumped back in her chair dramatically and replied with a dejected, "Yes."

"Sure I can't pick up a few cases for you?" I asked. "It's super slow this week."

I knew I'd offered so many times that I was leaning into the annoying range. But I couldn't help but feel like her load was a bit too hard to carry solo, especially when she was supposed to be on PTO.

"I appreciate the offer. But I'm good," she replied and then gestured down to the pile. "I've only got the rabbits left. I should be finished around lunch."

The skin around her eyes was tight, and I could tell something was still weighing heavily on her. Had Gerald decided to pounce on her instead of me this morning?

"Doing okay?" I asked, my concern getting the better of me.

To my shock, her eyes started filling up with tears.

I slid into her office, closed the door, and sat across from her. Here she was, just trying to get her work done, and I'd bumbled in, tearing open something that she'd been trying really hard to keep shut away.

I grabbed a tissue from the box on her desk and handed it to her.

The silence stretched between us.

"Want to talk about it, or do you want me to get lost?" I asked softly.

She used the tissue to wipe her tears. Her eyes were cast down at her desk, shoulders hunched.

"It's fine," she said, not really answering my question. She sighed, blowing the air out loudly through her lips. "The holidays are always rough."

I tried to hide my surprise at her answer. Sure, a lot of people were stressed out around the holidays. Not everyone liked their relatives, and some people felt obliged to spend time with them anyway. Plus, there was the pressure to buy presents regardless of whether someone could afford them. Travel in chaotic airports and on busy roads was the icing on the holiday shit-cake. Despite all of the baggage that came with the holidays, I still didn't understand Zoe's comment.

"Rough how?" I probed gently. "I thought you were going to Jayden's parents' place."

She waved a hand absently. "Yeah, we're going to Portland. It's not that. Jayden's parents are wonderful."

I kept my mouth shut, giving her space to tell her story. Something was eating her up inside, and I could see it all over her face. I just needed to give her a moment to get it out.

She fidgeted with the tissue, eyes cast down. "It's just hard being around all of the families. When we're out shopping, when we're at the airport, all of that."

Ohhhh. All of the pieces started falling into place.

"Does that mean…" I trailed off, hesitant to say it out loud.

The tears started again.

"Merry Christmas to me," she said with bitter sarcasm. "The jerks called a week before the holiday to let us know our application was denied. *Who does that*?"

My heart sank.

Zoe and Jayden had been trying to adopt a child for several years. They were both wonderful people with great jobs. And Zoe would be a fantastic mother. She was already a mother to all of the students who passed through her office, seeking the help that Admin failed to provide.

"Oh, Zoe," was all I could manage. I moved around the desk to give her a half-hug.

I didn't need to ask why they'd been denied yet again. I knew why: It was because the people running the adoption agencies were bigots.

Unable to help myself, I shook my head in disgust and returned to my seat. I leaned forward and reached across the desk for her hand. She clasped my fingers back.

"It's difficult seeing all of these couples with children, and we aren't allowed to have any. Especially when I see people shouting at their kids or raising a hand to them. There are so many children who need a place."

My heart ached for Zoe. In a state like Oklahoma, there wasn't much she and Jayden could do. It always amazed me how a Christian-majority state could be so hateful. What happened to "love thy neighbor?"

"Bastards," I mumbled.

Zoe released my hand and wiped her eyes again. "Sorry," she whispered.

"Psht." I waved my hand not unkindly. "Sorry for what? There's nothing to be sorry for."

She circled her hand in front of her face. "For losing it."

"Dude," I said firmly, feeling a bit indignant. "The way they're treating you and Jayden is awful. You have a right to be pissed. And be sad. And to vent. What they've done isn't right."

A sad smile tipped her lips. "Thanks, Josie."

My mind was racing for solutions. I wanted to spitball with her, think about surrogates, think about adopting in another state, that kind of stuff. But I knew that, right now, she needed to mourn the loss of the child the adoption agency had withheld.

I gave her hand another squeeze.

After a beat, she straightened her shoulders and said, "Enough of that. I need to suck it up and get these rabbits done."

Sensing the shift, I teased her a bit, saying, "Have fun with that."

She huffed. "Yeah. Not so much."

I made a fake magic wand gesture. "I bestow onto you oodles of coccidia and a speedy diagnosis."

Her smile grew a bit more, and she made eye contact. "Thanks again, Josie."

I knew she was thanking me for more than my mock blessing.

"Anytime." I gave her a supportive smile. "You sticking around for lunch? I'm sure Carol's got something sweet we can both stress-eat together."

That got a small laugh.

"Yeah, I'll see you at lunch," she said, this time sounding a tad better.

With that, I gave her another side hug before leaving her to her pile of glass.

As I walked back to my office, I couldn't shake the irony of having one friend in tears because she couldn't have a baby and another friend in tears because her parents were trying to force her to. What was up with people always telling everyone else how to live their lives? A woman's choice was just that: her choice. Everyone else needed to calm the fuck down and take a step back.

CHAPTER

TEN

The first half of Tuesday meandered by. The lack of cases forced me to complete my paper revisions, which felt great when all was said and done. Just before real boredom could set in, it was time for lunch.

I picked a spot at our usual breakroom table and set down my bag. As if a bell had rung, Dustin, Anna, and Carol joined me within less than a minute.

"Hello, y'all," Carol said as she sat down.

As usual, Carol laid a container of sweets to share in the center of the table. Today, it was chocolate chip bar cookies. When the lid popped open, the smell of the chocolate and brown sugar was overwhelming.

Seeing my face, and perhaps the drool, Carol nudged the box to me with a knowing smile. Even though I hadn't opened my lunch yet, I selected a cookie and started scarfing it down. I tried to eat healthy, but Carol's treats were like a drug, and she was my dealer.

"These are delicious," I half-moaned. "Thank you so much."

Dustin grunted his thanks as he chewed on his own cookie.

Carol beamed. "Y'all are welcome."

I wasn't sure how she managed to bake a new treat every night, but she did. Whatever delectable sweet she brought in was always amazing. It was something special she did just for our little friend group. I could practically kiss her for it.

After finishing his cookie, Dustin pulled out a giant sandwich with about an inch of meat squished between two thin slices of bread.

"What is *that*?" Anna teased.

"It's a BLT," Dustin said and took a giant bite.

"Pfft. Where's the 'L' and the 'T' in that bad boy?" I asked, grinning. There was no way a slice of tomato or lettuce dared to share a space with that giant wad of bacon sitting between those pearly-white slices of Wonder Bread.

Anna leaned forward and squinted at his sandwich. "Yeah, that's more like a BBB."

He held his sandwich out, studied it thoughtfully, and shrugged. "It's good belly bacon. I caught this hog a few months ago." He took another big bite, looking smug.

We snickered and settled into our meals.

"Is Dr. Smith coming to lunch?" Anna asked. "I thought I saw her this morning."

"I'm not sure," I answered hesitantly. "I know there were a few cases she wanted to button up before she left on PTO."

Plus, she may just not want to be around people right now, I didn't add.

"It was definitely busy last week," Anna reflected. "When is she leaving for Portland?"

"Tomorrow, I think?" I guessed, trying to remember.

"Hope she makes it out before the storm hits. Such a shame it's comin' in right at Christmas and all," Carol said. "I'll save her some cookies to take on the flight."

As if hearing her name echoing through the ether, Zoe swept in, looking exhausted. Between Carol's baked goods and the group's supportive vibe, I hoped we could help take her mind off things, even if we might not be able to cheer her up. I scooched over and swung a chair from an adjacent table into the open space.

She took a seat, offering a distracted "Thanks."

Carol pushed the cookies over to her. Zoe selected one and nibbled at it. Her normal zeal for Carol's sweets had been zapped, but she was trying to be polite. Carol noticed, and a flash of concern flitted across her face.

"All finished with your cases?" I asked, attempting to keep things light.

"Yes, the urgent ones, thankfully," she said with an exhausted sigh. "The rest can wait 'til I get back."

"That was a mighty big pile you were workin' on," Dustin mused.

"It was," she agreed. "But they were all pretty easy. The neuro goat had *Listeria*."

"Figured it was that when the rabies came back negative," Dustin said. "Whatcha find in the dog with the blood leakin' out its nose?"

"Streptococcal pneumonia," Zoe said and then tutted. "And the owner thought the boarding facility killed the dog."

Anna huffed. "They always think that."

"Or they blame the neighbor," I added. "And it ends up being a ruptured hemangiosarc."

"Sometimes bad things just happen," Carol said sagely.

Dustin's eyes grew dark. "Sure, most of the time, it's somethin' simple, but we still get nasty stuff. Oftentimes, it's just someone bein' stupid or neglectin' their animal, but I've seen my fair share of evil, too."

My heart clenched. I got the sense that his comment was based on experiences outside of work. He didn't talk much about his past, but from the bits I'd gathered, it seemed like his childhood had been rough.

I shifted uncomfortably. "The animal cruelty cases are tough," I admitted. "And sometimes the neighbor did actually do it."

"Yeah," Anna said sadly. "Like that one case you had, Dr. Harjo. The one where the neighbor put rat bait in some hamburger and threw it over the fence to kill that Rottweiler. Remember?"

I nodded, a wave of sadness washing over me. That case was so messed up that I'd tried not to think about it. If I did, I'd go crazy.

I picked at the edge of a second cookie, having suddenly lost my appetite.

"Did you ever find out what happened to the guy who did that?" Anna asked.

It took me a moment to answer. "I don't think anything happened to him," I said, unable to keep the frustration from my voice.

"Really? That's awful," Anna said, shaking her head sadly.

The injustice of it all boiled in my veins.

"Unless it's tied to a crime with a big punishment, like drugs, they usually don't even bother prosecuting cases of neglect or animal cruelty. They just walk away," Zoe added, her voice glum.

"And then the a-holes turn into serial killers," I snarked, feeling bitter.

I shot an apologetic glance at Carol for the half-curse. She reached over and patted my hand reassuringly.

Zoe sighed. "I'm grateful there wasn't anything malicious about the strep case. There was nothing the kennel could've done. It was just a particularly nasty bug taking advantage of the situation."

"Could the owners sue the kennel because the dog got sick there?" Anna asked.

"Maybe," Zoe answered slowly. "But sue for what? Animals are just property in Oklahoma. It's not like the dog was a purebred or specially trained or anything like that."

"That's so depressing," Anna said.

"Pretty much," I added with a frown.

Dustin made a *hmm* sound in agreement.

"Why do they bring the animals in for necropsy then? If the cops or the owners or whatever aren't going to do anything?" Anna asked.

"I don't know," I said in all honesty. "Closure, I guess?"

Silence spread across the table.

Having suddenly lost my appetite, all I could do was stare down at the half-eaten cookie sitting next to my unopened lunch box. The animal abuse cases always got to me; they got to all of us.

After a beat, Zoe waved her hand as if to brush away the bad juju. "Okay, everyone, that's enough depressing stuff," she said, not unkindly. "I've gotta brave the airport tomorrow, and it's gonna be awful. Let's talk about something fun. And pass me another one of those cookies."

With a smile, Carol nudged the cookies closer to Zoe.

It was enough to pop the bubble of tension, and everyone returned to their meals. I could finally peel the lid off my leftovers and force a bite of the pasta down.

"At least it's been nice and slow this week," Anna said, trying to bring some cheer to the table. "Just the one piglet."

"Yup," Dustin said. "And it was a fetus, too. Nice 'n easy." He took a large bite of his BBB sandwich, and his left cheek puffed out as he chewed.

"I expect it'll be that way for the rest of the week," Carol said. "It's always like this 'round Christmas and New Year's."

"People ain't gonna wanna drive in the storm either," Anna said, and then she turned to Zoe. "Speaking of which, when are y'all flyin' out, Dr. Smith?"

"First thing tomorrow," Zoe replied. "The storm is supposed to come in the afternoon, right?"

Carol and Dustin nodded.

"We should just beat it then," Zoe continued. "And we don't fly back until Monday. I think we'll be all right."

"Oh, good," Anna said.

Looking at Carol, I asked, "Think Fran'll close the lab given how nasty the storm's supposed to be?"

Carol raised her eyebrows and pursed her lips. She was too polite to say anything. But it was obvious that she didn't think Fran would do a damn thing about the storm. Given that Carol had been here longer than any of us, I didn't doubt her read on the situation.

Anna shifted in her seat.

I glanced around the table. "We can always slim it down to skeleton staff, right? Some people have long drives. It's not safe."

Carol gave me a reassuring look. "We'll figure it out, dear. We always do."

Not quite mollified, I decided to let it go anyway. I could tell I was headed onto a topic that everyone preferred to avoid: Fran.

Zoe saved me and asked, "So, you've really only had one case so far this week?"

"Yup. Just the one," I answered. "The piglet from yesterday."

"And with the storm, we ain't likely to get much else," Dustin added.

"Lucky. Everything that was sick must've died last week. You owe me," Zoe teased.

It was good to see her smile, even if it didn't reach her eyes.

"Yeah. Thanks for clearing everything out for me," I said with a cheeky grin. Feeling the urge to lighten things up, I turned to Dustin and sing-songed, "It's gonna get so *boooooring* this week. I think you and me'll have to play some tabletop games, Dustin."

A huge grin spread across Zoe's face, and her eyes lit up. "Yeah, Dustin. I heard you just *love* Arkham Asylum."

Dustin leaned back in his chair, and a smile twitched around the edges of his mustache. Sitting at a table for two hours playing a strategy game was torture for someone who spent most of his time outside.

"You can pretend all you want, Dustin," Carol said, her grandmotherly smile stretching wide. "You was in here playin' poker for half the day way back when during the big storm of—what was it—oh-six? Oh-seven?"

"What?!" I exclaimed at the exact same moment Zoe blurted, "Dustin was playing a card game?!"

Dustin snorted again. "Wasn't me," he insisted, holding his hands up to demonstrate his innocence.

We all laughed, and my shoulders relaxed. It felt good seeing my friends joke around. I picked up the cookie I'd been fiddling with and took a bite as I soaked in their smiles.

Just when I thought we were in a good spot, a loud throat-clearing cut through the laughter like a knife.

Carol looked up, focused on something behind me, and frowned. The hair on the back of my neck stood up, and my shoulders tensed. I turned slowly and found Gerald perched uncomfortably close to the back of my chair; I had to crane my neck to see him.

Zoe's face turned to stone. "Yes, Gerald?" she said, her voice icy cold.

Gerald narrowed his eyes at her and then looked back at me. "I wanted to inform you that, even though we are incredibly short-staffed, I have set up the cultures on case 43506859."

The comment was so matter-of-fact and awkwardly out of step from the group laughter just milliseconds before that all we could do was stare. His eyes danced around the others. A flash of longing crossed his face so quickly that I almost missed it.

It must be a lonesome life he's built for himself, I thought, feeling a confusing sense of pity. Then, I remembered all of the mean things he'd said and done, and that little sliver of compassion was squashed.

My back stiffened. "Thank you, Gerald," I said, unable to keep the lack of sincerity out of my voice. "I'll keep an eye out for the results." When he didn't leave, I added, "Was there something else?"

I could practically see the wall come down, and his expression grew mean.

"You should put more care into your cases," he almost hissed. "This could be the start of an abortion storm. Being lackadaisical could mean lives lost. Do you want to be responsible for more dead piglets?"

I felt my jaw drop. It was such a horrible thing to say that I had no clue how to respond.

Zoe tensed. "Stay in your lane," she said, her tone laced with a cool anger.

He crossed his arms, and a slight sneer twisted his lips as his eyes bore into her. It was a slippery slope between them, and I had a feeling this was going to get incredibly ugly extremely fast.

Just when I'd gotten Zoe to smile, Gerald had to come in and ruin it.

"Clearly, you don't understand the value of producing viable off-spring," he snapped.

My eyebrows crinkled in confusion. Gerald had a habit of taking random tangents, but this was so far out in left field that I wasn't following him at all. My eyes danced around the table; everyone looked equally confused.

Except Zoe.

The color had fled her face, and her body stiffened. He'd taken aim, and the arrow had struck true. Suddenly, all of the pieces fell into place. A cool sense of dread spread through me.

How could he possibly know what was going on with Zoe and the adoption?

My heart started to race as my eyes shifted between Zoe and Gerald. *Because the guy's a creeper. He knows everything.*

I had a flash of panic that maybe he'd overheard our conversation. An image of him standing outside with his ear pressed to Zoe's door appeared in my mind. Goosebumps spread across my arms.

I wasn't the only one who was mortified by his comment. The whole table continued to sit there in shocked silence. Not everyone knew the full story, but Zoe's shattered expression was enough to make it clear that the jab had been a fairly deep one.

The sound of Dustin clearing his throat was enough to help me get my shit together enough to respond. "What the hell, Gerald?" I said, shaking my head in disbelief. "That was totally random and unnecessary."

His eyes slid back to me, and his eyebrows furrowed slightly.

I couldn't tell what the hell he was thinking. And, honestly, it didn't matter what was going on in that messed up head of his. I needed to clear this damn landmine before someone lost a limb.

"Just go back to your office and leave us be," I said, frowning.

This time, he actually looked hurt, and the annoying, dichotomous twinge of pity returned. Before it could show on my face, I stuffed the feeling aside and turned my back to him.

"May I have another cookie, Carol?" I asked, pretending he wasn't *right fucking there*, breathing down my neck.

Carol licked her lips and slowly slid the box to me, eyes bouncing from me to Gerald and back. "Sure. Take as many as you'd like."

Gerald's glare felt like daggers in my back as I selected a cookie and took a bite. There was a sudden change in pressure, and then his footsteps echoed away from us.

After a beat, Dustin frowned and shook his head.

"That guy," I said, exacerbated, unable to help myself.

"He sure knows how to ruin a party," Anna said.

Zoe was silent, her shoulders tense and her face a mask.

I wanted to give her a hug or ask her if she was okay. But I knew she was doing her best to keep herself together. It was time to change the subject.

I finished my cookie in a second bite and brushed my fingers off on my napkin. "So, Dustin, what's this about you playing cards?"

Sensing my desire to bring the cheer back, Carol forced a low laugh and proceeded to tell the story of how Dustin trounced everyone at poker twenty-some-odd years ago when they were all snowed in at the lab.

And with that, the conversation drifted back to what games we might be able to get Dustin to play if the incoming storm kept things slow but Fran kept the lab open.

I couldn't help but steal glances at Zoe. She laughed at the right points, but her heart wasn't in it. I figured it was going to take some time for her to heal. She'd been hit with a whammy already this week, and traveling for the holidays was only going to pour salt in the wound.

After lunch, Zoe and I slowly walked back to our offices in silence.

"You headed out now?" I asked.

"Just need to clear out a couple of emails, and then, yeah," she answered, still sounding sad.

"Sorry for what happened back there," I fumbled as we stopped outside her office door.

"Nothing for you to apologize for," she said, voice soft but firm. "It's Gerald who should be apologizing. Really. I mean, an apology to anyone would do at this point."

"Hah," I snorted dejectedly. "Like that would ever happen. I wouldn't hold your breath."

Seeing the tears threatening again, I reached out to squeeze her hand. "But seriously, though. Screw that guy. Pack that drama in a tidy box and go enjoy your holiday with Jayden." Craning my neck to catch her downcast eyes, I smiled softly.

"It's more than just Gerald..." she started, and then her voice caught.

"I know, sweety," I said and folded her into a hug.

I ached to help my friend feel better, but I was at a loss for what to say. I wanted to shout to the world that she would be an amazing mother and encourage her not to give up. I wanted to tell her everything would be okay. I wanted the address of the adoption agency so I could go kick some ass.

Pulling away, I squeezed her hand again and said, "I'm here. Call or text if you want to talk, okay?"

She nodded.

"Give Jayden a hug for me," I added.

She nodded again.

With that, I let go of her hand, feeling her fingertips slip from mine.

I hoped beyond hope that Jayden's family would bring Zoe comfort and support this holiday as she worked her way through the loss of the child that she'd been denied.

CHAPTER

ELEVEN

Turbulent thoughts ping-ponged around in my mind, and I tossed my empty lunchbox on my desk with a huff. The crap that had gone down between Gerald and Zoe had really messed with my head. I was still trying to unravel what had happened. And unpack that weird sense of pity for Gerald.

I grabbed my lab coat and headed to the histology lab to try to distract myself. The bright fluorescent lights blazed in the windowless room, and there was a familiar sharp chemical smell. The only sounds were the faint whisking of a microtome cutting away at a paraffin block and the low hum of the fume hoods.

One of the histology technicians, Sally, was seated at the cutting bench, cranking the handwheel. When I entered, she looked up, and the bobbing of the block holder stopped momentarily.

I tipped my chin up in greeting and said, "Howdy, Sally."

She smiled in response and went back to cutting. Sally was pretty quiet and kept to herself, so I left her to it. She likely had an audiobook playing, and I didn't want to disrupt her work-groove.

I was glad it was her, and only her, working this week. Usually, there were three histo techs. But because the workload was so light with the holidays, Sally was flying solo. That was fine by me. I still harbored some hefty animosity for Noah after he'd set up the betting pool over the tiger and felt like I had to be fake with him.

Popping an earbud in, I queued up some old-school hip-hop and dropped my phone in my lab coat pocket. Snapping on a pair of gloves, I moved through the lab to the cart where all of the formalin buckets waited. Being the newest case, the small bucket for the piglet was right on top.

The tissues from the pig had only been sitting in formalin for about twenty-four hours, and they technically needed a tad more time to percolate. But I decided to give it a whirl. Even though the owner wasn't breathing down my neck for the results, I was getting anxious about the next storm coming in. I'd feel better getting this case closer to a final report before the weather changed.

If I was lucky, the tissues would be fixed enough that they could go on the processor tonight. I might even be able to report the case out tomorrow and button everything up before the storm.

I brought the jar over to the trimming hood and popped the lid open to have a peek. The tissues had already started to get the brown-tinge characteristic of fixation. But I suspected the formalin had only had enough time to penetrate the surface; the tissues had a plumpness to them that indicated the insides might still be a bit raw.

I used forceps to fish out a section of the friable liver, doing my best not to mangle it. I laid it on the plastic cutting board. With a scalpel, I made an exploratory slice. On cut-section, the liver had a red-tinged center.

Damn.

I paused, weighing my options. If everything could be trimmed into cassettes and sit in fresh formalin for the rest of the day, there was a very slim chance they could make it onto the processor tonight. If I waited, I probably wouldn't be seeing the slides until after the holidays.

I decided to throw caution to the wind, trim everything, and cross my fingers that it would fix in time. I'd trust Sally to make the call as to whether or not to put them on the processor before she left.

Rocking out to tunes, I made quick work of the fetal tissues. They were uniformly soft and underdeveloped. I made the sections as small and thin as comfortably possible, hoping the formalin would do its thing during the last few hours of the work day.

When I got to the brain, I paused.

The brain is one of the softest organs, and even gentle handling might damage it. Complete fixation firmed the neural tissue just enough to be able to cut it without trashing the architecture. Usually, a brain had to sit in formalin for at least a week, if not longer, before it could be trimmed in.

Fetal brains were another story; they would stay mushy no matter how long they were allowed to fix. The younger the fetus, the more liquid and unformed the brain. In some cases, I literally had to scoop bits of the brain into a cassette. Even though everything would look like soup under the microscope, it was still easy enough to spot the odd parasitic cyst or pick out inflammatory cells.

With the storm looming, I decided to press on and took representative sections. The cerebral shmoo slid off the razor blade into the cassette like Easy Cheese.

After everything was trimmed in, I plopped the cassettes into fresh formalin. The fluid didn't instantly turn pink, and I felt a sliver of hope. Maybe, just maybe, they'd get on tonight's run.

"Hey, Sally?" I asked.

Sally stopped cutting, pulled a glove off, and tapped her earbud to pause her audiobook.

"How can I help you, Dr. Harjo?" she asked pleasantly.

"I just trimmed the fetus from yesterday. It's still pretty raw, so I put it in a jar over there instead of in the fixation rack." I nodded to the hood. "I'm hoping it'll be fixed enough to run tonight. But don't worry if it's not."

"It's not a STAT case, right?" she asked.

"No, ma'am. Just thinking about the weather. And since we're closed Friday for the holiday...." I shrugged.

She nodded, filling in the blanks. "Understood. I'll see what I can do."

"Thanks," I said.

"I'm the only one in the lab this week, but things are slow. If they're fixed enough to process tonight, I'll try to get the slides to you tomorrow."

"I appreciate it," I said with a smile.

She nodded again before tapping her earbud and turning back to the microtome.

I left the histology lab feeling pretty good about where things stood. If it stayed slow the next few days, it was possible everything with the pig could be buttoned up before the storm swept in.

***

On my way back to my office, Gerald's open door caught my eye. He was hunched over his computer, intensely focused. His fingers sped across the keyboard.

He's gone plaid.

I felt a brief millisecond of confusion as to where that random brain fart came from. Then, I thought, *Yeah, he's definitely Dark Helmet.* A smile tickled the edge of my lips at the idea of him in a black spandex suit capped with a ginormous Darth-Vader-like helmet.

And Fran is definitely President Skroob.

This time, I had to stop myself before I blurted out a laugh.

Fucking Fran.

My footsteps passed Gerald's office and then slowed.

I couldn't get what occurred at lunch out of my head. I knew I'd have to confront him about it.

Whatever had happened between us over that damn tiger had subtly shifted the playing field. I'd defended him *and* confronted him during those chaotic weeks; I wasn't sure which of those actions had triggered the change. Maybe it was a little of both, or maybe it was neither. Whatever the impetus was, he hadn't banged on my car or lobbed a slur at me in ages.

There was a slim chance I might be able to get him off Zoe's back, and I wasn't sure poking the bear would be worth it. But I figured a slim chance was better than none at all.

I came to a stop just past his office, considering my next move. If I didn't say something, the whole incident would keep bouncing around my head, and I needed to purge that shit.

I made a U-turn.

When I knocked on his doorjamb, the typing instantly stopped, and he looked up at me, startled. A mixture of expressions sped across his face too fast to pick apart. He landed on a cautiously arrogant smirk, which wasn't a great start to the conversation.

I'd only been in his office to chew his ass once before. And—surprise, surprise—it was also over something nasty he'd said to Zoe. That time, I'd gone in with my anger licking like a raging fire and reamed him up one side and down the other. It'd felt good in the moment, but looking back, it hadn't done a darn thing to improve his behavior. I needed to try a softer approach.

"Have a sec?" I asked, trying to keep my tone neutral even though my heart was thudding.

He cleared his throat and gestured to the chair across from his desk. His sharp blue eyes followed me in, locked on target. He looked coiled and ready to strike. I couldn't help but feel like I was a rabbit entering a wolf's den.

His office was eerily sterile. Every surface was spiffy-clean and empty of clutter. There were no pieces of flare: no pictures, no art, no plants, nothing. I was sure he had books in his office somewhere, but they must've been hidden in one of the closed-door cabinets. There weren't even any pens or Post-it notes on his desk. The place was empty.

Like his soul.

Goosebumps broke out on my arms.

I took a seat, trying to cover up my fear. Even though adrenaline was pumping through my veins, I forced my body to relax in the chair. I crossed my legs casually and hung my arms along the armrests. I was hoping to channel an I-couldn't-give-two-fucks vibe, but I wasn't sure I'd captured it correctly.

He was frozen like a statue, gaze locked on me. His brown hair was slicked back, with not a hair out of place. His pressed button-up shirt and slacks were immaculate. He looked like he'd come straight out of an ad for an investment company.

"Yes?" he said curtly.

I fought another rush of adrenaline. Figuring the direct approach was the best one, I dove right in.

"What was that at lunch today?" I asked, barely keeping the anger out of my voice.

He pursed his lips and studied me, his eyes like daggers.

I tried not to squirm.

"I was just informing you that I took the initiative to ensure that our customers receive their results quickly," he said matter-of-factly. "This could be the start of an abortion storm. Your *laissez-faire* attitude could negatively impact this case and lead to more losses."

My hackles rose. I knew he was trying to bait me and avoid the real topic. I tried to let everything he was saying roll right off.

Like water off a duck's back, Aunty's voice whispered in my mind.

"I'm not talking about that," I said, keeping my voice casual. He knew exactly what I was talking about, and I let that fact settle between us like a stinking turd.

His pursed lips relaxed into a frown. A muscle in his cheek bounced as he clenched his teeth.

"What you said to Zoe was cruel," I continued. "What on earth made you think that was an okay thing to say to her? You should apologize."

His nostrils flared.

I realized I'd let my anger slip into my voice, and the schoolyard scrapper was starting to sneak out.

Trying to change tack, I said, "Look, if you want a collegial relationship with people at work, you can't say stuff like that. I'm just trying to understand what drove you to do that. It really hurt her. She's already having a rough time trying to process everything. She's gotta get her game face on for her trip, and you ripped the scab off."

A muscle under his eye had started to twitch. With a sinking feeling, I saw that I was royally screwing this up. I tried not to fidget; showing weakness would only trigger him.

The silence stretched, and the tension built between us. His eyes stayed locked on mine, and it took everything in me to not look away.

"She tried to pin the stolen tiger parts on me," he said, breaking first, his tone slightly petulant.

I felt a brief flare of victory and tamped it down. This was only the tip of the iceberg. I waited through the awkward silence for him to continue.

He crossed his arms, biceps flexing, and he clenched his jaw again.

Crap. Here it comes, I thought with a sinking feeling. *I know that look.*

"Why do you even care? You have your own problems. You should find a husband, settle down, and have your own kids. I'm sure there are plenty of men who like squaw women."

And there it is. Gerald is back in the building, folks.

A burgeoning sense of victory sparkled in his eyes, knowing he'd hit the mark.

It took everything in me not to jump up and lay a beat down on his scrawny ass. I gripped the armrests, deciding on my next move.

He's just a hurt little boy, Aunty whispered in my head.

I realized with a start that's exactly what he was. I was getting too close to the sore spot, so he lashed out at me. And pretty hard, too. I had no clue what to do next. My blood was raging. And if I didn't do something with all the anger, it'd turn to tears.

Stupid adrenaline. I hated the way it ran my body.

Deep breaths. Little steps. Eyes on the prize, Aunty whispered again.

I inhaled deeply and then said, "That was intentionally hurtful and a great example of what I'm talking about."

His chest deflated like a popped balloon. My response wasn't what he was expecting, and he looked a little lost.

Despite my best intentions, I knew I was too angry to finish this now. I needed to make a quick exit. I stood and pushed my chair in. "This is why people placed bets against you. This is why people don't want to talk to you. If you don't want to be alone, you should really think long and hard about how you treat people." It was probably the wrong thing to say, but I didn't know what else to do.

His face remained stony, but he didn't come back with a retort, which was something.

I left his office without another word and forced myself to not look back. As soon as I was out of his line of sight, I took a few deep breaths to try to calm my racing heart. I unclenched my fists and wiped my sweaty palms against my legs.

Inside my head, I tried to celebrate the fact that I'd faced the wolf and came out with only minor scratches. I couldn't help but wonder if maybe I'd finally put a dent in the dragon's armor.

CHAPTER

TWELVE

When I rolled up to Laila's place that evening, I'd shaken off the encounter with Gerald and was ready to face her folks.

I arrived five minutes early, figuring that was the sweet spot between respectful and obnoxious. The bouquet of flowers was clenched in front of me like a sword. Despite it being a winter wasteland, I'd managed to find a bundle of mixed flowers that was half-decent, even if it had taken three stops.

Laila answered the door before the chime finished announcing my presence. Her hair was slightly frizzy, with wisps escaping from her short ponytail. Her eyes were sunken with stress wrinkles tugging at the corners. She smiled weakly when she saw me, but it didn't touch her eyes.

She stepped aside to let me in. "Hey, Josie. Thanks for coming."

"Glad to be here. Thanks for inviting me." I gave her a half hug and a cheek kiss.

Despite the invaders, her house had a cozy feel. The smell of Indian spices tickled my nose, and my stomach grumbled. In the tiled entryway, I took my shoes and coat off, shifting the flowers from hand to hand as I did.

Rakesh was sitting in the living room, holding a tablet with his earbuds in. He didn't even acknowledge my presence. I couldn't help but frown at the troll as we snuck past.

We met Ishani in the kitchen. She had an apron over her sari, and her hair was pulled back in a tidy braid. She offered a polite smile.

I stepped forward, holding the flowers out to her. "Thank you for cooking tonight. These are for you."

Ishani gave an appreciative nod and said, "Thank you." Turning to Laila, she added something in Hindi.

Laila took the flowers and translated for me, "She asked me to put them in a vase."

"Dinner smells amazing," I said, practically drooling.

"I made *hara dhania cholia*," Ishani said, pointing to the large pot steaming on the stove.

"It's a chickpea curry," Laila added.

"I've never had that before." I peeked in the pot and inhaled deeply. "Thank you again. It smells delicious."

Ishani nodded her chin once, as if I'd said the right thing. Laila snuck me a slight smile, and I felt a sliver of relief that I'd done something right, even if it was small.

"I try to teach Laila these things," her mom tutted, waving her hand in the air. "She needs to learn how to cook for her family. It is a wife's duty to cook for her husband and children. I try to teach her, but she runs off every time. She will never get a husband this way. She disappoints us."

My shoulders stiffened defensively. I wasn't used to a family member talking smack like that. The casual way Ishani had delivered the barb had made it all the more irritating. She didn't even realize how much she was hurting her daughter.

Out of the corner of my eye, I saw a frown tug at Laila's lips. I bit my lip so nothing snarky would slip out. Now was not the time.

"Laila, when you are done with the flowers, please get the table ready," Ishani commanded.

The muscle in Laila's jaw jumped as she clenched her teeth.

"Here, I can help," I offered.

Ishani stirred the pot, clanked the spoon on the side, and rested it on a small dish on the counter. "No. You are the guest."

I shifted uncomfortably, unsure of what to do.

Laila tossed me a look that said, "Don't fight it," and pulled a vase out for the flowers. As hard as it was, I backed down. I needed to save my energy for later when the real monster showed up.

Ishani pointed across the island to the dining table. "You may sit," she directed me.

I shuffled over to the table, feeling completely out of my element, and stared stupidly at the chairs for a few seconds. I wasn't sure where I should sit and wondered if both ends of the table might be reserved for Laila's parents. I picked one of the middle ones, figuring that it was the best spot to park my ass without pissing anyone off.

As she set the table, Laila tossed me an apologetic look.

Her silence was freaking me out. If it had been just the two of us, we'd have already popped the tops off our takeout and flopped on the couch to watch a show. We'd be chatting about the day, and she'd invariably be cheering me up with her bright smile and witty jokes. Today, she looked like a trapped animal, wide-eyed and scared.

Rakesh was still hunkered down in the living room, which was probably a good thing. Laila seemed to be avoiding her dad like the plague. And it wasn't the cute fluffy version of the Black Death that was Yersi.

"Would you like something to drink?" Laila asked me.

The question was oddly formal.

"Water would be great, thanks," I answered cautiously.

She returned with two glasses of water and sat across from me.

At least I guessed right; her parents would be sitting at either end of the table.

"How was work?" Laila asked, her voice guarded.

"Meh," I replied, trying to relax. "Nice and slow. Just the one case yesterday. Except for Gerald, it's been pretty mellow."

As if forgetting the two monsters lurking in her home, she shook her head. "Psht. That guy. I'm tellin' you. At least it looks like you got out alive."

"Alive but not entirely unscathed," I joked. "He has a tendency to mind-fuck everyone long after the day is over."

With a start, I realized I'd dropped an f-bomb, and my eyes jumped to Ishani. She was busy chopping something and didn't seem to notice. I felt myself relax a tad. I needed to keep my game face on if I was going to be of any help to Laila tonight.

"I thought he was starting to be less of a jerk," Laila said.

I shrugged and sighed. "He's sort of been leaving me alone."

Are you kidding me? an evil voice whispered. *He lobbed a slur at you just a few hours ago.*

As if reading my mind, Laila asked, "Did something happen?"

My eyes jumped to Ishani again, and I wondered how much I could share. She seemed to be ignoring us, so I decided to lay it all out.

"He went after Zoe pretty hard," I said, voice low. "Her application to adopt was denied, and he must've found out somehow. He shredded her in front of everyone. It was ugly."

"Ouch." Laila cringed. "That's pretty low. I'm not sure those two will ever get along."

"There's definitely bad blood between them," I said, fidgeting with my glass. "I can see why Zoe gets so upset. Gerald always knows just the right thing to say to trigger people, and he saves the worst of it for her."

Laila frowned, looking down at her hands. "I don't understand why he doesn't just mind his own business. It takes so much effort to be mean to people."

"Right?" I huffed. I didn't understand him either.

Gerald was like the Lament Configuration. The desire to puzzle him out itched like a cilice, but I knew I'd unleash unholy hell once I solved that one.

The silence stretched between us as I slowly turned my glass, watching the water spin.

"I don't think he has much in his life besides work," I mused. "That leaves him with a lot of time and energy to be evil."

What I didn't add was that a part of me also believed that Gerald had to go through a shit-ton of pain to be such an asshole. That part of me felt sorry for the guy, and I was so ashamed of it that I couldn't even share those thoughts with my best friend.

Laila *hmmed*, and that sound spoke volumes. "People choose to be cruel. Imagine what the world would be like if they put that energy into something productive instead."

"I hear you," I agreed. "I guess that's why I'm trying to get him to cut it out. The lab would be a much better place if he stopped attacking people all of the time. I tried to talk to him in private about what he said to Zoe. I was hoping he'd see how much he'd hurt her and maybe even get him to apologize. Since the stuff with the tiger, I guess I thought he might listen."

"How did that go?" Laila asked, eyes jumping up to meet mine and one eyebrow raised in doubt.

"About as you'd imagine," I said. "He slipped right back into troll-mode. Talked some trash. Typical Gerald crap."

Laila pursed her lips and shook her head in sympathy. "Maybe he's beyond hope."

"Maybe." I shrugged. "But I can't see him leaving anytime soon. And the current situation is untenable. I think we might lose Zoe over it. I've gotta keep trying."

Laila shook her head sadly.

"At least work has been super slow," I said, trying to shift the conversation without being obvious about it.

"Do you think you'll close for the storm?" Laila asked, taking the bait. "It's supposed to drop a couple of inches. Maybe up to six."

My eyes went wide, my mind shifting completely away from Gerald. "Really? Damn. I'd heard it was going to be a big one, but that's a lot of snow."

A lot for Oklahoma, at least.

After I digested the information, I added, "Fran's away on vacation. I haven't heard anything about closing. But I may just push to close down regardless, to keep the lab staff safe and all. No one's going to bring in samples during a storm like that anyway."

"You should totally do that," Laila encouraged me.

She didn't know Fran as well as I did, though. If I closed things down without her blessing, it could bite me later.

Sick of thinking about the lab, I asked, "How 'bout you? How was work?"

Her eyes bounced quickly to her mom and back to me. I realized with a sinking feeling that I might have accidentally tread somewhere I shouldn't have.

"Fine," she said curtly.

Her eyes pleaded for me to drop it, so I did.

I thought about prattling on about my call to Armand but figured any topic related to relationships was probably best avoided.

Instead, I brought up fluff things, like the new Terraforming Mars expansion and the latest episode of *House of the Dragon*. Laila relaxed into it, and I even managed to get her to laugh a couple of times.

Before I knew it, dinner was ready.

Ishani called to Laila in Hindi, and together, they brought everything to the table. Ishani went to the living room to fetch Rakesh. He soon joined us at the head of the table and waited while Ishani served him. He grunted when she finished spooning the curry into his bowl.

I shot Laila a questioning look. She shook her head infinitesimally.

Ishani served the rest of us, and I thanked her. We dug in, using the naan as utensils to scoop up the curry. Soft slurping sounds broke the silence.

My eyes danced around the table, trying to get a read on everyone. The food was delicious, but the air of tension was palpable. I wasn't sure what to do, so I busied myself with eating, waiting for social cues from Laila.

Out of the blue, Rakesh looked at me intently and asked, "Why do you not help Laila find a husband?"

"Huh?" I answered, completely caught off guard by the question. Laila stiffened.

His eyes narrowed. "Laila needs a husband. You are her friend. You should help her find one. Yes?"

That 'yes?' was absolutely not a question. I felt a flutter of panic.

Ishani stopped eating, and her eyes danced between Laila and me.

"Um," I stammered, scrambling to get my game face on. I wiped my mouth with my napkin and tucked my hands under the table so he couldn't see me fidget. My sewing machine leg started up.

Rakesh dramatically rested his forearms on the table, one hand still holding a piece of curry-soaked naan. "Why does she not have a husband?"

A litany of snarky responses popped into my head, including telling him to mind his own business and fuck off. I bit them all back and tried to order my thoughts.

"Not everyone wants to get married," I said, figuring that was the politest of all the retorts that had been pinging around my mind.

It still wasn't the right thing to say. Ishani looked mortified, her face turning ashy. Rakesh sat statue-still, eyes locked on me with a withering stare. Out of the corner of my eye, Laila slowly bit her lower lip, eyes cast down.

Alarm bells started ringing in my head.

Rakesh leaned forward, like a lion slinking up on its prey. "Where is your husband?"

Fighting the thudding in my chest, I calmly said, "I don't have one." I tilted my chin up and met his eyes.

He stared back, unflinching. "I am certain your father is as disappointed in you as I am in Laila."

Now I was really pissed, and I couldn't hold it back anymore. "Guess it's a good thing he left before I was born then," I snarked.

Ishani let out a little gasp, and I realized that I'd gone a step too far.

"That explains much," he said coolly. He turned to Ishani and started talking in Hindi, voice agitated. He gestured to me and then to Laila. Ishani stared down at her food, taking it in silence. Laila shrunk in her seat.

He turned to me and gave me a look that could've overturned a mountain. "You are a bad friend." With that, he went back to sopping up curry with his naan.

I'd been dismissed. Unsure of what I was supposed to do with that, I glanced quickly around the table.

Shoulders hunched, Ishani slowly nibbled on her naan, eyes still cast down. Laila was pushing sauce around with her naan but not actually eating anything. She looked up quickly, met my eye, and shook her head so slightly that I barely caught it.

Fighting the post-adrenaline shakes, I tore off a section of naan and took a pinch of curry. The silence spread across the table.

Realizing I'd royally screwed the pooch, I kept my mouth shut through the rest of the agonizingly long dinner, trying to ignore the screaming lack of conversation. It was awful, and I couldn't imagine poor Laila having to deal with this all the time.

I'd grossly underestimated her folks, particularly her father, and I needed to rethink the situation. Her parents were dug in like ticks, and I needed to find a way to dislodge the buggers before Laila was forced to do something she didn't want to do.

*****

It was only a short drive home after dinner, but I spent the entire time running the brief conversation with her dad over and over again in my head. I couldn't help but feel like, in my efforts to make everything better for Laila, I'd only made them worse.

Her dad had stayed silent the rest of the meal and hadn't bothered to say goodbye when I'd left. Her mom had also turned icy, judgment wafting off her as the women worked together to clean up. As soon as the last dish was in the dishwasher, I'd been dismissed.

Laila had walked me to the door in silence. She'd given me a hug, but I could smell the defeat and disappointment on her. I knew we'd still be cool, but I couldn't help but feel like I'd let her down. I wished I had a time machine to go back and try to fix the mess I'd made.

It was pitch black when I got back home. Yersi was waiting at the door and greeted me with a *merf*, swirling around my legs. Even with all his attention, I was still agitated, unable to escape the feeling that I'd completely botched the evening.

My mind was occupied with self-flagellation, and I knew I couldn't sleep. I flopped on the couch to watch an episode or two of some fluff show on Netflix.

I surfed through the plethora of options, unable to settle on anything. I was stuck in an anxiety loop, and I couldn't pull myself out of the lapping conversations in my head. I'd wanted to do something to fix Laila's situation, but I'd only added fuel to the fire.

I picked up my phone to text her.

> Sorry about tonight. I think I made things worse.

I added a pleading face emoji.

She didn't reply right away. I wasn't sure if she was occupied with her parents or if she was mad at me.

> Call me if you want to talk. I'm here.

I put my phone on the coffee table, face down, and snuggled under the blanket. I was worried about my friend, but I didn't want to push her anymore. My hands were tied.

The inaction got my mind swirling. I couldn't understand why Laila's parents were so hard on her. A "family" didn't have to be a husband, wife, and two kids. There were so many different ways that people could form groups for mutual support and caring.

Didn't her folks see that they were crushing her with their expectations? What happened to live-and-let-live? Why couldn't her parents just let her be who she wanted to be? She wasn't hurting anyone. In fact, it was just the opposite. She touched the lives of every single student who crossed her path, she was a superstar at work, and, more importantly, she was happy.

Why mess that up?

Yersi jumped into my lap as if sensing my distress and started purring. I absently scratched him under the chin, trying to avoid the drool, and I felt the knot in my stomach relax just a tad. Yersi pushed his cheek against my hand, insisting on more pets, and started making biscuits.

I reflected on my own situation. I didn't have any close blood-kin anymore. It had been just me and my mom growing up. She'd passed when I was young, and Aunty had taken me under her wing. Aunty was my family now. My only family.

And Tessa, a little voice whispered.

Yes, Tessa is also family now.

I'd only known Tessa for a couple of months, but I already felt a momma-bear protectiveness over her. Aunty and Tessa were my found family, and I was eternally grateful for them.

Yersi had finally settled and was curled in a midnight-black donut on my lap, purring softly.

"And you, too, bud," I cooed at him. "You're the best kiddo a woman could have."

He replied with a content, slow blink.

CHAPTER
THIRTEEN

My eyes clicked open to the dark ceiling in my bedroom, and the cool air nipped at my nose. I hadn't had a drop of alcohol last night at Laila's, but I still felt puffy, and my mouth was dry. I wasn't sure what had woken me up well before my alarm, but my dry, scratchy eyes told me I should go back to sleep.

My buzzing brain vetoed that motion.

A *thud* broke the silence as Yersi jumped off the bed. I'd have about five seconds before he started begging.

Grumbling to myself, I rolled over to check my phone. The clock confirmed it was way too early to get up. There was also an eerie lack of notifications. I'd expected Laila to respond to my text last night, even if it was late. Something was definitely up.

It was early, but I sent her another quick text anyway.

> Worried about you. Let me know you're alive?

My phone locked without a response. I didn't want to be a nag, but I was genuinely starting to freak the fuck out.

I stayed in bed for a minute, chewing on my cheek. Yersi yowled from the doorway, reminding me of my duties as his royal attendant. I debated throwing a pillow at him.

Might as well get up, I whined.

Still feeling off, I robotically went through the motions of getting ready: feeding Yersi, feeding myself, getting dressed, and packing a lunch. Despite two cups of tea, I was still feeling sluggish. The only thing that penetrated the mind-fog was an endless loop of speculation about how Laila was doing.

Before leaving, I went outside to check on the chickens. My breath puffed out in front of me as soon as I stepped outside. The sun had risen, but it was still gray and gloomy. Low clouds stretched ominously across the sky. I could practically feel the weight of the pressure change.

The chickens were huddled close to the heat lamp, their feathers fluffed up. They greeted me with soft clucking but didn't leave the perch in their nesting box. Their water had frozen over yet again.

Crap.

Before I did anything else, I went back into the house to check the weather on my phone. Unfortunately, the forecast had gone from bad to worse. It was supposed to warm up ever so slightly. Just enough for those low, angry clouds to drop snow. And by the sounds of it, there was going to be a lot of it.

To my dismay, the timing of the storm's arrival had also moved up. It was now expected to roll in during the early afternoon, with the heaviest snowfall around three or four. The local authorities were encouraging people to avoid non-essential travel.

This was going to suck on so many levels.

Deep breaths. Little steps. Eyes on the prize, Aunty's voice whispered in my head.

First things first: I needed to get the chickens in the garage before the storm moved in. Then, I'd check in at work. Hopefully, Fran would see what was happening from her beach-side resort and close the lab for the day. If she was still unresponsive, I was going to try to move mountains to send everyone home. The alternative would put lives at risk.

I headed back outside. Thankfully, the Eglu that housed the chickens was an all-in-one, predator-proof, mobile chicken house. They were already tucked into the small nesting box, and all I had to do was slide the internal door closed to secure them before moving the whole kit and caboodle. I turned the heat lamp off, unclamped it, and set it to the side. Not wanting anything to spill, I moved the food and water containers out before tilting the contraption up on its rear wheels and rolling it to the front of the house.

With the movement, the clucking sounds picked up. But the girls had been carted around inside the nifty contraption often enough that they weren't frightened. I dragged the Eglu onto some collapsed boxes on the garage floor.

It was only a few degrees warmer in the garage, but the four walls and a roof would offer some shelter from the windchill and the heavy snow. I brought the heat lamp in, clamped it back onto the outer cage, and turned it on. I refreshed their water and filled their dish before sliding the internal door open. With all of the excitement, they ventured forth and began pecking at the food, clucking softly.

One task down.

With my girls sorted, I grabbed my stuff and headed to work to tackle the next mission.

***

The lab's parking lot was virtually empty. Some employees might be able to get to work, but they may not be able to get back home through the storm. I suspected we'd be getting a lot of callouts today.

After dropping my things off in my office, I checked in with Dustin. I was relieved to find him at his desk, reading the news on his computer.

"Morning, Dustin," I said and entered without knocking.

He looked up and flashed a small smile. "Mornin', Doc." He gestured to the computer with his chin. "Looks like it's gonna be a bad one."

"Yes, sir," I agreed. "Any news from Fran?"

"No, ma'am," he said and then chewed on his mustache.

"Who else is in today?" I asked, all business, my mind switching to action mode.

"Don't know for sure." He shrugged. "Anna was in when I got here. I saw Sally's car. And Dr. Richter's truck."

"Hmm," I said, my eyebrows furrowing. "I'll reach out to Fran. Maybe she'll close the lab."

Seeing Dustin's dubious expression, I said, "You never know," and shrugged.

He harrumphed.

"If I don't hear back from her, I'll make sure we still close down." I sounded more certain than I felt.

I could probably get away with excusing Dustin early. Maybe Anna and Carol, too. But the other departments were their own little fiefdoms. The other heads, Sandy, Manuel, and Gerald, would need to agree if I was going to play it safe. It might still be my neck on the line with Fran, but it'd be less bloody if I had the blessing of the other leaders.

Before I went to track them all down, I asked, "Anything come in?"

"No, ma'am," he replied. "Don't expect nothin', neither. I think people are hittin' the Homeland to stock up and hunkerin' down."

I nodded slowly. "Okay. Let me see what I can do to send everyone home early. If we get as much snow as they're saying, we'll probably need to stay closed tomorrow, too. I'll see what I can make happen."

He gave me a friendly salute and turned back to his computer.

My mind raced as I headed back to my office, making a mental to-do list. First thing, I needed to get everyone home, including myself. My Prius would definitely not make it on unplowed roads, and there was no way in hell I was asking Gerald for a ride home in his truck.

A snapshot of my virtually empty fridge popped into my head. Dustin was right; most people would be rushing around this morning, making sure they had enough food for the next two to three days. I quickly did a mental tally of what I had in my cabinets. Between the canned soup and pasta, I figured I could make it a couple of days if the town shut down. All the stores would be closed on Friday for Christmas either way, but Aunty would be feeding me that day. I figured I could last until Saturday and hit the store then.

At least the storm is coming now, I thought. *Maybe the roads will be clear by the holiday.*

I was crossing my fingers and toes for that one. A lot of people would be traveling that day, myself included. I was looking forward to seeing Aunty and Tessa. I didn't want to miss another day with them. My thoughts made a hard left to Laila, and a rush of concern washed over me.

She'll be stuck in her house with her folks.

My mind buzzed. I needed to make sure Laila was in a good spot, too. I stopped in the hallway, closed my eyes, and took a deep breath.

One thing at a time, Josie.

Right now, getting the lab closed was at the top of my list. Back in my office, I called Fran's cell. After several rings, it went to voicemail.

"Hello, Fran. This is Josie. I just wanted to make sure you're aware that there's a pretty bad storm moving in this afternoon. I was wondering if we could close the lab after lunch. Make sure people can get home safely before it gets bad. We might need to stay closed tomorrow, too, depending on the roads. Call or text me and let me know. Thanks. Bye."

I disconnected the call and laid my cell on my desk, not at all optimistic about her messaging me back. I wondered if anyone else in the lab had tried to contact her.

Sandy would know; she was the real matriarch of the lab and toxicologist extraordinaire. Of all of the doctors in the lab, she was the one with the most seniority.

I wasn't sure if Sandy would be in today, but I decided to give it a shot. If I could get her to support closing the lab at lunch, I was fairly certain the rest of the crew would follow. As luck would have it, she was at her desk, poking at her keyboard, reading glasses perched on her nose.

I knocked on her door. "Dr. Bishop?"

She looked up and smiled. "Good morning, Josie."

Sandy was close to retirement age, much to the dread of every vet in Oklahoma. She was heavyset with dark brown skin and short gray hair. Today, she was wearing thick, tan Carhartt pants and a comfy sweater. She pulled her glasses off, letting them hang around her neck, and turned to me.

"Morning," I said as I sat down across from her.

She leaned back, somehow managing to avoid knocking over the stack of papers behind her. Her office was cluttered but in an eerily organized way. If she was looking for something, she'd stare around the room for a millisecond, tapping her chin thoughtfully, and then miracle an article or a book from one of the myriads of paper towers around her small space.

"Ready for the holidays?" she asked.

"Meh," I said. "I like having a day or two off to spend with Aunty. But we're not too big on all the monetized craziness. We just hang out and eat good food."

"That sounds refreshingly simple," she said approvingly.

"You?" I asked. I was anxious to get to the meat of the matter, but Oklahoma etiquette required a bit of polite small talk first.

"We're keepin' it simple this year," she answered. "Just me and Walt. Walt's gonna barbeque goose."

My eyebrows shot up.

She cracked a warm smile. "Yeah, we might end up having to do it in the oven with this storm coming in. But he's been planning this since November. And you know him. Rain or shine, he'll be out there over the grill."

"Let me know how it goes," I said.

Walt was known for cooking some badass barbeque. I was still perfecting my technique and was curious to see how a goose would turn out. I didn't think the storm would let him outside to try it, though.

"Speaking of the storm," I continued, happy to find a natural segway. "Have you heard anything about shutting the lab down early today? Maybe keeping it closed tomorrow, too?"

She shook her head. "No, ma'am."

"I tried to call Fran to see what the plan was," I said. "But it went to voicemail."

Sandy was polite enough not to snort, but I could tell she wanted to.

"What do you think about closing the lab at lunch?" I asked. "I'm worried about people getting home. The chances of anyone bringing samples in once the snow starts are slim to none. I can ask Josh to start his on-call shift a bit early. He's got a big truck and lives close by. Should be easy for him to receive anything on the off chance someone can manage to get here. Over half the lab is gone already. It's not like many tests would even be run."

Sandy was nodding slowly. "I was thinking the same myself."

I felt a hint of relief. Sandy had some serious political clout. If she agreed, she'd provide some cover if Fran came down on me.

"The state offices already sent everyone home," she added.

"Oh, good," I said, the tension in my shoulders loosening ever-so-slightly.

Having the government buildings shut down only strengthened our position. Since the lab technically fell under the purview of the state and not the university, we were ultimately beholden to them. If a member of the public complained about the lab being closed, we'd probably be safe if the other state offices had also been shut down.

"What are they doing for tomorrow?" I asked. "Should we proactively stay closed tomorrow or play it by ear?"

Sandy pursed her lips, thinking. "I doubt the roads will be clear in the morning," she said, rocking back in her chair. "People are just gonna call out tomorrow anyway. I say we run it as an on-call day, starting after lunch today and through to end-of-day Thursday. Friday is already a holiday."

"Okay," I said. "Let me check in with Manuel and Gerald. We'll plan on shutting down at lunch and being closed tomorrow. Give the last stragglers a chance to get samples in this morning. I'll let you know if Manuel or Gerald disagrees. Sound good?"

"Yes, ma'am." She nodded. "Thanks for herdin' the cats."

I was sure she knew how much I did *not* want to talk to Gerald and appreciated that I was taking one for the team.

A smile tipped my lips. "All in a day's work."

I left Sandy's office with a wave and headed to the PCR lab. I knew I needed to get Gerald's buy-in, but I couldn't help but put that conversation off a tad longer. After yesterday, I figured he'd be in full-on shark-attack mode, and I didn't want to pull a Leeroy Jenkins. It would be better to garner support from everyone else first and then face him with a full arsenal.

I found Manuel at one of the PCR lab benches just inside the door, unpacking samples. One of the PCR lab techs, Beth, was sitting at a hood behind the glass of the enclosed prep room.

I technically wasn't supposed to enter without my lab coat, so I half-leaned across the threshold and called out, "Morning, Dr. Rodriguez."

He made his way over to me. "Good morning, Dr. Harjo."

Manuel was about my height with broad shoulders and a fit frame. He was clean-shaven with a military-style haircut. He wore his lab coat like he used to wear his uniform: ironed and neat.

"Most of your techs gone today?" I asked.

He nodded once. "Just Beth came in. I'll send her home as soon as she's finished the extractions."

"Oh, perfect," I said with a hint of relief. "I was coming to ask what your plan was. I was hoping to close pathology down at lunch. Sandy wants to close toxicology down, too."

"Has Fran provided any direction?" he asked, ever respectful of the chain of command.

I reluctantly shook my head. "I called her cell and left a message, but I haven't heard back. If we all agreed, I figured we could close and put a sign on the door just in case something trickles in. I'll ask Josh to start his on-call shift early."

He crossed his arms as he considered and said, "That's a solid plan."

"We're thinking about keeping the lab closed tomorrow, too," I added. "With the storm moving in late, the roads are likely still gonna be a mess in the morning."

"Makes sense," he said. "Will Josh be able to get in to receive urgent samples? What kind of vehicle does he drive?"

"He should be fine," I answered. "I don't think anything will come in, but if it does, he lives nearby and drives a truck. I'll ask him to call one of us if we get anything. He's pretty good at knowing what's what."

Josh had been working the on-call shifts for us for a while. He was great at triaging. On the weekends, he'd receive anything that came in and put them in the fridge for Monday. He'd scan the forms and call us if it was something urgent. For dead bodies, he'd call us no matter what and let the pathologist decide. Autolysis never stopped, even in the cooler.

"Sounds good," he said.

"I'll talk to Gerald," I said. "I'll let you know if the plan changes."

"Thanks for taking the initiative to get our employees home safely," he said.

I gave him a smile and a nod.

"Before you go," he added, "the PCR on the pig from Monday was negative."

In all of the chaos, I'd almost forgotten about the piglet.

"Remind me. What does the pig abortion panel include again?" I asked, not at all embarrassed that I'd forgotten.

Unphased by the question, Manuel said, "PPV, PCV, pseudorabies, and PRRS."

I nodded. "Not too surprised it came back negative. It was just the one litter. Probably isn't anything infectious. Thanks for getting it done when you're short-staffed, though. I appreciate it."

"Anytime," he said with a tip of his head.

With another "thanks" and a quick goodbye, I left to go find Gerald. I really didn't want to talk to him; I was still a bit salty after yesterday. But I could only put it off for so long.

Gerald's office was dark and empty. My eyebrows crinkled. If he wasn't stalking the hallways, he was usually squatting in his office. It was weird not to find him there.

I decided to check the microbiology lab. He typically only went in there to drive-by-bully the techs, but everything was a little off this week. To my surprise, I found him hunched at the lab bench, looking through agar plates.

Since I was still without a lab coat, I leaned through the door. "Good morning, Dr. Richter," I started, trying to be polite.

He put down the plate and turned to look at me but didn't come over. "Yes?" he called out.

Jerk.

I hated asking him for anything, and I kicked myself for not grabbing my lab coat before I'd come to his lab. "Um, I don't have my lab coat. Mind coming over here for a sec?"

He was too far away for me to catch his expression, but he put the plate down, took his gloves off, and made his way to the door. He *did* take his sweet time doing so. It was just another of his small gestures to exert control.

He stopped about two feet away from me, arms crossed. "Yes?" he said coolly.

"Do you have any techs coming in today?" I asked.

He stiffened.

With a sinking feeling, I realized I'd unintentionally picked at a sore spot. I quickly added, "I was trying to get a rough idea of how many people are in the lab. We haven't heard from Fran, and with the storm moving in and all...."

His glare chased away the rest of the sentence, and my adrenals kicked in.

"Um," I stammered, hating myself for it. "I've just been talking with Sandy and Manuel about maybe closing the lab at lunch."

"That's ridiculous," he interrupted. "Our customers depend on us to provide round-the-clock service."

"Yes, I understand," I replied, frustrated that the name-dropping hadn't worked. "But I don't think any cases will come in, and I'm worried about some people being able to drive home in the storm."

"Maybe if everyone didn't drive small, tree-hugging cars, they'd be able to do their jobs," he sniped.

Sweet baby Jesus, Gerald. Could you try not being a shitass? For just a millisecond? It took everything in me not to sigh audibly. This guy was impossible.

I figured we could still close the lab without his buy-in, but it would be messy. I had no idea how he would play it with Fran when she found out. If she came down on me for closing the lab, I'd have firmer ground to stand on if all of the department heads had agreed.

I tried another tack. "I know you're worried about the customers. We'll make sure they're taken care of."

He narrowed his eyes and pursed his lips. I could tell he doubted my ability to take care of anything, but he seemed willing to hear me out. The dark side of me wondered if he just wanted to see what I'd say so he could use it as ammo to tear me down later.

Fuck it. I had nothing to lose at this point.

"We'll make sure any samples that are dropped off are safely handled," I said, forcing confidence into my words. "I'll ask Josh to start his on-call shift early. He lives close by and can get here just fine. He'll make sure that any samples that are dropped off are stored appropriately until the staff can get in to process them."

To my surprise, Gerald actually seemed to be considering it.

"I'll ask him to call you if any microbiology cases come in," I added. That little nugget might be enough to get him to agree.

There was an uncomfortable beat of silence as he studied me. I felt like I was trying to take a bone away from a cranky, fear-biter of a dog. One misstep, and I was sure he'd maul me.

"Please?" I tried, hoping it didn't make me sound too weak. He tended to bite harder with the scent of prey on the wind.

"That would be acceptable," he said curtly, frown still tugging at his lips and eyes piercing me.

I practically fell to the floor in shock.

"Thank you, Dr. Richter," I blurted and then high-tailed it out of there before he could change his mind.

CHAPTER
FOURTEEN

I could practically feel the storm rolling in, nipping at my heels to get everything wrapped up. With the three department heads on board, it was just a matter of informing the rest of the staff, and I couldn't help but feel like it would be downhill from there.

The histology lab was the first stop. Thankfully, Sally was near the door at the embedding station. She was intensely focused on her work, forceps arranging the tissues in the hot wax.

I leaned in the door. "Morning, Sally."

She looked up. "Good morning, Dr. Harjo." She gestured to the cooling wax blocks with her forceps. "I was able to get your case on the processor last night. It should be ready around lunch."

"Oh! Thanks!" I said with a hint of surprise. I hadn't been expecting that, and in all of the storm prep, I'd completely forgotten that the histology was still pending.

"Um," I continued. "Because of the weather, the lab's closing after lunch today. We'll stay closed tomorrow, too. If you can get the pig case completed before we shut down, great. If not, don't worry too much. I want you to get home safe."

"I should be able to get it cut and stained for you," she said with a humble shrug. "Thank you for the update."

"Thank *you* for covering the entire histo lab this week," I replied with a smile.

With a wave, I left her to it.

I'd planned on telling Dustin next, but he wasn't in his office or on the necropsy floor. I figured I'd circle back and fill him in later. I moved on to hunt Carol and Anna down. As I rounded the corner to the receiving area, my stomach dropped.

Rachel Hoskins, the pig farmer, was standing in the reception area looking through the window and out onto the necropsy floor.

"Oh, there you are, Dr. Harjo," Anna said, putting the phone back in the cradle. "Ms. Hoskins has a litter for you."

My heart sank into my shoes. A "litter" meant multiple piglets.

A storm is coming.

Rachel turned to me, hands tucked in the pockets of her tan Carhartt jacket. She tipped her head in greeting, but her lips were twisted in a frown.

"Hello, Ms. Hoskins," I said. "Would you like to have a seat? I'll be with you in a moment." I gestured to the interview room.

With a slight, almost defeated nod, she obliged.

Anna handed me the submission form with pursed lips. "Looks like there are six of 'em."

Six! My shoulders tensed.

"Dustin is outside, gettin' 'em outta the truck," she added.

"Thanks, Anna," I said, taking the submission form and skipping the usual idle chit-chat. I was eager to get this unexpected case moving along so we could all get the hell out of dodge.

As I started to step away, I immediately swiveled back. Feeling flustered, I'd completely forgotten why I'd come down here in the first place.

"Oh, also," I said, catching Anna's attention again. "We'll be closing down at lunch and staying closed tomorrow, too."

She made a *whew* sound. "I was kinda anxious 'bout getting home after work."

"Can you let Carol know?" I asked and then tipped my chin toward the interview room. "I need to knock this out."

She nodded. "Yes, ma'am."

"Would you mind calling Josh, too? Make sure he knows we're closing down early?"

"On it," she answered.

"Thanks," I said, and she dipped her head in reply.

I glanced down at the paperwork before joining Rachel. The information was fairly threadbare; there was another aborted litter, and that was about it. Feeling a tingle of anxiety, I sulked into the room to interview Rachel for the second time.

Rachel's lips were pulled down in a deep frown, and her eyebrows were furrowed.

"Hello, Ms. Hoskins," I said, keeping my tone neutral as I sat across from her. I clicked my pen, ready to take notes.

"Dr. Harjo," she grunted with a nod. "No offense, but I was hopin' to never see y'all again."

I understood exactly where she was coming from and smiled sympathetically. "Looks like you lost another litter," I said. "Sorry to hear that."

She leaned forward, resting her elbows on her knees. "We were able to get more piglets this time, but the placenta was gone."

Bummer, I thought, but said, "It's okay. The more fetuses we have, the better. Thanks for bringing them all in. Has anything changed since the last time we spoke?"

"No, ma'am," she answered, sounding a bit prickly.

Rachel seemed to know her shit, but getting information out of her was like pulling teeth. I decided to start small and work my way up. "Did the sow show any signs before she aborted?"

"No," she replied curtly.

"Any coughing? Diarrhea?"

"No," she repeated, looking exacerbated now.

These were the same types of questions I'd asked on Monday, and I could tell I was annoying her. It didn't matter; I still needed to ask them. I couldn't help but feel like I was missing the sneaky foxtail, and the only way to get to the bottom of it was to keep probing the wound.

I pressed on. "Have you had a chance to take temps? Do any of the animals have fevers?"

"We took temps after the first litter was lost," she answered. "They were all normal. When we found the litter this mornin', I called Dr. Hughes to see if he could come out. His clinic is closed up for the storm. He won't be able to come out 'til after Christmas. We're doing our best."

"I know you are," I said with sincerity, feeling a tad chagrined. "I didn't mean to imply that you weren't. Sometimes, asking questions helps trigger a memory. You'd be amazed how thin some of the histories are, even the ones we get from vets. That's why we like to talk to people when cases are dropped off. Sometimes, we can pick out a nugget that might be useful."

She grunted, shifted back in her chair, and crossed her arms. "At least y'all are open today," she said as an olive branch. "I was a bit worried I'd make the drive and find y'all closed."

I cringed inwardly. If she'd come just a few hours later, she might've found the doors sealed for the next four days. I decided to bite my tongue and take the compliment.

"We'll get the necropsy done shortly and should be able to get some of the tests set up today," I said, trying to get us back on track.

She gave a slight nod of acknowledgment.

I looked down at the submission form and had a lightbulb moment. "Oh! Speaking of which. I'm not sure if the results have been released yet, but Dr. Rodriguez said the PCR on the first piglet you brought in was negative."

She looked up quickly, eyes sharp. "What's that test for?"

"Parvo, circo, pseudorabies, and PRRS," I answered, grateful I'd thought to ask Manuel that very same question less than an hour ago. Otherwise, I'd be looking like an ass.

She looked relieved, and I felt a tingle of apprehension.

"Just be aware that a negative result doesn't necessarily rule out an infection," I cautioned, watching her closely. "Normally, I wouldn't bat an eye and chalk the first case up to maternal factors. But the loss of an additional litter is a bit worrisome for something infectious."

Rachel pursed her lips and fidgeted with her beanie. "The sows are vaccinated for all those 'cept for pseudorabies. They stopped vaccinating for that in oh-three when it was eradicated from commercial farms."

My eyes widened just a tad; Rachel really and truly knew her stuff. I felt a burgeoning respect for this gruff woman. She was obviously worried about her herd, and she'd done everything she could to protect them.

"I haven't checked on the bacterial cultures yet," I said. "But we should know today if there is any growth or not. I'll give you a jingle when I know more."

"Thank you, ma'am," she responded.

I tapped my pen on the table, considering what else could wipe out multiple litters. "You're all-in, all-out if I remember correctly. Right?" I asked.

She nodded. "Our biosecurity is locked up pretty tight. Employees are assigned to specific barns. We got coveralls and boots they gotta wear. Footbaths. That kinda thing. We also got good rodent control. Every once in a while, we'll find a stray rat or somethin'. But we got it locked down as best we can."

I nodded, impressed.

"We talked about feed and water before. Still no changes, right?" I asked.

"No, ma'am," she answered matter-of-factly.

"I know the storm is coming in. But do me a favor. Put some of the sow chow in a big plastic baggy for me. Save some of the water, too."

She looked at me doubtfully.

"Just in case," I added with a shrug. "Sometimes mycotoxins can hide in feed that otherwise looks right as rain."

She considered and then nodded. "I'll ask the guys to do that as soon as I get back."

One more question was tickling the edge of my mind, but I couldn't fish it out of my brain. I paused to noodle some more. My thoughts shifted back to the Shadowhawk case and the sketchy farmhand. My skin prickled.

"What's your staff like?" I asked.

Her eyebrows furrowed. "What do you mean?"

Feeling like I'd misstepped again, I fumbled around, trying to explain myself. "Any disgruntled employees? Anyone new? Anyone not following protocol? That kinda thing."

Her frown deepened to something that was edging on a scowl.

I held my hands up in surrender. "Not saying anything bad about your employees," I conceded. "I just know stress can do this kinda thing, too. Pigs are sensitive. And smart. This storm coming in today is following pretty closely on the heels of the last one, and it may have unsettled things, even with them being inside. Having someone new taking care of them may've been enough to tip one or two of them over the edge."

Her frown softened, and she looked to be considering what I'd said. She sighed and nodded slightly. "Yeah, could be. Weather 'as been pretty bad this year, with all them swings in the barometer."

She leaned forward again, holding her leathery hands in front of her, and picked at her short nails. She stared at the ground, thinking.

"We got one new guy in the pregnant sow barn," she said. "I'm usually in the farrowin' barn and not with 'em much in the other buildings when they're workin'. I'll ask Tommy when I get back. He's the supervisor. See what he thinks." She shook her head. "I'm not sure 'bout that but doesn't hurt to check, I guess."

I still felt like I was missing something, but I was drawing blanks and couldn't think of what else to ask. It was time to get Rachel back on the road and start working on the piglets.

Standing, I said, "I think I have all I need, Ms. Hoskins. I'm sure you want to get back home before the worst of the storm hits."

"Yes, ma'am," she agreed, rising.

She followed me out to the vestibule, and we shook.

Worry was still etched in her face. Losing two litters might be a fluke, and a part of me wanted to reassure her. I decided to leave it with the shake. I didn't want to offer hope that may prove false.

After parting ways with Rachel, I made a beeline for the necropsy floor. My mission was to get these piglets done as quickly as possible. The impending storm was breathing down my neck, and I wanted to get the samples to the various labs with enough time for the techs to process everything. It was going to be tight.

The faint sounds of Hank Williams crooning "Never Again" drifted through the necropsy door. I slid my arms into the sleeves of the starchy lab coat and put on shoe covers before passing through the door. The smell of disinfectant was strong as I stepped over the footbath.

Dustin stood at one of the small animal tables, whistling along. He looked up from labeling containers.

"Howdy, Doc," he said in greeting.

"Howdy." I moved to his side, snapped my gloves on, and looked down at the six fetuses laid out on the table. "Welp. I think I jinxed us.'"

"Nah," he said and waved a hand, Sharpie still between his fingers. "This ain't nothin'. Least it ain't a neuro horse."

I snorted a laugh. He was absolutely correct.

Even though there were six piglets, they were small and in various stages of mummification. Other than that tidbit, I already knew I wouldn't find much on gross examination. This was going to be a simple matter of sample collection.

"Are we pooling samples for micro and PCR?" Dustin asked.

It was a somewhat rhetorical question, but Dustin always liked to double-check with the pathologist.

"Yeah, if we find something, it won't matter which pig it's in," I said. "Want to divide them up? We each do three?"

He nodded slightly. "Sounds good. That'll let us get 'em to the labs before lunch."

"Speaking of which," I said. "I came by to tell you earlier: We're closing the lab at lunch and staying closed tomorrow. So, the faster we can get them to the labs, the better."

"Glad to hear. Thanks for workin' your magic, Doc," he said.

As Dustin divided the piglets to either side of the small animal necropsy table, I picked one up to examine. Its skin was dry and brown-tinged, pulled tight over its bones, just like an Egyptian mummy.

I examined the rest of the litter.

The size of the piglets varied, and some were in more advanced stages of mummification than others. Sows tended to hold on to their piglets *in utero* even after death. This meant that one piglet might die in the womb and stay there. Sometimes, the remaining piglets would be just fine. Other times, the remaining piglets would die at different stages of gestation. When the latter happened, there'd be a litter of piglets that looked just like this.

I felt my stomach tighten.

This meant that, whatever this was, it had been around for a while, picking piglets off one by one. Even though I'd asked Rachel to grab feed and water, I had a hunch that this wasn't caused by a toxin. I had a horrible feeling that something infectious was making the rounds at Rising Sun Farms.

"Let's get these done quickly," I urged. "Dr. Rodriguez probably can't set anything up today with the storm and the holiday, but they might be able to get the extractions done so the PCR can be run on Monday. I'm not sure what'll happen with the cultures."

The microbiology testing was another bag of beans. Gerald might decide to set up the cultures and come in on Christmas to check on them, especially if he knew how serious this might turn out to be. For all his faults, he did take care of customers.

"Are we collectin' for histo?" Dustin asked.

"Yeah, we probably should," I answered. "I don't think I'll see anything given the mummification, but this is the second litter they've lost. I'm kinda worried that we're on the edge of something exploding here. I wouldn't feel right not trying."

"Roger that," he said. He grabbed six small formalin buckets and labeled them "A" through "F," one for each piglet.

Once everything was laid out, we got started on the necropsies. With scalpels in hand, we made quick work of the fetuses, collecting bits and bobs for the Petri dishes and formalin jars. The stomachs were shriveled raisins, and we weren't able to collect stomach contents. But I was crossing my fingers and toes that we might get something out of the internal organs on culture or with PCR.

Other than the mummification, the necropsies were relatively un-remarkable and went quickly. Even though I wasn't surprised, I still felt a twinge of disappointment. I'd be leaving Rachel hanging over the long weekend, and I strongly suspected there'd be more losses.

As we were cleaning up, I had a flash of brilliance. Removing my gloves, I went over to the paperwork. Next to the "Abortion Panel Profile" box, I wrote, "Plus Lepto."

I'd need to triple-check Kirkbride's book back in my office, but I had a nagging feeling that leptospirosis could cause fetal mummifi-cation in pigs. Leptospirosis was most often associated with kidney infections, and people often forgot that the bacteria could wreak all sorts of havoc once they hit the bloodstream.

I called to Dustin, "When you drop the samples off to Dr. Ro-driguez, can you please ask him to add a Lepto PCR to that first piglet from Monday?"

"Yes, ma'am," he replied.

"Thanks," I said absently.

I racked my brain for any other differentials. Something to test for that I might've forgotten. I needed to get as many tests ordered as possible before everything shut down. I still felt like I was missing something, but damned if I could put my finger on it. Frustrated, I stomped through the footbath.

CHAPTER

FIFTEEN

With the necropsies done, I headed back to my office, distracted. I couldn't shake the feeling that I'd overlooked something with the pigs, and it was eating at me.

Focus, Josie.

I took three deep breaths.

My computer woke with a mouse wiggle, and I pulled up the scanned paperwork from the first case. I'd written down the vaccine brands but hadn't followed up. At the time, it hadn't seemed all that important because infectious causes of fetal loss were so rare in well-run operations like Rising Sun Farms. Now that a second abortion had occurred, an infectious etiology seemed more likely, and knowing what the sows had been vaccinated against might be vital to the case.

After a quick internet search, it was clear that Rachel had a top-notch vaccination program. A hefty number of infectious organisms were covered, including but not limited to parvovirus, *Erysipelothrix*, multiple serovars of *Leptospira*, circovirus, *Mycoplasma*, *Pasteurella*, and PRRS. I couldn't help but feel like I'd reached another dead end. In a weird, backward way, I was a tad disappointed. A slam dunk was what I wanted this week. It was what I *needed* with this damn storm breathing down my neck.

Even though the pigs were vaccinated, there was a very slim chance that one of the tests could still pop with a positive. With a new employee around the farm, it was possible that a batch of vaccines had been left at room temp or a group of animals was missed. Sometimes shit just happened.

I pulled out Kirkbride's tome and flipped to the chapter on abortion in pigs. Sure enough, there was a laundry list of infectious causes, and several of them resulted in fetal mummification. However, the pigs at Rising Sun Farms had been vaccinated for the majority of them.

Well, so much for that.

My finger slid down the table, and I noticed the list only included infectious causes. There were still plenty of other things that could cause fetal death, like maternal factors, environmental factors, and toxicoses. I flipped through the next few pages. Those things were discussed in paragraph form, but the information lacked detail. It wasn't clear if any of the non-infectious causes could result in fetal mummification.

With a sinking feeling, I realized it was entirely possible that other sows had lost their litters, and the farmhands didn't know about it. If it was early enough in gestation, the fetuses could've been reabsorbed. Or, if the sow had aborted late-term fetuses, it is quite possible they'd been eaten before the employees found the evidence. The employees might not even know the fetal loss had happened until the sows went into heat again.

This could be bigger than we thought.

According to Sally, I'd have the histology slides from the first case before lunch. Even though I wanted to bug out before the worst of the storm hit, I knew I'd be sticking around for those slides to come off the coverslipper.

I closed the book, and my fingers sped across the keyboard. I quickly checked the results on the first piglet. As Manuel had said, the abortion panel PCR was negative.

I scrolled down to the microbiology results, and a big, fat "pending" stared back at me. I cringed. Gerald was going to be salty when he saw the PCR results had been reported before his were; he had a weird chip on his shoulder when it came to the PCR department. He also tended to take his frustration out on others, and I didn't like the idea of being the target of his ire.

Figuring out what was happening at Rising Sun Farms was more important than worrying about any backlash from Gerald, especially with the lab closing in a matter of hours. We were on the edge of something, and I couldn't in good conscience leave anything hanging over the four-day weekend.

Focus.

There were only two possible reasons why Gerald hadn't entered the culture results yet: Either there was some growth on the plate that needed to be worked up, or he was so busy he hadn't had time to enter "no growth" into the system.

I grabbed my lab coat and tried his office, only to find it dark. With trepidation, I headed to the microbiology lab, where I found him perched on a lab stool, hunched over the same bench as before. He looked lonely and small in the empty space.

Hearing me come into the whisper-quiet lab, Gerald looked over his shoulder, his expression unreadable. He quickly turned back to his work.

"Yes?" he asked curtly.

I moved over to the lab bench.

"Hey," I said tentatively. "I know you're busy. Sorry to bother you. Are there any results yet on the piglet from Monday? Another litter just came in from the same farm."

"Yes, I am aware," he snapped. "Dustin brought the samples in thirty minutes ago."

My eyes narrowed at his snark. He hadn't answered my question, and I wasn't sure how to ask it again without pissing him off.

I landed on saying, "Thanks for handling those," and then added, "Any growth on the first one? I know it's early, but...." My voice trailed off as he stopped what he was doing and slowly turned to me.

His steely stare shot laser death rays at me. Fighting a rush of adrenaline, I stuffed my balled fists in my lab coat pockets, plastered on a fake smile, and waited for his answer.

"There's no growth on any of the plates from case 43506859," he snapped

I assumed 43506859 was the first piglet. Gerald was a true Rain Man when it came to numbers. My mind tended to slide right over them, and I'd have to check my log if I wanted to look a case up in the system.

"The aerobic results will be entered today," he continued. "As you should know, the *Brucella* cultures cannot accurately be reported until Monday."

I did know that; I didn't just fall off the turnip truck. Those bugs were slowing-growing bacteria, and most diagnostic labs let the plates sit at least a week before sticking their neck out to call anything "no growth." But I also knew that snarking back at him wouldn't accomplish anything.

My smile started to feel strained. "Thank you," was the only polite response I could muster.

"I will be plating case 43506865 as soon as I've finished this one." He gestured to the three agar plates in front of him on the lab bench.

I felt a jolt of surprise.

In most labs, if there was a four-day closure, they'd just store the samples in the freezer and plate them when they returned. If he plated them today, he'd need to check them on Friday at the latest. Otherwise, the agar plates had the potential to be completely swarmed with colonies, and he'd have to start all over again.

I wasn't sure how I felt about Gerald coming in through the snow and on a holiday to check on one of my cases. A sliver of appreciation and respect bubbled to the surface, which also made me want to vomit.

"Thanks for doing that," I said, forcing the words out. "I know it means you'll have to come in on Christmas."

He stiffened. Gerald wasn't used to people being nice to him. And, if I was honest with myself, I wasn't used to it, either.

"This is the second abortion in the same week. This could be the start of something serious," he said, echoing my own thoughts.

Goosebumps broke out on my arms.

"It is our duty to protect the agriculture in this state," he added.

The mixture of emotions I was feeling only swirled faster. "I agree," I had difficulty saying.

This conversation was so weird and so unlike Gerald that I didn't know where to go next. Normally, he would have said something nasty to me by now, and I'd be fuming. Instead, he'd kept it professional, albeit exceedingly awkward.

To my horror, I found that I wanted to involve him in the case, and I wasn't sure what to do with that.

Screw it, I thought and dove right in.

"The abortion panel PCR was negative on the first piglet," I said. "I just added Lepto. I assume that'll have to wait until next week. But the pigs are vaccinated for Lepto, so I'm not optimistic about that one. Histo on the first one comes back this afternoon."

There was a short, uncomfortable silence. Through the pause, he didn't say something mean, mock me, or snap at me. He just sat there, silently working. I think I shocked him as much as I'd surprised myself. It was still awkward as all hell, but at least he wasn't being a malevolent turd.

I fidgeted with the Sharpie in my lab coat pocket. "Thanks again," I stammered.

He didn't reply. Instead, he kept flaming the loop and selecting colonies to streak, like I hadn't said a damn word.

I slowly left the lab, looking back over my shoulder and chewing my cheek. Out in the hall, I realized I'd started to sweat from the adrenaline dump, and my pits were wet beneath my lab coat.

It had been an exceedingly odd encounter with Gerald, and I was frazzled. He hadn't bullied me, and for some reason, that had shaken me more than him being a shitass. Trying to shake off the heebie-jeebies, I turned my focus back to the piglets.

"No growth" didn't mean much. It was like the negative PCR results. It just meant we hadn't detected anything infectious in that particular fetus from the narrow list of organisms we tested for.

I needed to get some more eyes on this case.

Manuel first. Then Sandy.

My mind circled through the differentials as I made my way to the PCR lab. Thankfully, Manuel wasn't in the clean room, and I found him entering results at the computer station in the lab.

"Hello again," I greeted him.

He gave me a small, tense smile.

"Everything okay?" I asked.

"It's hectic. Beth and I are doing our best to ensure that most of the cases are reported before we leave. The majority of them will be released today." He thumbed the neat stack of papers next to the keyboard. "Dustin brought over your samples. We'll get the extractions completed before we leave, but we won't be able to run anything until Monday."

He looked up at me; the slight crease between his eyebrows was the only clue that he was truly concerned.

"That's okay," I said, trying to hide my disappointment. "Can't control the weather."

"We'll add the Lepto PCR to both cases, but we won't be able to run them until next week," he added.

I nodded slowly, unable to hide a slight frown. I knew it would be impossible to run the Lepto PCR on the first case today and still get out by lunch. But a person could hope.

"Can you think of anything else we should be looking for?" I asked.

He leaned back in his chair and tapped his fingers on the desk, thinking. After some consideration, he answered, "Other than the foreign animal diseases, I can't think of anything."

My heart lurched. *Foreign animal diseases?! There's no way I'd get a foreign animal disease over winter break with a big storm moving in.*

The powers-that-be had to truly hate me for a hot mess like that to drop in my lap.

It can't be a foreign animal disease. I refuse to let it be that.

But the universe didn't care about my opinion. Biology did what biology wanted to do.

"Foreign animal disease?" I repeated back cautiously, testing the words.

He leaned forward, resting his elbows on the lab bench, and laced his fingers. His eyes were unfocused as he sifted through the annals of his experience as a military veterinarian.

"When I was deployed in Poland, we were providing assistance to control an outbreak of swine fever that had extended into Germany," he said.

I couldn't help a sharp intake of breath. Classical swine fever could cause fetal mummification. I'd just read that in Kirkbride's less than twenty minutes ago.

His eyes quickly bounced to me, and he must've seen the look of horror on my face because he added, "Didn't mean to worry you. The chances of swine fever popping up again in the US are slim."

He leaned back again, muscled arms flexing as he braced them on the lab bench. "I'm sure it'll be something simple. It might not even be infectious. We'll see if anything shows up on the next round of samples."

I couldn't shake the thread of concern. "Should we be testing for anything else?"

Considering, he rolled his lips in and then said, "I think you're all good for now. We'll run the Leptos. I'm certain Dr. Richter has the *Brucella* cultures incubating. And you've got the histo pending. Something will pop up, or it won't. You know how these abortion cases are. We might never figure out the cause."

He was right, but I still felt like I had to bird-dog this one.

"Okay," I conceded, knowing there wasn't much more I could do at the moment. "Please let me know if you think of anything else."

"Yes, ma'am," he answered with a nod.

"Thanks," I said. "Drive safe and happy holidays."

"You, too," he said, returning to his data entry.

I'd gone to Manuel hoping to feel a bit better about the case. Instead, he unintentionally sowed a seed of fear. Now, I was feeling more lost than ever.

Foreign animal disease.

His words bounced around my mind like a curse. I tried to shake them off, but they clung to me like crazy glue. I needed to talk to Sandy. She would help me feel better and chase the bad vibes away.

I found her in the lab, helping Eva get through the last few cases. Lab coat on, I joined her at the lab bench. "Hey."

She smiled at me. "How can I help you, Josie?"

"Have a minute to talk through a case?" I asked.

"Sure." She dipped her chin to the stool next to her. "Have a seat." She put her pipette down and took her safety goggles off, giving me her full attention.

"Thanks. I appreciate it," I said as I sat down.

Sandy was awesome; she always made time for everyone, and I never felt like I was putting her out. I wanted to give her a hug of appreciation.

"I'm working up two abortion cases, both from the same farm," I started. "The owner brought in just one piglet from the first litter on Monday. No placenta. It was in pretty good shape. No gross lesions. Micro and PCR came up negative. I added Lepto PCR, but won't get those results back until Monday. I should get histo back on that one today, but I'm not holding my breath."

She pursed her lips as she listened, and I could see her mind working through the differentials like a flip book.

"Today, a second litter came in," I continued. "Six fetuses. Mummified. Various stages of gestation. Again, no placenta. I won't have anything back on them until next week."

She grunted in sympathy.

"The owner runs a tight ship. It's an all-in, all-out facility with what sounds like fairly good biosecurity. The sows are vaccinated. The buildings are heated. They're on city water and mix their own rations."

"Did she bring any of the food or water in?" Sandy asked.

I cringed inwardly. "With the piglet on Monday, I didn't think to ask. I figured it was going to be one of those maternal-factor things. I'm pretty sure the owner was thinking the same thing. You know how fetuses are; we often don't find anything. We both kind of brushed it off. When the owner was in today, I asked her to collect feed and water samples. But she lives fairly far away. I don't think we'll be seeing those samples until Monday at the earliest."

Sandy nodded. "Understandable." She leaned back in her chair, rocking slightly. "Could still be maternal factors. If not, it's likely to be infectious, even with the negative results. If you hear hoof-beats, think horses, not zebras."

"Yeah," I said, nodding, even though I'd been moving the zebras higher on the differential list less than an hour ago. "Maybe there's a false negative floating around on that first case."

"Could be," she said, her tone neutral. "As for reproductive toxicoses, they are extremely rare in commercial pigs. This time of year, carbon monoxide poisoning from faulty ventilation or heating systems can cause abortion in pigs. With the last storm, it's possible that the heaters finally kicked on."

She raised an eyebrow in question.

"I don't know," I responded doubtfully. "The owner really knows her stuff. Because of the setup, she said she's not in every building every day. But I can't imagine them not catching a faulty heater. I can ask, though."

"That'd be unlikely anyway, I guess, especially with the mummified litter. In the rare reports of carbon monoxide exposure, all of the sows aborted around the same time." She paused to consider. "Nitrates in the water can cause abortion. But being as they're on city water, that's pretty unlikely. Plus, I haven't heard of that causing fetal mummification. You said she's bringing in some water?"

I nodded.

"We can check the nitrate concentration. It's a quick and easy test. Just to cover all the bases." She didn't sound convinced.

"Worth a try. I'll make sure to add that test once the water comes in," I said, making a mental note even though I wasn't convinced either. "Anything else? I thought about mycotoxins. We can check the feed she brings in."

Sandy tilted her head and pursed her lips as she noodled over everything. She was like a walking PubMed, and I let her do her thing. I couldn't help but hope that she'd pull a miracle out of a magic hat.

"Of course, zearalenone is a cause of reproductive disruption in pigs," she continued after a moment. "But I think of swollen vulvas, pseudopregnancy, and failure of implantation with zearalenone. I'm not sure about abortion of mid to late-term fetuses, especially mummified ones."

She shook her head. "I don't know, Josie. I gotta feeling this one isn't toxic. If several sows aborted the same week without any mummification, I'd feel a lot better about runnin' all the tox tests. But I'd rule out all of the common infectious things first."

I chewed my cheek, unsure whether I wanted to hear the answer to the question that was sitting on the tip of my tongue. Unable to help myself, I spilled it. "What about a foreign animal disease?"

Her eyebrows lifted slightly. Those words were like dropping a grenade in the room.

After a beat, she answered, "Foreign animal diseases always need to be on our radar. But I'd still rule out the common things before you head down that road."

I sighed, a tad relieved. Whether she knew it or not, Sandy had just given me permission to not freak the fuck out.

"Cool. I'll just wait and see what Manuel and Gerald find. I might even see something on histo," I said without any real hope. "I'll send the water and feed over whenever she brings it in. We can run the nitrate, but I'm thinking we just hold the feed for now."

She nodded in agreement. "Let me know what you find."

"Will do," I replied, standing to leave. "Drive safe and happy holidays if I don't see you before then."

"You, too, Josie."

With a wave, I left the toxicology lab, unsettled. I hadn't been super hopeful that Sandy could hand me a diagnosis, but she had somewhat alleviated the seed of fear that Manuel had planted.

Less than five minutes later, I was back in my office, slumped in my chair, staring at the phone. I needed to call Rachel, but I wasn't feeling it. I didn't have anything useful to share with her, and if I was honest with myself, I was slightly embarrassed.

Ruling stuff out is just as important as figuring out the cause, a previous faculty member's voice whispered in my head.

Yeah, unless it's fifteen hundred pigs at risk as I faff about trying to figure out what the hell is going on, an evil part of me replied.

I grabbed my pen and started tapping it on my desk.

I decided to call Rachel's vet, Dr. Hughes, first. She'd mentioned that they were closed. But there was a chance they had an answering service or a number to call for emergencies.

After several rings, the call went to voicemail. The message informed me that the clinic was closed and routed all emergencies to another location. It said voicemails would be returned on Monday.

Damn.

It wouldn't be worth calling an emergency clinic in this case. I needed to brainstorm with another veterinarian familiar with the farm, which seemed impossible at the moment. I left a quick message and asked for a return call, leaving my cell number. There was a slim chance someone was still checking voicemails even if they were closed.

After hanging up the phone, I started tapping my pen again. I still had to call Rachel, and I wasn't looking forward to it.

Might as well just get this over with.

Resigned, I dialed Rachel's number.

"Rising Sun Farms," she answered. The sound was a bit muffled, and I realized she was probably still driving home and talking to me on speaker from the road.

"Ms. Hoskins?" I asked.

"Yes, ma'am."

"This is Dr. Josie Harjo from the diagnostic lab. I wanted to give you an update. Is now an okay time to talk?"

"Thanks for calling," she replied gruffly. "Go ahead."

"Other than the mummification, I didn't find anything significant in the fetuses you brought in today. As I mentioned earlier, the abortion panel PCR on the first fetus was negative. Word of caution: That doesn't completely rule anything out. It just means we didn't detect that narrow list of bugs in that fetus. The aerobic cultures have no growth. Nothing's growing on the *Brucella* plates either, but they need to wait until Monday before they can call it. I added a Lepto PCR to both cases. But I'm not putting all of my eggs in that basket. You have a good vaccination protocol on your farm."

"Okay, thank you for the update," she said, disappointed.

I felt a twinge of guilt that there was nothing more to share. My pen continued its tapping.

"Once the roads are clear and it's safe to drive, please bring in the water and feed samples," I reminded her. "The toxicologist, Dr. Bishop, doubts it's anything toxic. But we'll run a nitrate on the water and hold the feed just in case we need it later."

"Yes, ma'am," she answered matter-of-factly. She sounded a bit relieved to have something she could do.

I chewed my cheek, trying to figure out the best way to broach the next subject without offending her.

"One last thing," I pressed on. "I don't think it's likely, but I'd recommend checking the ventilation system and the heaters. Carbon monoxide can cause abortions. I'd expect more widespread fetal loss with something like that, but still. Just one more thing to check off the list if it's easy."

I paused with bated breath, hoping I hadn't unintentionally insulted her.

"They don't call it the 'silent killer' for nothing," she replied. "I'll look into it."

My shoulders sagged in relief. I was starting to like this practical, non-nonsense pig farmer.

"With the storm and the holiday, we won't know more until Monday. But I will call you as soon as I have any more information," I said. "Stay safe, and happy holidays."

"You, too, Dr. Harjo."

I hung up the phone, still feeling off. My pen continued its tapping on my desk. I knew if I put it down, my sewing machine leg would start up, or I'd chew a hole in my cheek. I needed to do something but damned if I could figure out what it was. Not knowing what was causing the abortions was eating at me, and I wouldn't be able to relax until I'd solved it.

CHAPTER
SIXTEEN

Dark clouds hung heavy in the sky. The pressure had changed, and it felt like the storm would blow in at any moment.

I slumped in my chair, mind still whirling. I caught sight of my cell on the desk, and my heart dropped. I'd been so wrapped up in work that I'd completely forgotten about Laila. I picked up my phone, and the screen unlocked with Face ID. I opened up my messages and found a reply to my earlier text.

I'm alive.

I slid my thumb down for more, and the screen bounced. That was it. No additional texts. No gifs. Nothing. Just a simple but frustratingly vague "I'm alive."

My fingers sped across the screen.

Are you going to be okay with the storm coming? Want me to come by?

I waited for the ellipses of a reply to start bouncing across the screen. After thirty seconds, my phone's screen darkened, and it locked without an answer. Leaning back in my chair with a *harumph*, I set my phone down and started fidgeting with my pen. There wasn't much I could do until she texted me back.

With the storm pressing in, the roads would only be clear for another two or three hours at most. After that, it would be sketchy trying to get anywhere in my Prius. Whatever I decided to do, I needed to get a move on.

Antsy, I grabbed my lab coat and headed to the histology lab.

The hallways were whisper-quiet, and I didn't see a soul. In the lab, Sally was pulling racks off the automatic coverslipper and setting them into the hood to dry. She looked harried but moved with precision, working with practiced ease.

As I walked over, she looked up and gave me a nod in greeting.

With my hands stuffed in my lab coat pockets, I said, "How's it going, Sally? Need any help?"

"Almost done," she answered. "I had to triage." She nodded over to the cutting bench. "There are about forty or fifty blocks left to cut. But your case is finished. Everything else can wait until Monday."

I was impressed at how much she'd managed to complete. Just yesterday, there had been a mountain of work, enough for two or three people. She must've seriously hustled to get everything done.

"Thank you, Sally. I appreciate it."

"You're welcome," she replied.

The last rack was removed and placed in the hood. She pulled out a few slides and tested the coverslip glue by lightly tapping her glove on the edges.

Seemingly satisfied, she said, "If you wait a minute, I'll put the slides in a flat for you."

Flashing a smile, I said, "That would be amazing. Thanks again."

I grabbed some cardboard flats from the adjacent bench and handed them to her. She fished through the racks, finding the slides from my case and laying them into the flat. She quickly did a quality control check against the paperwork and handed the slides to me.

"Be careful. The coverslip glue is still wet," she advised.

"Yes, ma'am. Thanks again," I said. After a beat, I added, "Sure you don't need any help?"

"I got it," she said and shooed me out with a friendly gesture. "Go read the case and get yourself home."

"Will do. Drive safe and happy holidays, Sally."

"You, too, Dr. Harjo," she answered as she turned to pull the rest of the racks off.

I made a beeline back to my office. I set the cardboard flat on my desk, slid into my chair, and clicked on the microscope. I flipped open the cardboard covers, revealing the eight freshly stained and cover-slipped slides from the first piglet.

When I picked up the first slide, the edges stuck slightly to my fingers. Sally hadn't been kidding; the glue hadn't dried completely. If I wasn't careful, it would smear all over my microscope stage, or even worse, one of my objective lenses. That was a serious faux pas in the pathology world, and I'd never live it down.

Slide after slide skated across the stage. As each piece of glass scraped across, I felt a building sense of disappointment.

Everything was completely, heart-wrenchingly normal.

A heavy, tired sigh escaped. *Damn it.*

Leaning back, I rocked slightly in my chair and chewed on my cheek. I hadn't really expected to find anything; it was a fetus, after all. But *still*. The situation at Rising Sun Farms was gnawing at me, and it would continue to nibble away through the next four days.

This stupid case. It was supposed to be an easy fetus, I huffed to myself.

I didn't want to leave everything hanging ahead of one of the heaviest snowfalls in the last five years, but I didn't have a choice. I couldn't magic a lesion from the ether, as much as every pathologist wanted to do just that at some point in their career. I couldn't help but feel like I was on the edge of the cliff, and one small nudge would push me knee-deep into an abortion storm.

And I couldn't do a damn thing about it.

Resigned, I went through the motions of writing the report. Typing "within normal limits" was its own special level in hell reserved for frustrated pathologists.

When I got to the comment section, the cursor flashed malevolently. Usually, this was the section where the pathologist would tie everything together in a succinct narrative, looking like a superhero. I didn't have squat to tie together. It was like trying to knit a scarf with two-inch yarn scraps; it just wasn't happening.

The cause of abortion remains elusive, I typed.

The cursor blinked at the end of the sentence, laughing at me. In my head, it sounded like the obnoxious kid from *The Simpsons*. I deleted the crappy sentence and tried again.

There were no histologic changes within the sections examined to explain the cause of abortion in this case.

That felt a little bit better. Still not great. But it would do. I continued typing.

Infectious organisms were not detected with aerobic culture or routine PCR testing. *Brucella* cultures and *Leptospira* PCR are pending.

Normally, I'd just finalize the report, dust my hands off, and be done with it. But I had that second case hanging over me. I felt like I needed to say more, but there was a battle raging inside.

Only report what you are certain of, the voice of one of my mentors whispered in my ear.

I brushed the thought away. That was an ivory-tower way of thinking. Real life—real cases—they just didn't work like that. I scrolled my mouse back up to the part about the negative test results and clicked. The text cursor blinked at me.

Screw it. Follow your gut, Josie.

Given the presence of additional fetal losses at the facility (reference case 43506865), the possibility of an infectious etiology cannot be entirely ruled out. Test results should be interpreted in the context of clinical findings. Consultation with your veterinarian is recommended to determine the next steps in this case.

I released the report, feeling a bit dissatisfied. I always hated signing off on a report that said virtually nothing. But at least I'd been able to reference the second case and add a warning about a potential infectious cause. It was all I could do at this stage.

I frowned at my computer. The Rising Sun Farms cases continued to taunt me. I'd done everything I possibly could have, but my hands itched to do more. Feeling frustrated, I shut my computer down and locked up my office.

Pausing in the hallway, I checked my phone.

Laila still hadn't replied to my offer to stop by, and I was left considering my next move. Since I didn't know if she'd gone to work today, I wasn't even sure where to find her. I hadn't done much to help at dinner last night; I'd probably made things worse. Maybe she didn't even want me around.

Give her some space.

It was always hard for me to do nothing, but I figured that was probably the best course of action in this situation.

I dropped my phone into my purse and did a quick survey of the building. The histology, toxicology, and PCR labs were dark. Gerald was still hunched over a bench in the microbiology lab. I thought about ignoring him and then reconsidered; it was a bit too impolite, even if he was a prick.

I peeked in through the door. "Dr. Richter?"

He turned his head in acknowledgment but didn't stand up.

"I'm going to send the last few stragglers home," I said from the threshold. "Are you going to be a while?"

"Yes," he snapped. "It's our responsibility to ensure our customers get their results regardless of a little snow."

My knee-jerk response would've been too mean. Instead, I said, "I'll put the signs out and lock everything up. Will you set the alarm when you leave?"

"Yes," he said sharply, turning back to his work.

On impulse, I added, "Happy holidays," and skated out before he could ruin it.

I gathered my things and headed to the receiving area. I found the last few stragglers, Anna, Carol, and Dustin, sitting in the front office, chatting casually.

Seeing me come in, Anna asked, "Ready to close up?"

I nodded. "I think so. Dr. Richter's still working. I let him know we'd put the signs up and lock everything down. He'll get the alarm when he leaves."

"Thanks for arranging everything so we could get out early," Anna said, grabbing her things.

Sure, I'd "arranged" things, including getting buy-in from my peers, but Fran still hadn't called me back. I wasn't sure how she was going to feel about this, and she could come down on me pretty hard if she thought I'd made a bad decision.

Keeping everyone safe is worth it, I thought, even though I was still dreading Fran's response.

Dustin stood and put his coat on, Carol grabbed her purse, and we huddled up. We turned the lights off and taped the early-closure notice to the entrance.

Before stepping out into the cold, the four of us exchanged hugs with words of "Drive safe" and "Happy holidays." We all piled into our cars just as the wind had picked up and large fluffy flakes began to drift down.

I started my Prius, blasting the heat. Thankfully, I only had to drive a few miles to get home. I rubbed my hands together and placed them on the icy steering wheel. Before backing out, I glanced once more at the lab.

At least four more days I'd have to wait. At least four more days *Rachel* would have to wait. All I could do was hope the two abortions were a fluke. Otherwise, I'd return to find a stack of dead piglets waiting for me.

I pulled out of the parking lot, a tight knot sitting in my stomach.

CHAPTER
SEVENTEEN

It was only a short drive back home, but the weather went from inno-cent, fluffy flakes to angry flurries lickety-split.

By the time I parked my car in the driveway, the snow was coming down at a steady rate. It was obvious that the precipitation would be leaning on the heavier side of the predicted six inches, and my car would soon be covered. Until they plowed the roads, I'd be well and truly trapped.

The cold bite of the air and damp flakes chased me into the house. I bustled through the door with a shiver, kicking my shoes off and hanging my jacket up. The thick clouds had dampened the midday sun, and there was a gray, dusk-like gloom outside. I was grateful I'd brought the chickens inside and that we'd closed the lab early.

Meoooowww, Yersi insisted, rubbing against my legs.

After dropping my keys and purse on the entryway table, I squatted down to give him snuggles. The chin scratches did the trick, and a throaty purr started up. Satisfied, he sashayed over to the couch, tail swishing languidly, and nestled into the blanket.

Using the door through the kitchen, I headed into the garage to check on the chickens. They clucked softly in greeting. It was definitely cooler out there, but the water wasn't frozen. I tossed them some extra food, reassured that they'd be okay for the night.

Even with the chickens settled, I still felt restless. My stomach kept reminding me that I hadn't eaten lunch yet, but I was too worried about Laila to deal with that. Once I was back inside, I fished my phone out of my purse to text her.

How are things?

The message went out into the ether, and there was no immediate response. It was so unlike Laila not to text back right away, even if with a simple tag. I felt a bit lost and fidgety. Being trapped in the house only made it worse. A chaotic mess of thoughts swam through my head: the pigs, Laila, missing Armand, and the weirdness with Gerald. I couldn't handle having so many unresolved issues in my life. The itch to fix something—anything—was driving me nuts.

Keeping my phone handy, I grabbed my uneaten lunch from work and settled on the couch. I unpacked the container of pasta and popped the lid. The smell of the tomato sauce made my stomach rumble. Though it would have been exceedingly more delicious after a quick zap in the microwave, I was feeling too grumpy to get off my ass and ended up snarfing it down cold.

My stomach gurgled, initially thankful for the calories and then somewhat resentful that one of Carol's desserts hadn't joined the mix. Even though it was miserably cold outside, I knew I'd be popping a pint of ice cream before the day was over.

Leaving my dirty dishes on the coffee table, I rechecked my phone. I hadn't heard the ping of a text, but it was one of those obsessive reflexes I couldn't shake.

I set the phone back down with a huff and grabbed a book. When I tugged on the blanket, Yersi shot me a glare, and then he decided my lap would make a better spot anyway. Once the blanket was pulled over my ice-cold feet, he sauntered across the couch and started making biscuits on my lap. He settled down with a content, low purr. All was still not right with the world, but my shoulders relaxed ever so slightly.

Cracking the book open, I tried to get lost in the story. The words twirled across the page, and I kept re-reading the same paragraph, trying to focus. My mind just couldn't slow down enough to even digest a fluff novel.

An exacerbated sigh escaped, and I slapped the book closed. Yersi, startled from his meatloaf position, gave me a cat side-eye and flicked an ear back before curling into a ball, nose tucked under his tail.

Then, like manna from heaven, my phone dinged. My heart lurched, and I quickly leaned over to snatch the phone from the coffee table. With an exacerbated *merf*, Yersi hopped down from my lap and stomped away, tail twitching irritably.

Ignoring him, I unlocked my phone, thrilled to find a text from Laila.

> Can you call?

Relief washed over me. Instead of texting back, I dialed her number, and she answered on the first ring.

"Hey, Josie," she said, half-whispering. "Thanks for calling."

My stomach dropped at the thread of worry in her voice. "Everything all right?" I asked, even though I already knew it wasn't.

She snorted a quiet, sarcastic laugh. "Not at all."

The knot in my stomach tightened. A quick glance outside told me all I could do was listen. There was no way I could get my Prius out of the driveway at this point.

Snowshoes? a sarcastic voice echoed in my head. If she needed me, I'd find a way to rescue her, no matter hell or high water.

"What happened?" I asked hesitantly.

"I didn't think it could possibly get any worse, but it did," she said, voice still low. I couldn't help but picture her locked in a bathroom or closet, curled into a seated position with her knees pulled up to her chest, holding her hand over her mouth to muffle the sounds.

My apprehension built up a notch.

"My father went on a rampage this morning," she continued. "It was awful, Josie."

This was followed by a long pause. I knew her well enough to guess that she was probably fighting tears, and I gave her space.

"They found a new match for me. My parents sat me down, told me all about him, and showed me pictures. You'd be proud, Josie.... I said no. It was so, so hard, but I still said no."

She was right; I *was* proud that she'd stood up for herself. But I was also still incredibly worried. I wasn't sure how long she could keep this up, no matter how strong I knew she was.

She paused and sniffed through tears. "My dad was angry. Like furious. He started shouting at me, and then he turned on my mother. And my mother...she just sat there and took it. My dad has been in the living room all day, and I'm scared to even go in there. My mother just follows me around the house, trying to change my mind. Constantly. Like I have to go to the bathroom to get away. Between the two of them, I'm not sure I can take much more of this."

A sympathetic "damn" was all I could manage.

My heart sank further as my mind raced. With the storm, she'd be trapped in the house with them. She couldn't even go to work to blow off some steam. And I couldn't go over there to protect her, either.

"All this pressure...I just can't take it," she continued. "My father's a monster. I just can't."

My heart ached to help her. "I'm so sorry that this is happening. I can't imagine what it's like to be in your shoes right now."

The problem was that I *could* imagine what it was like for her; I'd watched enough shows with wackadoodle dads that my mind drifted to dark places. I tried to pull myself out of the swirl of negative thoughts.

Laila replied with a sniff.

"It's gotta be rough. But please. You're one of the strongest women I know. Please don't let him bully you into anything," I half-begged.

"How many more times can I say no, just to have him railroad me over and over?" she said, dejected. "I can't live like this, Josie."

"We just have to find a way to say no that he'll listen to," I said, trying to sound more confident than I felt.

"Yeah," she said, voice doubtful. "But how?"

"Um," I hesitated. Her family had a way of working that was completely new to me, and I had no clue how to navigate it. "What do you think would get your dad off your back?"

"Just shut up, get married, and have children," she sassed bitterly.

"Besides that. *Obviously*," I sassed back, a smile tugging at my lips. Laila still had a fire in her. I could work with that. "Can you just tell them you don't want to get married instead of just saying no to matches?" I pressed.

"Not really," she said. "They'd just say that it doesn't matter what I want. It's about duty. My mother wants grandchildren. Like yesterday."

"Hmm." I wasn't used to being in a family where you couldn't be honest about your feelings.

"The way my parents grew up.... Women are supposed to find husbands and start a family. The only reason they sent me here for school was so that I could find a better match. They never expected me to do anything with my degree. And they certainly never thought I'd be single into my thirties."

She'd shocked me into silence.

"It's expected that I get married," she continued. "It doesn't matter that I don't want to. That's why they keep trying to match me with different men. They think I'm just being ridiculously picky."

"And you can't tell them to lay off a bit?" I asked, even though I knew the answer.

"Uh, no," she answered curtly. "They're dead-set on seeing me engaged. And, honestly, Josie, I just don't know how much more I can take. With them in the same house, they're wearing me down. At this point, I want to say yes to some random match just to make them go away."

She was stuck between a rock and a hard place. I couldn't see a way out for her. I could practically see her shaking her head and worrying her lip like she always did when she puzzled over a difficult problem.

"Are you going to be okay with the storm and all?" My question was a bit off-topic, but I was really starting to worry about leaving her trapped in her house with her parents.

"Yeah," she answered quietly, sounding unsure. "I'll just say I have to work and lock myself in my bedroom."

"When the roads clear up enough, you can come here. Or I can try to come there," I offered.

I wasn't sure my car would make it, but I would get there if she needed me, no matter what gauntlet had been thrown in my path.

"Thanks, Josie. I might take you up on that. We'll see how it goes tonight at dinner."

"Call me anytime, okay?" I offered.

"I will. Thanks again."

We said our goodbyes and hung up.

I wasn't feeling great about Laila being stuck at home with her folks. Even though she was a tough cookie, I was unsure that she could withstand the constant pressure from her parents. I didn't want to see my friend come out the other side of this storm engaged to some rando from an arranged marriage service.

I glanced out at the darkening sky, unable to shake the feeling that the storm was mocking me.

CHAPTER
EIGHTEEN

In a moment of typical Josie brilliance, I'd forgotten to turn my alarm off, and the blaring sound woke me up bright and early on Thursday. Heart thudding, I fumbled in the dark to silence the wailing.

Even with the little heater chugging away overnight, the cold air pressed in. I snuggled deeper under the covers, not wanting to get out of bed. I closed my eyes, under the delusion that sleep could be found again. Pulling the covers over my head, I enjoyed the last few moments of burrito-blanket bliss before I was summoned by the fur demon.

A pitiful, drawn-out *meow* came from the doorway. The way he made it sound, my title should have been The Evil Withholder of Food.

I flipped the covers back with a shiver. That plaintive first meow was just the start of a magnum opus. If I didn't bow to his command, he would make it abundantly clear that he would simply die of neglect if he wasn't fed within the next five seconds.

Wrapped in my robe, I shuffled into the kitchen, fed Yersi, and put the kettle on. The quiet of the house was broken only by his slurping as he chowed down on his wet food.

A surprising sense of loneliness pressed in. I usually enjoyed living by myself—preferred it, actually. All I needed was Yersi and the chickens. I didn't know if it was the snow-white wasteland crouched outside or my feelings of helplessness over all of the drama going down outside of my tiny home. I had no clue what triggered that feeling. All I knew was that I wished with all of my heart that Armand was here so that we could eat a warm breakfast, cuddle on the couch, and spend a relaxed day indoors.

Fourteen more days.

I checked the time on my phone and did some mental math. It was early afternoon in Romania, and I figured he was probably busy wrapping the last few things up at work before the holiday. Since the storm had kept me out of the lab today, I could still catch him when he got off.

As I waited for the water to boil, I texted him.

> Snow day today. Have time for a call when you get off work?

He responded almost instantly with a thumbs-up.

> 10 AM your time?

> Perfect. Miss you.

Unable to help myself, I added a kissy face emoji, and he responded with a heart.

Feeling infinitesimally better now that I had made plans to call later, I set my tea to steep and slipped into my poofy slippers to check on the chickens.

The garage felt like a different planet. The air was frosty and damp, and my breath puffed out in front of me. The sharp tang of chicken waste hung in the air.

The girls were on their perch under the heat lamp. When I turned the garage light on, they started clucking softly. Gertrude leaped to the ground to greet me at the Eglu door.

Ice rimmed the surface of the water bowl, but thankfully, it hadn't gotten cold enough in the garage for the water to freeze completely. I scattered fresh feed, and the other three joined Gertrude to peck at it, their clucking now more conversational. It was a good sign that they'd all left the sanctuary of the heat lamp to eat.

Despite the smell, the amount of feces peppering the floor wasn't too awful. It was still too dark to see what unholy hell the clouds had dropped on Stillwater overnight, but the temp alone made it clear that the chickens needed to stay in the garage for at least one more day. I figured I'd pulse check again tomorrow. If the weather was still too nasty to move them outside, I'd do a quick splatter clean-up.

Back inside, I shucked off my slippers with a shiver, still feeling the nip of the cold from the garage. I busied myself by making breakfast and eating it slowly at the counter, a book in one hand.

About an hour or so later, the sunrise revealed a winter wonderland. About six inches of pristine snow blanketed everything in sparkling white. It was beautiful in a barren, harsh way.

I was grateful we had proactively closed the lab today. Even though we were already down to a skeleton crew for the holidays, most of the threadbare staff wouldn't have been able to get out of their driveway, myself included.

Shuffling back into the bedroom, I grabbed my phone and flopped on the couch, wanting to check in with everyone. I started with Tessa.

> Hey! Just checking in. You doing okay with the storm?

Unsure if she'd be awake this early on a snow day, I rested the phone down. I pulled my blanket across my lap and propped open my book. Yersi immediately jumped up and claimed his spot. Less than a page in, my phone binged with her reply.

> Doing good. Hunkered down at my place.

> Dr. Anderson sent everyone home early yesterday and told us to stay home today. I'm supposed to check in on Saturday.

I sent her a thumbs up.

He's such a great guy.

She hearted my text.

He's an awesome boss.

I smiled inwardly. Maybe, just maybe, my plotting would come to fruition. If she had to spend some time working in a rural vet clinic to get her loans paid off, Willow Park Vet was the place to be.

Do you have enough supplies at your place?

Part of Tessa's emergency housing plan from back in September had included a cafeteria card. But most of the places to eat on campus had closed for the holidays. And the two that were open for "holiday hours" were likely closed with the storm. Thankfully, she texted back:

I grabbed some cans of soup on the way home yesterday.

I sent a thumbs up.

Because she lived in the dorms, she didn't have a full kitchen. But they did have a microwave. If she had canned food, she could make it for a bit.

Do you know if the vet school hospital is open?

> It's closed except for the ER and ICU.

I thumbs-upped her text, feeling a thread of relief at the news. If the hospital had closed, it would be even harder for Fran to come down on me for closing the lab. Fran still hadn't called or texted me back, and I didn't know what that meant. Hopefully, it meant she didn't have cell service.

Despite showing a strong front, I was still nervous about how she'd react to us closing down the lab without her explicit permission. She could be a bit unpredictable and petty. If anyone made her look bad, she'd throw them under the bus, and I definitely didn't want to be *that* person.

Another message from Tessa dragged me out of my thoughts.

> Did the lab close?

> Yep. At lunch yesterday. We're closed today too.

> How are things at your place?

Physically, everything at the house was just fine. It was the damn thoughts buzzing around my head that were such a mess. Not wanting to drag Tessa down into the rabbit hole, I focused on the good stuff.

> The girls are settled in the garage and Yersi's on my lap. As long as the power stays on, we'll be good.

It was her turn to send a thumbs up.

> Looks like a lot of snow dropped. If the roads clear up later, you're welcome to come join us if you want.

I was eager for a distraction, and I hoped she'd take me up on the invite. But I also knew the roads were likely to be a mess for most of the day, if not longer. Stillwater wasn't known for its snow control.

The ellipses bounced for a bit as she texted her response.

> Everything here is completely buried. I don't think I can get my car out.

I tried to brush the disappointment aside.

> I figured. I'm not sure I can get mine out either.

> It should be okay by tomorrow, right? I don't want to miss Aunty's again.

I sent a shrug emoji.

> Not sure when they'll get the roads clear.

It was a non-committal text, but I didn't want to offer false hope. I wasn't sure what the roads would look like in twenty-four hours. The storm had come and gone, but it had left its mark.

She replied with a sad face emoji.

My feelings echoed hers. I'd already missed Aunty's last weekend to go to the airport with Laila. I didn't want to miss seeing her for the holiday. That was just too much. I needed my weekly dose of Aunty.

Throwing caution to the wind, I texted back.

> Don't worry. We'll figure out a way to get there.

Tessa hearted my text.

> See you tomorrow?

Yup

She sent a gif of two women dancing in a car.

A smile tickled the edge of my lips, and I added a laughing tag.

It felt good knowing Tessa was safe, both physically and mentally. Just a few months ago, she'd been the exact opposite. After losing her place, she'd been sleeping in her car, severely depressed, and considering suicide. We'd worked hard to get her back on track. She was now settled in campus housing with a meal card. That would be enough to get her through the end of senior year. She still had a bumpy road ahead. But I was confident she'd make it through okay.

I texted Aunty next.

> Checking in. You doing okay?

Within seconds, my phone binged with a reply.

> Hello, sweety. Yes. Chula and I are good. The chickens are in the shed.

> How are you?

> We're good here.

I took a quick pic of Yersi curled on my lap and sent it to her. She hearted the image.

> We got about six inches here. What's it like down there?

> About the same. The library is closed today.

> The lab is closed too. We shut down yesterday after lunch.

> Glad you're home safe. How's Tessa?

Her question gave me the warm fuzzies. She'd only known Tessa for a few months, but Tessa had fit right into our little family. She was like my sister-from-another-mother. Even though none of us were related by blood, we were thick as thieves, and Aunty and I were both fiercely protective of her.

> She's good. She's in her dorm but has plenty of supplies.

Glad you are both home.

…

…

I want to see you both on Friday but if the roads are bad you should stay home.

My heart sank. Aunty and I didn't celebrate Christmas for the same reason that most Oklahomans did. But we took advantage of the day off to eat good food and enjoy each other's company. I did not want to lose this day with her, especially since, for the first time ever, we would have someone else joining us: Tessa.

I can practically hear you thinking, Josie.

I read her text with the playful chiding that was intended. She knew I'd be there tomorrow, even if I had to rent a snowmobile to get there. I chuckled.

We'll play it by ear. I promise I won't drive there unless we can make it in one piece.

She hearted my text.

We can make up for it on Sunday if we can't get together on Friday. The roads should be clear by then.

I sent her a thumbs up to reassure her, even though I didn't mean it. It would take more than six inches of snow to keep me from driving to Ada on Friday.

Stay warm. Love you.

Love you too.

It felt good knowing that Tessa and Aunty were both safe at home, but that knowledge hadn't done a damn thing to calm my buzzing mind. Picking my phone back up, I texted Laila.

Checking in. How are things there?

My phone locked without a reply.

I chewed my cheek, considering. She'd been oddly slow to respond to my texts since her parents had arrived. I still couldn't tell if that was her way of telling me that I was in her face too much or if she just truly couldn't get to the phone.

There wasn't much I could do to help her if she didn't text me back. Even if I wanted to go over to check on her, there was no way in hell I was getting my car out of the driveway.

Trying to distract myself, I picked up my book and let the story draw me in. Yersi's slow purr rumbled from my lap, and my shoulders slowly relaxed as I got lost in the story.

About thirty minutes before my call with Armand, the reminder on my phone chirped, drawing me out of the book. Yersi hopped from my lap, stretching his back in a tall arch before disappearing into the kitchen to check for any bits that might have fallen on the ground.

I quickly changed and braided my hair, making my top half presentable for the video call. I refilled my mug and curled back under the blanket. Yersi immediately returned to his spot on my lap, purring softly. I logged in, and within a few minutes, Armand's face appeared on the screen.

At the sight of his crooked, shy smile, all of my feelings for him bubbled to the surface. Because of all the other drama with Laila and at work, I'd stuffed that lonely ache deep down inside. Seeing him practically tore my heart from my chest.

"Hey," he said, voice soft. His chin was tucked down slightly, and he looked up at me, soft curls dancing over his forehead.

Damn.

That look got me every time, and my toes curled.

"Hey, babe," I replied, a love-drunk smile appearing.

The thousands of miles between us yawned. He was so far away, and all I wanted to do was hug him and smell his aftershave.

As if reading my mind, he said, "Fourteen more days."

"Yeah, fourteen more days," I said, still feeling the long stretch of time between us. Two weeks felt like eons. "Has Ileana caught on?"

"I don't think so. I've only packed the things in my apartment. I haven't started packing my suitcases. When I do, I'll have her watch me put her toys and leash in there so she knows that she is coming too."

"Aw," I said, my heart melting. "That's sweet."

You can always see into the soul of a person based on how they treat their furred friends.

My thoughts drifted to picking him and Ileana up from the airport. With a quick flash of panic, I realized that I might not be able to fit the crate and his luggage in the back of my Prius, even with the seats folded down.

I shook away the thought. We could figure that out later. I'd rent a bigger car or borrow Laila's if I had to. Right now, I just wanted to be as close to Armand as I could with several thousands of miles separating us.

"It's nice seeing you today, *iubita mea*," he said, voice soft. "I'm glad you texted."

"I'm glad you were free. Miss you." Feeling particularly sentimental, I added, "I kinda wish you were staying here." My cheeks grew warm, embarrassed that I'd let a private thought slip.

He tilted his head slightly, eyes sharp.

Despite the warp-speed progression of our relationship, the topic of him living at my place during his six-month stint hadn't even come up. After getting the grant and having his visa approved, he'd just found a place that allowed him to bring Ileana and had paid the deposit. I wasn't sure if he hadn't asked because he didn't want to live with me or if he was worried he'd be stepping on my toes.

Or maybe it didn't even cross his mind, a self-flagellating part of me whispered.

All of this swirled through my mind, and I felt myself visibly swallow.

We're moving too fast. Slow down, Josie. This is how you get hurt.

He was still studying me, expression soft.

I fumbled, "Of course, Yersi would probably make Ileana his bitch. We couldn't have that." I forced an uncomfortable laugh.

He arched an eyebrow and smiled. "Ileana bows to no one."

"I don't know," I sing-songed. "Yersi is the Great Slayer of Canned Food, third of his name, ruler of Casa Harjo."

We shared a laugh, my original awkward comment blessedly ignored like a fart in a room. Things were getting serious between us, and I wasn't sure how I felt about that.

You don't have to cross that bridge today. Just enjoy this time.

"How's Laila?" Armand asked, shaking me out of my loop.

Grateful for the distraction, I jumped right in. "Things are messy over there," I started and then shared the story of the exceedingly awkward dinner with her folks, leaving out any personal details involving Laila's situation.

"Wow," he said, shaking his head.

"Yeah, and I only had to have dinner with them," I said. "I can't imagine poor Laila trapped in her house with those two." I sighed. "Anyway, I'm just hoping we can find a way to send them home sooner rather than later."

"What is their return date?" he asked.

"They don't have tickets booked back home yet."

His eyebrows shot up.

"Yeah. Exactly." I frowned. "I don't know how long they plan on staying."

"Can she not talk to them? Ask them to leave by such-and-such date?" he asked.

The words were flippant, even though his tone wasn't, and I couldn't help feeling a thread of irritation.

"You'd have to meet her parents to understand," I said. "I'm not sure the direct approach is possible in that family. When I spoke up at dinner, I thought her father was going to lunge across the table and choke me."

"Still. She should just tell them what she wants," he pressed.

I bit back a snort. Armand hadn't met her parents. I got the impression that Rakesh might lose his ever-loving mind if Laila dared to speak up. And Rakesh was a lot bigger than Laila.

"We'll see how things go," I said, trying to shake off the dark thoughts.

"Laila is a strong person," he said. "It will work out."

I *hmmed* noncommittally. After a beat, I said, "The whole mess has me thinking. Zoe wants kids, and the adoption agency won't let her have them. Laila doesn't want kids and is risking her relationship with her parents over it. I just don't get it. Why do people care so much about whether or not someone has kids? All it does is hurt people."

The questions had been rhetorical, and Armand knew it. He just nodded his head sadly and said, "I feel bad for both of them."

With a start, I realized I might've overshared.

Too late now, dumbass.

"I just don't know how to help either of them," I said, trying to nudge the conversation in a different direction.

"I think all you can do is listen and be there for them."

He was giving good advice, but it didn't make the helpless feeling go away. I looked down at the snoozing Yersi in my lap, seeking comfort.

"Do you want kids?" His question came out of the blue, and I jerked my head up. He had a kind expression, but curiosity danced around in his eyes.

I didn't know the right answer in this situation, and I felt a bit trapped. Sure, I'd thought about kids, and it wasn't just the thought of diapers that had stopped me from having them. Raising a kid right took a lot of time and energy, and I wasn't sure I had enough of either to do it well. The moment had just never felt right. Yersi and the chickens were all I needed right now.

I decided that the truth was the best answer. If my opinion tainted our relationship, it would be what it would be.

"I'm not sure," I answered hesitantly. "I don't feel the burning urge and the thought of diapers.... I get my fair share of gross stuff at work. But never say never, right?" I studied his face, checking his response. His expression stayed soft and open. "How about you?" I asked, still feeling tense.

"I'm not sure either," he replied. "But if I found the right person and I was settled, that might change."

He locked eyes with me, and I felt my gut clench. I couldn't tell if it was from nerves or happiness. I would need a couple of days to unpack the flurry of emotions.

Feeling the weight of the moment, I tried to lighten things up by saying, "You just want an all-Varoujan soccer team."

He smirked. "*Football* team," he corrected playfully. "An all-Varoujan *football* team."

We both snickered, and from there, the conversation shifted to lighter topics. After about an hour, we said our goodbyes and signed off with an air kiss. Even after we'd said goodbye, my mind whirled for hours with thoughts of motherhood.

***

Resigned to being trapped in the house alone with my thoughts for the day, I did the weekend chores a few days early.

I read.

I watched Netflix.

And I got really, really bored.

By the early afternoon, I was so antsy my skin was crawling. Laila still hadn't responded to my text, and the stress was chewing me apart.

Figuring that some time outside might distract me, I bundled up and then paused at the door. With the garden shut down for the winter, my options were shoveling snow in the front or shoveling snow in the back.

Well, that sucks.

Even though shoveling snow was the last thing I wanted to do today, a shot of endorphins would help, so I bundled up and trundled outside.

They didn't exactly sell snow shovels at the local Wal-Mart in a place like Stillwater. So, I grabbed my garden shovel and figured I'd give the front path and driveway a go.

It was crystal clear outside, the bright sun glittering across the snow. The cold nipped at my cheeks. The street itself was still unplowed, with a single row of large tire tracks marring the road.

I warmed up quickly as I cleared the sidewalk and dug my car out. I didn't want to be spending another day trapped at home. Alone. Without Aunty or Tessa.

Loneliness knocked at my door.

I tried to ignore it.

With the egress cleared as much as possible, I stomped back inside. I figured now was a good a time as any to check back in with Laila. I had a nagging worry and couldn't tell if it was about Laila or something else.

Once out of my cold-weather gear, I grabbed my phone and flopped on the couch. As soon as my ass hit the cushion, Yersi hopped in my lap. He butted his head against the phone, insisting that I love him instead of the stupid black box I was focused on.

I texted Laila again. If she didn't reply, I'd call. I set my phone to the side, intending to focus on His Royal Highness for the next few minutes.

A few seconds later, my phone binged with a response from Laila.

Can you talk?

That's not a good sign, I thought.

A tingle of worry spread up my spine as I hit the call button.

"Hey, Josie," Laila answered after the first ring. Her voice was an odd mixture of worry and resignation.

"What's up? How are things?" I replied, trying to sound casual and supportive.

She sighed. "I'm not sure I can make it trapped inside my house with my parents all day. They're driving me crazy."

My brain shifted instantly to problem-solving mode. "Have they cleared the roads by you yet?"

"Nope," she said, voice bitter. "I could try to go out, but what excuse would I make? I left something in the lab?"

"Do you have to give them a reason?" I asked.

She huffed. "I think I'll just have to hide in my room 'working' until I can make an excuse to go out."

"Want me to come over there?" I offered. "The roads are pretty bad here, but I can try to get out. We can play a game or something."

"No, that's okay," she answered. "I'm not sure your Prius can handle it."

Normally, she would have teased me a bit with that comment. Instead, it came out as a resigned statement.

I thought about trying to get a Lyft or something and quickly brushed the thought away.

"Well, if the plow comes by, I'll text you," I said. "Maybe if the roads clear, you could go to the grocery store or something."

"I could try," she said, sounding doubtful.

"You could say you need to grab a few things before everything closes for Christmas," I nudged again.

"Shit!" she exclaimed. "I'm going to be trapped with them another day tomorrow! How the hell did I forget about the holiday?"

"Blocked it out, maybe?" I tried to joke.

"Shit," she repeated, this time hushed. "It would be better if I could chase my father out of the house, but I'm not sure I can. He's being so weird about everything. I'll have to come up with some way to get out of here. I'm going to go nuts."

My heart ached for my friend. The vibe was terrible with her folks right now. I couldn't imagine being stuck with that black cloud in a house for two days. Realistically, she couldn't even go for a walk; the snow was too deep on the sidewalks.

"Want to come with us to Aunty's tomorrow if the roads are clear? Get out of the house?" I offered.

She sighed. "I don't think they'll let me."

Her choice of words struck me. The thought of someone having enough control over Laila to not "let" her do something was a bit of a shock. I wanted my fierce, strong Laila back. It killed me to see her like this.

"Well, I'm here if you need me," I offered for the umpteenth time. "I can still try to make it over."

"It's okay, Josie. I'll manage. I just don't want to do this. And I have to. It sucks."

Yes, it truly does, I thought.

"Sending hugs," I said, feeling weak.

"Thanks," she sighed.

"Deep breaths. Little steps. Eyes on the prize," I said. "No matter what, we've got this. Green?"

She caught the movie reference and replied, "Super green," with a hint of a smile in her voice.

CHAPTER

NINETEEN

As soon as my eyes clicked open Friday morning, I was out of bed and at the front door, checking the state of the roads. Even though it was still dark out, there was enough light from the streetlamps to illuminate the freshly plowed streets.

A giddiness took over. If my little street was plowed, there was a good chance the rest of the roads to Ada were clear. I couldn't wait to see Aunty.

I bustled around the house, getting Yersi and the girls sorted. I had a quick snack of yogurt, just enough to hush my screaming stomach until I could bury my face in Aunty's feast. Grateful that I didn't need to impress anyone, I put on a cozy sweater and jeans. I brushed my hair and let it hang free over my shoulders.

Around eight-thirty, Tessa's beater rolled up, and my excitement built. I didn't realize how much I needed this day.

I bustled her inside the house, gave her a hug, and took a good look at her. Her long black hair was pulled into a neat ponytail and was covered with a beanie that Aunty had knitted for her. Her clothes were well-worn but clean. She wore a huge smile.

Tessa had transformed since September. She had started to put on some weight, and her skin had a healthy sheen. More importantly, her bags had virtually disappeared, and her step seemed lighter. She looked *happy*.

I beamed. "How was the drive?"

It was only a couple of miles from her place to mine, but the state of the roads beyond my little fiefdom was unknown.

She shrugged. "Not bad. Most of the roads are plowed."

"Awesome," I replied, feeling optimistic. "I bet the highway is clear then. Shall we?"

Merf, Yersi replied at my feet, as he swirled around my leg.

Tessa squatted down to give him scratches. "Not you, little man. You need to guard the house from that evil neighbor kitty next door."

He brushed his cheek back and forth across her leg. A throaty purr started, and he put his two front feet on her knee like he was trying to crawl into her lap.

"Aww," Tessa cooed. "Sorry, bud."

A feeling of contentment washed over me. Yersi was my Tessa barometer. When she was in her darkest place, he'd been wary of her. He'd followed her around the house and watched her with his tail tap, tap, tapping on the ground like Poe's raven. It had been creepy as fuck. But when she was on her true path, like she was now, he was a complete love bug around her.

I slipped my shoes and coat on. With one last scratch for Yersi, Tessa stood and helped me with the books by the door. We headed out into the cold morning and bundled into the car.

Blasting the heater to clear the last vestiges of ice off my windshield, I asked, "What do you want to listen to?"

She considered and said, "Let's go old school. How about 2Pac?"

"Fabulous," I said with a grin. Our shared love of hip-hop was just one more thing that had brought us together.

I fiddled with my phone and queued up the playlist. "All Eyez On Me" filled the car as I pulled out onto the street, the tires only sliding a tad on the slippery driveway. There was a comfortable lack of conversation as we wove through the streets to West 6th Avenue. I was hyper-focused since the roads still weren't great. But once we were headed south on the highway, I could feel the tires grab and was able to relax into the drive.

As the playlist shifted between songs, a thread of worry still itched at the back of my brain, chewing into today's happiness. I wondered how Laila was doing, trapped at home with her dad. I fretted over the unsolved cases at Rising Sun Farms. An annoying part of me was even uneasy about Gerald being all alone in the lab today, working on a day that should be spent with family and friends.

Who says even he has any? an evil part of me snarked. I felt an instant wash of guilt.

As if reading my thoughts, Tessa asked, "You good?"

"Umm, yeah. Just worried," I hedged. I still hadn't put all of my thoughts in order. Plus, the empathy I was feeling for Gerald was frankly embarrassing. I hadn't totally unpacked that shit and wasn't sure I even wanted to.

"What's on your mind?" Her question was casual, and I could tell she was trying not to push me too hard. She was just trying to create a space for me to talk if I wanted to. With a start, I realized I needed to. But not about Gerald. Not yet, at least.

"There's just a lot of stuff going on," I said, unsure where to begin.

"Work stuff or life stuff?" she asked.

I frowned. "Both."

"Sorry. That sucks," she replied with honest sympathy. She'd definitely been around that block before.

"It's not super bad," I said, taking one hand off the wheel to wave it dismissively. "Just a lot of little things swirling around in my noggin."

After a beat, I decided to start with something easy. "We had a couple of cases from the same farm this week. Fetal pigs."

She groaned in sympathy.

"Yeah, I know," I said.

"I take it you didn't find anything?" she asked.

"Not yet. The abortion panel on the first case came up negative, and there was nothing on histo. With the storm, I won't get anything back on the second case until Monday at the earliest. It could be nothing. But...." I shrugged, leaving the thought unfinished and acting more nonchalant than I really felt.

She gave me a reassuring smile. "You've done your best. What else can you do right now?"

"Nothing, I guess. The four-day weekend in the middle of it all is throwing me off. It's hard to let it go until Monday. I'm sure it'll be fine, though," I replied unconvincingly.

"You're worried because you're good at your job and you care. But there's truly nothing else you can do today. So, take advantage of your time with Aunty. Eat her amazing food. Enjoy yourself."

I smiled. "Yeah."

She stayed quiet, giving me space to collect my thoughts. I wanted to talk through the stuff with Laila, and it needed to be with someone who wasn't my current love interest. The awkward shifts in conversation with Armand had dredged up feelings I definitely wasn't ready to unpack yet. Plus, he was going to be her coworker for six months, and I couldn't help but feel like I was talking smack. The baggage with Armand wasn't there with Tessa, so I decided to give it a try.

"There's also some stuff going on with Laila," I started.

I tasted the story on my tongue, seeing if it felt like gossip. Tessa knew Laila, but they weren't super tight, and they only knew each other in passing. Laila certainly knew about Tessa, though. I'd shared all the dirt when Laila was helping me fumble my way through that hot mess back at the start of the school year.

My desire to talk it over won out, and I said, "Laila's folks are in town."

She nodded. "Yeah. I remember you went with her to pick them up on Sunday."

"They're here to marry her off," I continued. "Her mom's all 'husband this' and 'grandkids' that. Her dad's all creepy-weird about it. Her folks are hardcore bullying her to get engaged."

"Geez," she said, voice hushed and eyebrows raised. "I take it she doesn't want any of that?"

"Nope," I replied. "Definitely not now, and maybe never."

"And they flew all the way here just to see her get hitched?" she asked, incredulous. "That's messed up."

"Yeah, it is," I said. "She keeps rebuffing proposed matches. But they are coming down on her pretty hard. Telling her that she should give up the Chair position and focus on finding a husband."

Tessa frowned.

"I could tell it was bad when we picked them up at the airport," I continued. "But I didn't realize how awful it was until I was over there for dinner. Her dad started laying into me."

"Really?" Tessa interrupted, slightly aghast, turning to me.

"Yup," I said, nodding but keeping my eyes on the road. "Like I was a bad friend for not helping her find a husband. Like I was a bad influence for not having a husband of my own."

"Wow," Tessa said softly, shaking her head in disbelief.

"I'm pretty sure I'm *persona non grata* with her folks now," I said. "But in the whole scheme of things, that doesn't matter. I'm more worried about Laila. She keeps turning away guys, and her folks just shove new ones in her face. I think there might even be a matchmaker involved somehow."

"I didn't realize that was still a thing," she said.

I snuck a glance at Tessa to gauge her reaction. She was looking down at her hands, fidgeting with the edge of her sweater.

Her eyebrows crinkled. "Can't she just tell them she doesn't want to get married? That she doesn't want kids?" she asked hesitantly.

"According to her family, it's her duty to do both," I replied. "I'm not sure women are even allowed to say something like that in her family."

"Still," she waffled. "After what happened to me, I'm a firm believer in 'honesty is the best policy.' That might be her only way out of it, even if they end up coming down hard on her."

Her words bounced around in my head, and it took a minute for me to digest them. I hadn't really thought about it like that. But I also wasn't sure being direct and truthful with a monster like Rakesh would work.

"I hate leaving her alone with them today, trapped in that house," I said regretfully. "Maybe she can at least get out for a walk or something to escape her mean-ass dad."

The silence stretched between us.

I was feeling oddly vulnerable. Even though I'd picked away at what I thought was bothering me, there was something deeper hiding in there.

"The situation with Laila is dredging up all sorts of baggage," I said, feeling myself choke up a bit. "You know. Like motherhood and stuff. And people who want kids and can't have them. And people who don't want kids and are forced to have them. And Armand's half a world away. And I feel like we're on the verge of a big shift in our relationship. And...."

My words caught in my throat, and tears pressed in. I still hadn't gotten to the root of it. After a beat, the words finally spilled out. "It's hard this time of year without my mom."

There, I finally said it.

Tessa sighed softly. Her hand reached across the console and squeezed my arm.

I glanced over. She was looking out the window at the barren miles of snow-covered pasture broken only by the black hash marks of barbed wire fencing.

"I miss my mom, too," Tessa said sadly. She looked down at her hands and started picking at her cuticles. "It's like there's a piece of my life missing that's just normal for everyone else. She won't be there for my graduation or to meet a partner or to hold my kid if I ever have one." She sighed. "I sometimes wonder if she'd be proud of me, and it sucks that I'll never know."

Her words echoed true, and it was like a punch to the gut.

"That empty space...it's hard." She looked up with a sad, soft smile. "I'm glad I've got you and Aunty, though. Y'all are life-savers. Thanks for letting me crash your party."

I took a hand off the steering wheel to give hers a squeeze.

***

The tires crunched on the residual snow on Aunty's driveway. I could tell she'd been out shoveling, and the space was wide enough for me to park.

Tessa noticed, too, and said, "Awww. Aunty cleared the snow."

My heart warmed.

"Yes. She's pretty damn awesome," I agreed.

We piled out of the car and grabbed the stack of books from the backseat. Since Aunty and I didn't celebrate Christmas, today was going to be super chill. Just good food and family. We didn't have to worry about carrying presents. And knowing Aunty, there'd be so much food that I didn't bring any.

We made our way to the house, winding along the shoveled path. Chula peered through the window, two front feet on the windowsill. She had a happy-dog smile, and her airplane-ears were perked.

We clanged through the front screen, and the warm air kissed our cheeks when we opened the door. Chula skittered over in excitement, nails clicking on the wood floor.

"Who's my girl?" Tessa cooed, squatting to pet Chula.

Chula responded with happy licks to Tessa's face, her tail thumping loudly on the floor. She loved Tessa and could barely contain herself.

"If I ever get a place that would let me keep dogs, I might have to request visitation rights," Tessa joked.

It was positively wonderful to see Tessa happy. It meant so much to me that she had found a family with me, Aunty, and Chula.

And Yersi.

He'd come around eventually; Tessa just needed to put her spirit in the right place.

I laid the books on the table by the door, noting the new stack for us to take home. It felt good to have someone always thinking about me. I figured it made Tessa feel good, too. She deserved it. She didn't have any blood-kin, but we were her family now.

"Hello, ladies!" Aunty called from the back of the house. "Come in, come in."

We made our way to the kitchen, Chula trotting behind us.

The place smelled amazing. Aunty had gone all-out this year and cooked her made-from-scratch maple and pecan cinnamon rolls. The smell wrapped around us, and I felt myself start to drool.

"Aunty," I sighed in ecstasy. "You made cinnamon rolls."

She couldn't help giving us a self-satisfied smile as she wrapped us in hugs.

"They smell delicious, Aunty," Tessa breathed.

"Come sit," Aunty instructed.

She buzzed around the kitchen, making us herbal tea with honey. I wrapped my hands around the warm mug and inhaled. The smell of the jasmine was pleasant, and every muscle relaxed.

"Thank you so much, Aunty. This is such a treat," Tessa said.

Aunty beamed, simply happy because she had made us happy.

"The cinnamon rolls will come out any minute. How hungry are you? I was thinking of making some bacon to go with them."

Now, I was really drooling. There was something about the way the maple sweetness of the cinnamon rolls and the saltiness of the bacon came together. It made me mime a chef's kiss.

"If it's not too much trouble. That would be fabulous," I answered.

Tessa nodded with a smile. "Can I help?"

"No, no," Aunty said. "You ladies relax. I'll get it whipped together in no time."

The conversation was casual and relaxed as Tessa shared stories of working at Willow Park, and Aunty talked about her time at the library.

I listened, chiming in when appropriate, and avoided the topic of my week like it was an armadillo with leprosy. I could tell that Tessa knew I wanted to stay away from it, and she was helping guide the conversation. I suspected it would come up eventually. Aunty had a way of sniffing these things out. But it was nice to just enjoy the moment.

About an hour later, we were sitting around the table, content and stuffed. I'd practically licked my plate clean. This batch of cinnamon rolls had been particularly delectable, and I'd managed to snarf down two; they were best when they were fresh out of the oven.

With our teas topped up, we moved into the living room to sit by the fire. Chula took up a spot at Tessa's feet. Tessa reached over to gently scratch Chula's floppy ears, and Chula's tail thumped lightly on the floor.

Aunty settled herself in the recliner and looked at me, eyes sharp. "You've been quiet this morning," she observed.

Tessa's eyes bounced to mine and then quickly away. She continued her worship at the altar of Chula, eyes cast down.

Shifting in my seat, I said, "There's just a lot of stuff going on at work and with Laila. I'm a bit distracted."

I wanted to add an apology and stopped myself. Aunty always chided me for saying sorry all the time, especially when there was nothing to be sorry for.

"I take it that it didn't go well on Sunday?" she asked.

I shook my head. "Laila's family is...oppressive." It was the only word I could think of, but it still seemed to fit.

Aunty grunted with sympathy.

I was suddenly verklempt, and the words stuck in my throat.

Tessa softly interceded, "Laila's parents are trying to force her to get married and have kids. It sounds like she's stuck between a rock and a hard place. Right, Josie?"

I nodded.

Aunty tutted. "People should be free to be their true selves and make their own decisions."

"The pressure to become a mother is pretty intense," Tessa said. "Vet students get it all the time. But then, when students do become mothers, Admin shakes a finger at them. Remember the class two years ahead of me?"

I nodded, frowning. "The 'making babies class.' Yeah, I remember."

Six of the hundred or so women in the class had decided to have children during vet school. Admin was so put out that they had labeled them the "making babies class" and openly mocked them.

"It's like society just wants us to stay home and have kids," Tessa continued. "If we go to school and don't have kids, we're selfish bitches. If we have kids during school, we're stupid or slutty. It sucks."

"What about the male students?" Aunty asked.

Tessa and I both snorted.

"Admin couldn't care less whether or not guys have kids. They don't even pay attention to them," I said bitterly.

"They assume their wives will take care of everything," Tessa added with the same level of bitterness.

Aunty sighed and shook her head. "Your mother had you and was successful. And she did it all on her own."

My heart clenched. We hardly ever talked about my mom. It hurt too much. Aunty knew that, and I was surprised she brought it up. I bit the inside of my cheek, trying not to cry.

Aunty looked at me with love in her eyes. She knew bringing my mom up had hurt a bit, but that I also needed to hear it.

Tessa noticed I was uncomfortable and shifted the conversation. "At the end of the day, it's the woman's choice. People need to mind their own business and stop judging everyone else all the time."

Thankful for the reprieve, I said, "I just feel bad for Laila. I don't know how to help her."

"Keep doing what you're doing," Aunty advised. "Be there for her. Support her decision. That will help her face her parents."

"Yeah," I said. "It's just hard not being able to *do* anything."

"Like load her parents in the car and drive them to the airport?" Tessa quipped.

I snorted. "Exactly."

After a beat, Tessa said, "I can't believe arranged marriages are still a thing."

From there, the topic of conversation drifted, and Tessa and Aunty did most of the talking. I stared into the fire, thoughts stuck on my mom.

I had grown up an only child. My dad had left before I was born and essentially disappeared. My mom had worked full-time to support us. It had been rough financially, but the love and support I received from her had more than made up for it. My mom had been my everything. When she passed, she'd left a gaping wound that could never be closed. Even Aunty, as much as I loved her, could never fill that void.

Do I want to be a mother? Be there for someone like my mom was there for me?

I was a bit like a mother to Tessa, helping her through her a rough spot. But our ages were less than ten years apart, and she seemed more like a sister than a daughter. It still felt good to look after someone. Support them. Be there for them.

A laugh jerked me out of my thoughts.

"What? I missed it," I said.

Still chuckling, Tessa said, "Aunty and I were debating whether what women go through is more like *The Handmaid's Tale* or *Mad Max: Fury Road*."

"Oh, damn," I said, horrified. "How about neither?"

That got another laugh, and the conversation drifted as we tried to find a movie, series, or book that reflected how we wanted the world to treat women and motherhood.

It took a long time, and we never found a perfect fit. But the three of us did find support and friendship during that conversation. The power coursing between us made me feel strong enough to tackle anything.

Several hours later, I felt stuffed full of food and love. Tessa and I packed the books and some leftovers into the car, hoping to get home before the sun started to set. Tessa spent a good fifteen minutes saying goodbye to Chula, who had rolled on her back for belly scratches.

Aunty folded me into a big hug. "Will you be back on Sunday for brunch?"

I flashed a grin. "Couldn't keep me away."

She held my shoulders and looked deep into my heart. "I love you, Josie. I know I am not your mother; I could never fill her shoes. But I am your aunty. You are still like a daughter to me."

Tears filled my eyes, and I pulled her in for another hug.

"I love you, too," I sniffled into her hair. "Thank you for—" the words caught in my throat "— for everything."

We released each other from the hug, and she smiled at me, eyes soft. "You are all the woman your mother could have ever hoped for."

***

The drive back home was pleasant. The roads were relatively clear of both travelers and snow. Tessa and I listened to music in comfortable silence.

The tires crunched through the residual snow as I pulled into my driveway. I helped Tessa load her books and a to-go plate of cinnamon rolls into her car.

"Glad you could come today," I said, folding her into a hug.

"Thanks for inviting me," she said with a smile. "I love Aunty and Chula."

There was much left unsaid between us. But it didn't need to be said. I knew she appreciated having people to be with on the holiday. She also knew we loved having her as part of our family. It was a nice, comfy place to be.

"If you get bored on Saturday and want to hang out, shoot me a text," I offered, knowing that an empty dorm could get pretty lonely over the holidays.

"Will do," she said. "I think I'll be busy at Willow Park, but I'll keep you posted. Say hi to Yersi for me."

With another hug, she got into her car. After seeing her safely pulled away, I grabbed my stuff and headed up the path. Fumbling with the keys, I unlocked the front door.

Yersi greeted me with a casual *meow* as he wove around my legs. I set my books from Aunty down on the end table and brought the leftovers into the kitchen.

Excited, Yersi followed me. I plopped a can of cat food in his dish before heading back into the living room to collapse on the couch. I'd had a lovely day with Aunty and Tessa. But I still felt heavy. It was hard work lugging around oodles of unpacked thoughts.

I turned the TV on and started flipping through the streaming platforms, trying to find some fluff to watch. Holiday shows were everywhere—*Elf*, *A Christmas Story*, *Scrooged*—all the classics. They were good movies, but I wasn't feeling it. I decided to rewatch *Mindhunter*...because...who doesn't want to watch a show about serial killers on a holiday?

CHAPTER

TWENTY

My Saturday started with cleaning up shit. Literally.

A high-pressure system from the south had followed on the heels of the storm, and the snow had already started to melt into a brown, sludgy mess. Though I normally welcomed a shift in the weather, the warmer temps signaled that it was time to move the chickens out of the garage, a task that I was not looking forward to. It's astounding how much feces four chickens can paint onto the ground in two days.

Before I ventured in, I opened the garage door to air out the acrid, burning smell of ammonia. Taking a deep breath of the fresh air outside, I rolled the Eglu to an area near the house that had been cleared of snow and made sure the girls were settled. Excited by the movement, they hopped out of their nesting box to peck at the fresh food.

Next on the list was getting the garage back in order. The poop-covered cardboard boxes went straight into the giant compost pile. After a once-over with the mop, the garage was looking and smelling like its old self.

With that horrible task done, I showered and slipped back into a pair of comfy sweats. I spent the rest of the day snuggled on the couch with Yersi, alternating between watching TV and reading a book.

Even though there wasn't much left to do chore-wise, I was still feeling restless. I had thought about texting Laila—several times, actually—and had put the phone back down without sending a single one. I didn't want to be a nag, even though waiting in the dark made me uneasy.

After dinner, I still hadn't received any word, and I was fidgety. The worry buzzed in my skull. Something was off, and I just couldn't shake it.

The same uneasy feeling was still there when I woke up Sunday morning. I tried to distract myself by getting ready for brunch at Aunty's, but the joy I normally felt about seeing her today was dampened by the worry over Laila.

Unable to hold back any longer, I sent Laila a text.

> Just checking in. How are things?

I waited with my phone in my hand for a few minutes, expecting a quick reply. It didn't come.

Unable to leave my phone behind, I put it in my back pocket and went to check on the chickens. It was gray and gloomy outside, but the temperature was still warm-ish. The forecast said it would be just dandy today with no more snowfall. I gave the low, threatening clouds a side-eye.

Oookay.

The chickens clucked quietly in doubtful agreement.

They'll be fine, I tried to reassure myself. I decided to trust the forecast and left their Eglu outside. I'd check again when I returned from Aunty's and move them back into the squeaky-clean garage if it looked like the weather would get ugly again.

As I waited for Tessa to arrive, I busied myself around the house and tidied the kitchen for the millionth time, my anxiety getting the better of me. Yersi sat perched in a kitty-loaf position on the chair at the kitchen counter, watching me intently. I was pretty sure he thought I was nuts for going after the small brown spot in the grout for the umpteenth time. He demanded a well-kept lair, but I could tell from his judge-face that I was taking this cleaning thing a step too far.

About fifteen minutes before nine, Yersi perked up and hopped from the chair. A second or two later, there was a knock at the door.

I popped my head up from my task like an alert meerkat. "Coming!" I shouted, quickly stashing the cleaning supplies like a guilty secret, and hustled to the door.

Yersi meowed at me to hurry up. He stepped back as I swung the door open.

"Good morning," I said with a smile, waving Tessa inside.

"Hey," she answered, a bit breathless. She stomped her feet to get the last bit of slushy snow off her shoes and stood in the entryway. Yersi swirled around her with a friendly *merf*.

Bending down to greet him, Tessa cooed, "Hey, buddy."

He purred loudly in reply.

"Ready?" I asked as I grabbed my coat and my purse.

Meow, Yersi responded in the negative. Tessa and I exchanged a look and laughed.

"Sure," Tessa said. With a final scratch, she stood, and Yersi rubbed his face against her jeans.

As I grabbed my keys from the entryway table, my phone binged from my back pocket.

Laila. My heart lurched.

"Just a sec," I said, pulling my phone out.

The notification that filled my screen was not the one I was expecting. It was from Josh, our on-call student. I chewed on my cheek as I opened the text chain.

> Good morning Dr. Harjo.

> A case just came in. Want me to put it in the cooler for tomorrow?

Yes, was my knee-jerk reply. I didn't want to miss brunch with Aunty, and I definitely didn't want to crawl into work to do a necropsy on a Sunday. My rational side kicked in, and I knew I needed to know more about the case before I responded.

"Everything okay?" Tessa asked.

"Not sure," I answered vaguely as I texted Josh back.

What kind of animal is it?

A dog who died from cancer would chill just fine overnight, and I could hop in the car and head to Ada. A sudden-death cow could mean the start of an outbreak and would require me to schlep my ass in. I did *not* want to get knee-deep in blood and guts today.

Please don't let it be a cow.

The ellipses bounced as Josh texted his reply.

It's an aborted litter.

The floor dropped out from underneath me, and I felt a trickle of acid escape into my esophagus.

Tessa caught my expression, and her eyebrows furrowed. "Is it Aunty?"

Shaking my head distractedly, I replied, "Work." My heart was sinking so fast it would soon fall straight through my toes.

"Hmm," she said and crouched back down to pet Yersi.

My phone binged with another text.

Here's the form.

Like the prophetess Cassandra, I knew what it would say before the image even popped up in the text chain. Bile crawled up the back of my throat as my eyes jumped from the submitter to the history, confirming the feeling of portent.

Ms. Hoskins.

Rising Sun Farms.

Two fetuses and a placenta.

Fuck.

There was no way that I could, in good conscience, toss the piglets into the cooler to wait until tomorrow. Even though there was only a very slim chance a gross lesion would be present, I needed to get eyes on this case. Plus, if I did the necropsy today, all of the samples would be ready for testing first thing tomorrow morning.

Sigh.

A selfish part of me was petulant that I would miss brunch with Aunty and Tessa, and I tried to find any reason to push the case off. But I was certain this was an outbreak now; I couldn't convince myself otherwise. Though I absolutely did not want to go to work today, I knew I needed to.

Quit your whining, I self-flagellated. *At least you're not in Rachel's shoes.*

With another heavy sigh, I texted Josh a reply.

> This is the third case from that farm. I'll need to do them today.

> When are you coming in?

Usually, the on-call student would stay to help out, especially with the larger species. But it was the holiday weekend, and I felt guilty asking Josh to hang around for a couple of fetuses I could quickly crank through on my own.

> I'll be there in about twenty minutes. You don't need to stick around. Just leave them out on the table.

> Are you sure? I can stay if you want me to.

He was being polite, and I appreciated the gesture. It really wasn't safe for someone to be working alone with sharps in the lab. Accidents happened, even to the best of us. Tom had given himself a nasty cut that had required stitches about five years back. Since then, Fran was mighty prickly about people working solo on the necropsy floor.

It took me less than a second to decide.

Screw it.

I was probably already going to be on Fran's bad side for closing the lab early. What was one more thing?

> I'll be fine. Go home and enjoy the rest of your holiday.

> Thank you. I'll get everything set up for you and leave the alarm off.

> Happy holidays.

I sent him a thumbs-up before locking my phone. Tessa was watching me expectantly.

"I'm going to have to go in. I'm sorry," I said dejectedly.

She frowned in sympathy. "That's okay. Want me to come help?" she offered.

I shook my head. "No, no. You go to Aunty's. It'll be fine."

At least we all got to hang out Friday, I thought, trying not to feel disappointed and a tad jealous.

As if sensing my thoughts, Tessa gave me a side hug. "Want me to bring a plate back for you?"

"I'm good," I waved her off, not unkindly. "Go on, or you'll be late. I'll let Aunty know."

"It won't be the same without you," she said sadly.

We said our goodbyes. I closed the door behind her and allowed myself a minute to mope before I texted Aunty. It felt weird having Tessa go without me. I knew my relationship with Aunty was rock solid. I was also certain that Aunty would welcome her with open arms. But a small, evil part of me couldn't help but feel like Tessa was replacing me today. I didn't like the twinge of jealousy I was feeling.

Trying to shake it off, I messaged Aunty.

An urgent case just came in. I won't be able to make it today.

Tessa is still coming tho.

The bing of my phone shook me out of my self-pity.

We'll miss you. Be safe.

She added a heart emoji.

Unsure how to unpack all the messy feelings surging through my head, I grabbed my purse and headed to work.

***

The lab was dark and foreboding. I didn't often go in when no one else was there, and the emptiness echoed through my bones.

I left my purse and phone on the ground just outside the necropsy room door, not bothering to stop at my office. After putting on my lab coat and shoe covers, I headed out.

Goosebumps prickled across my arms. The necropsy floor was horribly creepy when the lab was empty. Shadows loomed in the corners. The faint outlines of the two piglets were visible on the nearest small animal table. I quickly flipped the switches, and the lights buzzed on across the large room.

The submission form was resting on the counter. Next to it was a bag of feed and a jar of water. Rachel had remembered to grab the other samples, even with the holiday, the storm, and the stress of another aborted litter. My respect for her grew.

My shoe covers scraped across the epoxied floor, echoing in the room. Even though I wasn't really a fan, I had half a mind to play Hank Williams just to chase the creepy-crawly feeling away.

Cut it out, Josie. You're acting like a spooked child.

If I focused, I could get this done lickety-split and get the hell out of dodge. I snapped on a pair of gloves and sprayed the table down before starting the external examination.

The piglets from the latest aborted litter were fairly well-developed and were probably just a week or so from full term. Both fetuses were about the same size and appeared to be the same gestational age. There was no evidence of mummification or external fetal anomalies.

I opened the plastic bag with the placenta, grateful to finally have one to examine. Lifting the organ out of the bag, I placed it on the table.

The condition of the organ was surprising. Usually, placentas from livestock were messy wads of flesh with bits of hay and dirt stuck to them. The fact that this placenta was pristine confirmed that the sows were being raised on cement with excellent cleaning protocols. Given the level of biosecurity, I just couldn't reconcile the possibility of this being an infectious disease outbreak.

I gently hosed down the placenta and used the tips of my fingers to carefully spread it out. Diffuse placentas were beautiful organs, and the entire surface looked like a low-pile carpet. I leaned over to get a closer look.

A tingle of excitement traced down my spine. I reached up to turn on the surgical light that was hanging low over the table.

I wasn't sure if I was imagining it or not, but there seemed to be very faint white dots pitting the chorionic surface. They were so subtle that they could easily be artifact. I wouldn't know for sure until I had a look at it under the microscope, but I couldn't shake the feeling that there was something there.

Using scissors, I snipped away sections of the placenta and dropped them in formalin. I added fresh sections to the Petri dishes labeled for microbiology and PCR. If those tiny white dots were real, it was a million times more likely that we were dealing with something infectious, and it didn't bode well for Rising Sun Farms.

But how did an infectious disease make it into a facility that was so tightly locked down?

I couldn't help but feel like I was still missing something. Unfortunately, I wouldn't know more until the samples made their way through the various departments for testing.

Reluctantly, I moved the placenta to the side and started in on the fetuses. The necropsies of the two piglets were unremarkable. Given the blush of a lesion in the placenta, I was hopeful I'd find something in the internal organs, but I was left wanting.

Chewing on my cheek, I surveyed the fetuses one last time, running through everything in my head. At this point, the differential list was almost as long as it was with the first case. I was fairly certain it was an abortion storm, and I was leaning toward something infectious. But if the placental lesion was an artifact, it could still be a toxin or some herd-wide environmental factor like carbon monoxide.

With dismay, I realized I still had nothing helpful for Ms. Hoskins, and my heart sank.

Not much I can do now except wait, I thought dejectedly.

My shoulders slumped. I kept telling myself it was worth missing brunch to have the samples ready when everyone came in tomorrow, but I'd still lost precious time with Aunty.

My shoe covers whisked across the necropsy floor, sending another eerie shiver up my spine as I placed the samples on the counter near the feed and water. I still had to venture into the cooler to grab an offal bin and clean up, and I did *not* want to go in there. The icy tomb was unpleasant on a good day.

Suck it up, buttercup.

The large cooler door snapped open with a *thunk* and a slight breath of air. The cooling fans hummed, and the cold air brushed my skin, sending goosebumps across my arms. Despite being squeaky clean, the smell of rotting meat tickled my nose.

To the right, large hooks hung from clunky chains. I was glad it had been slow, and there weren't any gutted carcasses adorning them. I could handle dead bodies. It was my job, after all. But there was something about going into a cooler with disemboweled bodies hanging from the ceiling that gave me the heebie-jeebies.

Keeping it quick, I grabbed an offal bin and rolled it out onto the necropsy floor. The bin's wheels skittered on the ground as I guided the barrel to the small animal table. I dropped what remained of the piglets and the placenta in the bin. Wanting to get it over with, I pushed the bin back into the cooler and gave it enough of a nudge that it slid inside without me having to step over the threshold again. The door clanged shut, closing off the scent of refrigerated death.

Still feeling slightly skittish, I washed the blood from the table, the sharp tang of the disinfectant chasing away the last of the cooler smell. Not wanting to leave a mess for Dustin, I made sure everything looked amazing and then grabbed the samples before skedaddling off the necropsy floor.

When all was said and done, the necropsy had taken less than an hour. I bussed the samples to the receiving department, which was significantly less spooky.

I placed the microbiology and PCR samples in the fridge and the feed and water samples on the counter with the submission form. Realizing that I hadn't taken a close look at the toxicology samples, I picked up the jar of clear water, opened it, and had a sniff. It seemed fine, but only Sandy could tell me whether or not a toxin was hiding in there.

I opened the bag of feed, running the mash through my fingers. The earthy smell of grains hit my nose. The feed consisted of rolled bits of corn and finely chopped bits that were likely some type of grain byproduct, like chaff or hulls. The feed looked fresh with no suspicious wet clumps. The color also looked right. Again, only Sandy could tell me if there was anything suspicious in there.

Closing the bag, I pursed my lips. This didn't have the feel of a toxicology case. But without an answer, all the options were still on the table. I marked the requested tests on the form: porcine abortion panel, plus Lepto and nitrates. I tucked the form under the toxicology samples.

I wove back through the dark hallways to grab my purse by the necropsy door. I still hadn't been able to shake the spooked feeling. For a millisecond, I thought about hightailing it out of there. But I owed it to Rachel to give her a verbal update.

When I passed Gerald's shuttered office, my stomach turned. The guy always seemed to be lurking around every corner, and I half-expected to see him there, hunched at his desk in the pitch dark, the flash of light reflecting off his eyes as he tracked my path down the hall like a hunter. Feeling spooked, I fast-walked into my office and shut the door.

Heart thudding, I took a few deep breaths.

I tossed my purse down and booted up the computer. I toyed with the idea of pushing the gross report off until tomorrow; I wanted to get out of the lab. Plus, it wasn't like I'd made an earth-shattering discovery on this latest round of necropsies. But I suspected Gerald would be up in my face tomorrow morning if he found samples waiting to be processed and no gross report in the system. I didn't want to deal with that.

I quickly typed up yet another boring report, adding a comment that I was suspicious of a subtle lesion in the placenta, but histology would be required to confirm it. The report didn't tell Rachel or the vet a damn thing. Once again, a feeling of helplessness washed over me. After signing the report, I picked up the phone to call Rachel.

She answered on the second ring.

"Ms. Hoskins? This is Dr. Harjo from the diagnostic lab."

"Yes, ma'am. Thanks for comin' in on a Sunday," she said matter-of-factly.

"I just released the gross report, but I wanted to give you a verbal update," I paused, trying to figure out the best way to tell her that I had no answer.

Yet. No answer yet.

"Find anything?" she asked, filling the space.

"Thanks for bringing the placenta in. I think there might be a lesion there. It's hard to tell on gross. I'll have to look at it under the microscope to be sure. Otherwise, I didn't see anything notable."

She sighed heavily.

I wasn't sure if she was frustrated with me or the situation. I picked up my pen and started tapping it.

"I'm extremely worried that this is the tip of the iceberg," I said. "I've flagged all of the samples as STAT. Toxicology should be able to check the water for nitrates first thing tomorrow. We should start getting the infectious disease results back from the litter last week and this litter on Tuesday. I might be able to look at everything under the microscope by Tuesday if I push it. Wednesday at the latest."

"Okay," she said, voice flat.

My pen tapped faster.

"Do you want me to send the feed off for mycotoxins?" I asked. "That test can take a while, and it's kind of expensive. We can send it off in the morning or hang on to it until the other test results come back."

"We've got good feed, and nothing's changed."

That doesn't mean a damn thing, I thankfully didn't blurt, my mind flashing to the Shadowhawk case.

"But I can't afford any more losses," she continued. "Please go ahead and send it off."

"Yes, ma'am. I'll make sure that gets ordered for you."

"Thank you, Dr. Harjo. I mean it," she said. "Sorry for bein' salty. I know you're doin' your best. I'm just worried about my pigs."

It was such a thoughtful thing to say and so out of character for most owners that I felt a jolt of surprise. I was worried about her animals, too. *Really* worried at this point. But saying that wouldn't help anything.

"We'll figure this out," I said, trying to reassure her. "I'll give you a call as soon as more results come in."

"Thank you, ma'am."

We said our goodbyes, and I slowly placed the phone back in the cradle. There wasn't much more I could do today. I loved my job, but sometimes, the waiting really wore away at me.

I grabbed my purse and locked up my office. On my way out, I added mycotoxin testing to the form. I set the alarm and fled through the door, unable to shake the feeling that I'd escaped the wolf's maw.

***

Back at home, I couldn't help but sulk.

I'd missed brunch at Aunty's, and for what? A dead-end necropsy?

I didn't care how cold it was outside. I decided lunch would consist of a pint of ice cream on the couch, watching rerun episodes of my favorite shows. Yersi, sensing my mood, curled up on my lap.

Two episodes in and the pint of ice cream polished off, I still wasn't feeling any better. I was worried about the pigs. I was stressing about Laila. I was worried about Zoe. I was missing Armand. There was too much drama bouncing around my head.

Laila still hadn't replied to my text from this morning. I wasn't sure if that was because she was respecting my time that I should've been with Aunty. Or if something had gone seriously wrong.

Why wouldn't it be going well? Maybe they're all sitting around enjoying a cup of tea together.

I snorted to myself. Yersi cracked his eyes open in a warning. The staff was not allowed to disturb His Royal Highness' slumber.

Reaching for my phone, I texted Laila again.

> I got called in this morning and missed Aunty's. I'm around if you need anything.

I held my phone for a beat, waiting to see if she would respond. The three bouncing dots were elusive, so I set my phone back down.

Everyone I knew was away on holiday or busy. I felt restless and alone.

Helpless, more like.

Yersi repositioned himself, circling his head under his paw, reminding me I wasn't entirely alone.

Taking three deep breaths, my shoulders relaxed slightly.

I needed to enjoy these moments of quiet. I was on duty again tomorrow, and things could get pretty ugly fairly fast. I couldn't help but feel like tomorrow was waiting for me, and it was holding a bat.

CHAPTER
TWENTY-ONE

Monday morning was a smack in the face. When the alarm screeched, I fumbled for my phone to silence the evil mechanical beast.

It took my brain a moment to process the missed messages filling my screen. Angling my phone so the Face ID would work, I saw with deepening dread that every single text was from Laila.

I jolted up, and Yersi hopped off the bed with misguided gustatory anticipation. He wailed a drawn-out *meow* from the doorway.

Trying to ignore him, I opened the text chain. The first text was sent around 10 PM the night before.

> Are you still awake? Can you talk?

Even though I knew it was unwarranted, I felt awful that I hadn't been there for her.

About thirty minutes after the first text, she'd added:

> Things exploded with my parents. I'm freaking out.

And then a bit later:

> Please call me.

I couldn't imagine how the situation with her parents could get any worse. What did "exploded" even mean? I couldn't help but picture Laila hiding in her closet, her father stalking the house with an ax like Jack from *The Shining*. I shook off the random, dark thought. Acid trickled up my esophagus as my empty stomach clenched.

Around midnight, she'd sent the last two texts.

> I guess you're asleep already.

> Call me when you wake up. Things are really bad. I don't know what to do.

My heart thudded in my chest with the first trickle of adrenaline. I wasn't sure if I should cold-call her this early in the morning, but I had to do something.

I scooted up in bed to lean against the pillow and dialed her number. Yersi, seeing the movement, let out an excited *meow*. I picked up the spray bottle and threatened him with it. He cat-laughed just out of range and meowed again. I scowled at him as the ringing tone trilled in my ear; I didn't have time for his whining.

Laila picked up on the third ring. "Josie," she said, her voice subdued.

My heart slunk down to my stomach.

That single "Josie" said oodles. She sounded like she'd been up for a while and had resigned herself to her fate. It was possible she hadn't even slept at all.

"Hey, Laila. You okay?" I asked, feeling frazzled. It was a dumb question. I knew she was absolutely *not* okay.

She sighed and said quietly, "Things were awful last night."

I felt a surge of protective adrenaline. "Awful, how?" I asked quietly, my tone hushed and laced with a hint of I'm-gonna-kick-some-motherfucking-ass. The type of tone that made people flinch.

A horrible realization dawned on me. "Did he hit you?"

"No. Nothing like that," she said quickly, but after a beat, she added, "He took it out on my mother."

What does that *mean?*

I sat up straight, back stiff and hyper-alert. "Are you safe?"

"From physical abuse? Yeah." Her voice was sad and defeated.

I wasn't sure how to feel about that. On one hand, I was grateful her dad hadn't raised a hand to her or her mom. On the other hand, I knew that emotional abuse could be equally painful, and I hated the fact that she was going through this. My hackles lowered a tad.

"Start from the beginning," I prompted, circling my hand impatiently even though she couldn't see me.

Yersi let out another plaintive wail. I shot him with my eye daggers, to which he was immune. His tail jittered in irritation at my lack of compliance.

"I went shopping with my mother on Saturday," Laila began. "She was really hounding me about wedding dresses and stuff, but I just rolled with it. It was uncomfortable, but it didn't get really bad until after that."

"What happened then?" I asked,

Laila sniffed through quiet tears, and her voice picked up speed as she pressed on. "My father said he'd arranged a call with a guy the matchmaker found. I disappeared for the first call. When I hid for the second call, my father completely flipped out. He said I was an impossible daughter and a disappointment."

When she paused, I asked, "What was your mom doing during all this?"

"At first, she was quiet and just looked profoundly dismayed. But as my father got increasingly angry, she shriveled."

"She didn't say anything?" I asked, horrified that her mom hadn't stood up for her. Protected her. That's what moms were supposed to do.

"No, she didn't say a single thing," Laila said bitterly. "I guess I should've expected that. She's never defended me. I think she's too scared of my father. Plus, she wants this marriage to happen as much as he does."

"Damn, Laila," I half-whispered.

"He kept hounding me," Laila continued. "And then he turned on my mother, blaming her for everything and shouting at her that it was her fault that I was a failure. It was really hard watching him do that to her. He started ranting about how horrible I was and that I had a duty to be obedient. Then, he just stormed off. It was only later that night that he started up again, yelling at my mom. I could hear them through the walls. He was awful to her. The things he was saying to her were...they were horrible. I know I'll eventually have to leave my room this morning. Face them. But I...."

I'd never heard her sound so defeated. Laila was usually the one who stood up to the douche-bags at work and fought tooth and nail to advocate for others. But when her parents were around, it was like they sucked all of the strength out of her.

"Do you want to come to my place?" I offered. "I'm worried about you staying there."

I was met with thoughtful silence.

"I'm not going to let him chase me out of my own house," she said, her voice icy cold.

There's my Laila.

Grasping at straws, I offered, "Want me to come be your backup? What can I do?"

"I think..." she started. "I need more time to process all of this. Maybe we can meet for lunch today?"

"Yes," I said, relieved to have some way to help her. "When and where?"

"I think I need Buffalo Wild Wings. That okay? Noon?" she half-begged.

I was a bit surprised by the suggestion. That was her greasy-spoon, soul-food place. Lately, she'd barely been eating. I wasn't sure if it was a good sign that she was eating again or if we'd reached rock bottom.

"I'll be there," I said. "And, Laila, call me anytime. Seriously. And if it's ever unsafe, just come over. Okay? You have a key. Just come."

"Thank you, Josie," she replied, choking up.

***

After the call with Laila, my anxiety was climbing through the roof. I went to the lab in a half-zombie state, distracted and frazzled.

As soon as I passed through the front doors, I could sense the shift. More people were around the lab this week, and everything just felt a tad busier. I passed James in the hallway with a nod, too preoccupied to make small talk. I dumped my stuff in my office and made a quick U-turn at my desk to check in with Dustin.

And, of course, as if the universe hadn't already thrown me enough curve balls, I smacked right into Gerald.

"Geez, Gerald! What the hell?!" I exclaimed, startled, and stepped back. It took everything in me not to brush the cooties off.

He looked at me shrewdly, arms crossed, forming a blockade at my office door.

My heart sank. This body-blocking routine reeked of the old Gerald, and I wasn't sure I could deal with his drama today.

"More pigs came in over the weekend," he said, stating the obvious. "From the same farm."

"Yes, Gerald." I was so tired, annoyed, and anxious that I couldn't muster up anything better to say.

"It's an outbreak," he said, standing firm.

"Yes, it seems so," I said, crossing my arms defensively.

"There was no growth on the *Brucella* cultures from the first case. The aerobic cultures from the second case also have no growth. Are you sure Dr. Rodriguez didn't miss something? I am certain this is viral. If you didn't rely so much on PCR, these cases would be solved by now."

Yep, the old Gerald has definitely slithered back in.

I shook my head in dismay, dropped my arms, and clenched my fists. "Look, dude. Back up."

His eyebrows wrinkled in confusion.

I waved my hand up and down at him. "This whole blocking-the-doorway thing. It's creepy. Back up."

He looked hurt, and I felt an uncomfortable shred of guilt like I'd kicked a dog.

Why do I feel bad? The nasty part of me whispered. *This guy is a complete shitass. Fuck him.*

My exhaustion and stress got the better of me, and I sniped, "If you didn't do this weird stuff all of the time, maybe people wouldn't hate you so much."

I regretted the words as soon as they left my mouth. It was a horribly nasty thing to say and wasn't much better than some of the things that Gerald had said to me.

His face completely shuttered, and he tilted his chin up.

"Well, Pocahontas. Whenever you're ready to do your job and help the client, I'll be in my office." He flashed his Manson lamps and stormed off.

Instead of the usual surge of anger, I felt like I'd had the wind sucked out of me. Everything was bubbling up at the same time, and it was overwhelming.

I can't deal with this shit right now.

Eventually, I'd need to puzzle out the Gordian Knot that was Gerald. But not today. I had way bigger fish to fry. Trying to shake off the altercation and get back to business, I made my way to Dustin's office, where he was at his desk, nursing a steaming cup of coffee.

I knocked on the doorjamb and said, "Good morning." Taking a deep breath, I tried to fight off the shaky hands that followed a surge of unspent adrenaline.

He looked up, smiled, and waved me in. "Mornin', Doc. You all right?"

I tossed a hand up dismissively. "Just Gerald."

Dustin's eyebrows lifted. Gerald had certainly done Dustin dirty, too. But Dustin wasn't one to gossip and would only lend an ear if needed. He could sense I didn't want to give the shitass an ounce of my waning energy, so he let it pass.

After a beat, he said, "Saw you got 'nother batch of fetuses yesterday."

"Yup," I said and flopped in the chair across from him, shoulders sagging.

"Find anything?" he asked, leaning back in his chair, cradling his mug in both hands.

"Nope." After a beat, I corrected myself, "Well, maybe placentitis, but it was so subtle it could be nothing."

He frowned in sympathy and rocked a bit in his chair.

"How about you?" I asked, desperate to change the subject. "Have a nice holiday?"

"Yes, ma'am," he said. "The storm kept us in, but we were ready for it. Dolores made her chicken fried steak."

"Chicken fried steak? For Christmas?" I teased, feeling the first smile of the day dance across my lips.

"Yes, ma'am," he said with a resolute nod. "Wouldn't have it any other way."

"Well, her chicken fried steak is pretty damn good," I conceded.

He leaned back in his chair, his mustache titling up with a smile. "How 'bout you?"

"The roads were clear enough that Tessa and I were able to make the drive to Aunty's. She cooked her famous cinnamon rolls."

"Cinnamon rolls? For Christmas?" He parroted back playfully, lifting an eyebrow as if to question whether Dolores' chicken fried steak or Aunty's cinnamon rolls would win in a showdown.

"Come on," I said with a grin. "Maple pecan cinnamon rolls? With bacon?"

"Well, if there was bacon...." He held his hands up to concede the match.

We both chuckled.

"I'm just glad we could still get down there," I said. "With the storm and all, I wasn't sure we could make it. The fact that I got to see them Friday made it easier to miss brunch yesterday."

With that, he gave me a look. "Josh said you sent him home and did the case on yer own. You shoulda had him stay."

I shrugged, slightly chagrined. "It was a holiday weekend."

He lifted an eyebrow in friendly doubt.

"It wasn't like I was working on an adult horse," I added.

He huffed a laugh at the reference. When a fellow pathologist, Tom Lang, started about five years ago, he'd come in on a Saturday to do a horse necropsy. It was the weekend before finals, and being the nice guy that he was, he'd told the on-call student that he could manage it alone. He'd managed it all right. Managed to give his hand a pretty gnarly slice with his necropsy knife.

"Still coulda gotten hurt," Dustin chided, not unkindly. "And it's pretty damn hard to stitch yourself up."

It was my turn to laugh. After that fateful event, Tom had called me in to help. I'd driven to the lab and found him dripping blood everywhere, looking about ready to faint. At first, I was glad he called me; I wasn't sure he could have driven himself to the emergency room. Then, to my horror, I quickly realized that he hadn't called me there to drive him anywhere; he'd called me there to suture him up. Right there. On the necropsy floor.

"He should've just let me drive him to the hospital," I said, shaking my head with a grin. "Asking a pathologist to put in a tidy line of sutures. I mean, come on."

"Meh," Dustin said with a slight shoulder shrug. "It healed pretty well."

Tom still had a scar, but it was, to my immense surprise, a tidy one. It might've been something I could be proud of if I hadn't gotten in so much trouble over it. Since then, Fran was pretty insistent that nobody went out on the floor alone. Period. Even though she'd made the rule to protect herself from liability, it was still a smart rule to protect employees.

"Just be careful out there, Doc," he said. "I've gone ass-over-tea-kettle once or twice myself. It's easy enough to have things go real bad, real fast."

I nodded slightly to acknowledge the advice, a solemn cloud pressing over me. There had been a pathologist at another lab who'd slipped, and by some random, very unfortunate chance, his knife had hit his femoral artery, and he'd bled out right there on the necropsy floor.

"Plus, if Fran finds out...." He gave me a look that finished the sentence.

I sighed and shrugged. Fran was the least of my worries. "I'm probably already on her naughty list for closing the lab early. What's one more thing?"

A hint of worry flitted across his face. He shifted in his chair and changed the subject. "Don't want to jinx us or nothin', but it should be slow again this week. We got nothin' for today so far. The pigs from yesterday might be all ya get."

My shoulders sagged slightly in relief. "I sure hope so."

I didn't have much work today, but between Laila and the unsolved Rising Sun Farms cases, my mind was a whirlwind. The thought of another case, even an easy one, was just too much.

"I'll give you a jingle if anything changes," he said with a friendly nod.

"Sounds good. Thanks," I said, standing. "I'll let you get back to it."

He gave me a friendly salute. "See ya later, Doc."

Back at my desk, I looked up the results to-date on the three pig cases. It wasn't that I didn't believe Gerald; it was more about trying to put all the pieces together. See everything in one spot. Plus, it distracted me from all the other stuff.

A quick scroll through the completed test results confirmed everything Gerald had said: There was no growth on the microbiology plates, making it unlikely that it was anything bacterial. I leaned back in my chair, tapping my pen on the desk. Something about the placentitis was niggling at me, and I couldn't put my finger on it.

With a huff, I pushed away from my desk and went to find Sandy. Maybe talking through the case with her would help.

She was in her office, reading glasses perched on her nose, plunking away at her keyboard. I knocked lightly on the doorjamb.

"Good morning, Dr. Bishop. Have a nice holiday?" I asked as I took a seat.

She looked up at me, smiled, and took her glasses off, letting them hang around her neck. "Yes, ma'am. And you?"

"Yep," I said, somewhat truthfully. I leaned forward, cutting to the chase. "I need to pick your brain. It's about those pigs."

"Oh, yes. I saw the feed and water. We'll test the water for nitrates and send the feed out for mycotoxins today. Don't put all your eggs in that basket, though," she advised.

"Thank you." After a beat, I added, "I'm pretty sure it's infectious. But everything has come up negative so far."

She leaned back and rested her arms on the armrests. "Walk me through it."

My sewing machine leg bounced as I ordered my thoughts. "The first piglet had no gross or histologic lesions. There was no growth on the aerobic and *Brucella* cultures. The abortion panel PCR was negative. I added Lepto. It's still pending. The second set of piglets were mummified, but no other gross lesions. I need to trim them in today. There was nothing on the aerobic and *Brucella* cultures on them either. PCR, including Lepto, is pending. Yesterday, I got a third round of piglets. I also got placenta on the third case."

"Oh, that's good," she interrupted.

I nodded and continued, "There were some really subtle changes in the placenta. It could be nothing. Obviously, I don't have any test results back on them. They'll be setting everything up today."

Sandy pursed her lips and tapped one arm of her eyeglasses against them. "Placentitis. I'd be thinking bacterial."

"Yeah, but there's been no-growth so far," I said, feeling doubtful. As much as I disliked Gerald, his lab put out results I could trust.

She shrugged. "On the fetal tissues, sure. But maybe something will pop on the placenta."

I cringed at the potential delay. They'd be plating the placenta today. It would be at least a day or two before we'd know if there was any growth. Then, they'd still have to work it up. Plus, placentas were fairly dirty. Even if there was growth, they'd have to pick through the contaminants to find anything significant like *Streptococcus suis*.

"I wonder if we should do virus isolation, too," I mused. That would take forever, and it hurt just to say it out loud, but I couldn't help but think we were missing something.

As if she sensed my inner turmoil, Sandy said, "Sorry I couldn't be of more help. I know this is weighing on you. I think you're just going to have to ride it out. Wait for the results."

Unable to accept my fate, I grasped at straws. "Maybe we should do a farm visit?"

Her eyebrows shot up in doubt. "I thought I remember you saying they ran a pretty tight ship?"

I nodded, already knowing where she was headed.

"I doubt they'd let us out there until all the testing comes back negative," she added.

"Yeah," I conceded. "I'm just feeling a bit desperate. They have a pretty big operation. I don't want them to lose any more animals."

Her eyes softened with sympathy. "I know." Leaning back in her chair, she added, "I'm sure this'll all be sorted by the end of the week, and then you can start the new year with a clean slate."

I said my thanks, even though I lacked her confidence, and then left her office feeling worse than when I'd first come in. Something about the placenta kept nagging at me. Back in my office, I pulled Kirkbride's book off the shelf. Maybe I'd missed something.

I flipped to the chapter on pigs and ran down the list, trying to identify an infectious disease that caused mummification and placentitis. Unfortunately, the list was about as long as it was before. To make it all the more frustrating, the tests I'd ordered should've caught the more common stuff.

Maybe Sandy was right. Maybe culturing the placenta would give us the answer that culturing the fetal tissues hadn't. I put the book back in its spot, feeling defeated.

It's a fetus. Those cases rarely get solved.

I wasn't sure if I was trying to reassure myself or make excuses. Unable to shake the feeling of incompetence, I let out a heavy, defeated sigh. I had samples from three separate litters in an abortion storm. Of all fetal cases, I should get an answer with these simply based on sample size alone. I had to get an answer.

Feeling stir-crazy, I fled to the histology lab to trim in the tissues from the two recent cases. There was little else I could do, and I couldn't sit at my desk for a moment longer.

CHAPTER
TWENTY-TWO

A few hours later, I pulled into the Buffalo Wild Wings parking lot, relieved to see Laila's car already there. With the students still away on winter break, it was easy to find a parking place, and I pulled in right next to her Subaru.

The restaurant somehow managed to be both loud and empty. But it was blessedly warm, and the smell of fried food made me drool. Wiping the residual snow off my shoes, I took my coat off and glanced around the place, trying to find Laila.

She was stashed in a corner with her back to the wall. Catching her eye, I raised a hand, and she replied with a weak smile. Even across the room, the stress was visibly etched on her face.

I made my way through the relatively empty dining area and hung my jacket on the back of the chair.

"Hey," I said, giving her a supportive smile and leaning over for a half hug.

"Hey," she echoed. She seemed reflective, her voice soft.

As soon as my ass hit the seat, a server appeared from the netherworld to take our orders.

"Boneless wings with honey barbeque sauce, a side of onion rings—make that two orders of onion rings—a root beer, and a chocolate fudge brownie," Laila said without batting an eye.

My eyebrows shot up in surprise. I wasn't sure where she was going to put all of that food. But I wasn't one to talk. I'd consumed my fair share of food-therapy.

"Anythin' else with that?" the server chirped reflexively.

"That's it," Laila answered.

I bit back a snort.

"And you, ma'am?" the server said, turning to me.

I ordered a chicken tender wrap and water. The server collected our menus and left with a swirl.

Laila rested her chin on one palm, and her shoulders sagged. "How's work?"

I arched an eyebrow at her attempt at small talk. "It's fine," I lied.

There was no way in hell I was going to chit-chat about work with the giant elephant's ass taking up the entire room. Tossing out any modicum of Oklahoma charm, I took a direct approach, knowing Laila would forgive me.

Leaning forward, I said, "Laila. What the hell is happening with your folks? I'm legitimately worried about you being around them."

She sighed and frowned. She started spinning the salt shaker in slow circles.

I reached out and squeezed her hand. Her eyes jumped to mine and away again as she fought tears.

"Laila," I started, softer this time. "Is he hurting you?"

She shook her head. "He doesn't hit me," she finally answered, somewhat defensively.

"Well, at least there's that," I huffed. "But Laila. Seriously. There's more than one way to hurt someone. Constantly yelling at someone is also a form of abuse."

Her face grew stony, and I realized that I'd pushed it a bit too far.

"Sorry," I backpedaled and tried another tack. "Tell me the whole thing from the start."

Our drinks arrived just at that moment, lurching us out of the conversation. Laila leaned back as the server put the drinks down and thanked them absently. She stared down at her root beer with a slight grimace, hands tucked in her lap and throat bobbing.

"What happened on Saturday?" I nudged.

"We went shopping in OKC, just my mother and me," she started, voice shaky. "Even though the mall was crazy, she seemed to enjoy herself. She kept nagging me about getting married, but otherwise, it wasn't too bad. The usual level, you know?"

Even though I had no clue what a "normal" level of nagging was, I nodded to keep her talking.

"She was even kind of nice to me," she said, shrugging slightly. "Anyway, when we got back home, my father didn't even let us put our bags down before he jumped on us."

"Jumped on you how?" I took a sip of water to cover up how much I disliked her father.

She looked down at her folded hands. "My father said he'd scheduled a call with a man the next morning. The matchmaker arranged it all. I tried to make excuses, push back, you know...but my father just bullied me until I acquiesced." Her eyes bounced to mine, gauging my reaction.

"No judgment. Go on," I said, even though, in my head, I was still doling out heaps of judgment on her dad.

She paused and fiddled with her straw. "Then, yesterday, I went to get groceries before they could stop me and 'accidentally' missed the call."

My eyes went wide. "Oh, dang. How did that work out?"

She huffed. "About as you could imagine. My father was so angry. He said he'd rescheduled the call for that night and basically sat with me all day until it was time."

"What the hell?" I said, voice soft, slightly aghast. I couldn't imagine a parent treating their adult daughter like that.

"Yeah," she said sadly. She paused, fighting tears. "I was just about ready to go through with it. I figured I didn't have much of a choice. But right before the second call, I chickened out and locked myself in the bathroom,"

"That's not chickening out. That's protecting yourself," I asserted.

She shook her head. "Not really. He was furious and...."

She paused for what felt like forever.

"It's all my fault," she barely whispered.

"What is?" I asked softly.

"Him taking it out on my mother," she said, shaking her head. "He was so enraged about my avoiding the call twice that when I finally left the bathroom, he pounced on me. He said I was a shame on the family and that I'd probably lost the match. He called me a *pathabhrashṭa*."

"What is a *pathabhrashṭa*?" I interrupted, completely mangling the pronunciation.

"Um. It's like someone who lacks morals." She waved her hand, slightly frustrated. "More than that, though. Like a deviant. Someone who is defective. Anyway, he ranted that only someone as lowly as me would shun a good man. Then, he went all quiet...like the scary kind of quiet...and he turned on my mom. The things he said to her...they were awful. And it's my fault he got mad at her."

"Screw that noise," I grumbled. "Your dad coming down on your mom isn't your fault. That's his fault for being a total dick."

A dozen expressions crossed her face so quickly that I couldn't gauge her true feelings.

"Sorry for talking bad about your dad," I said, voice low, and then my back stiffened. "Wait. I take that back. I'm sorry if I hurt *you* by saying that. I'm absolutely *not* sorry for calling a spade a spade."

I paused, watching her. Her eyebrows were furrowed with worry, and she kept her eyes cast down.

"You aren't responsible for how your dad treats your mom," I pressed. "It's like blaming yourself for Ian Murray's douche-bag-ery."

That chased her frown away for a second, and my heart lifted slightly.

I huffed before continuing. "Women are so quick to accept responsibility for bad shit that is done to us. People say things like 'guys whistle at you because of how you dress' or 'you got raped because you were flirting.' It's literally ingrained in how we think. I get it. But please don't shoulder other people's rotten behavior. It's not your fault."

She looked down at her root beer, considering what I'd said.

"When I'm Chair, it *will* be my fault," she said softly.

It felt so good to hear her call herself "Chair." At that moment, I knew that no matter what her folks threw at her, they wouldn't crush who she truly was at her core.

"Sure, you'll be responsible for setting the tone in the department," I conceded. "Setting the culture. But you won't be responsible for other people's behavior. It all depends on how you react to it. If you don't address the bad behavior, toxic environment, whatever, then it's on you as a leader."

Laila nodded, processing everything.

I took a deep breath. I was pretty passionate about this topic, but now was not the time to soapbox. I needed to focus.

Before I could shift gears, the server came with our meals, interrupting my train of thought. I gave them a distracted smile and a thanks.

After the server left, Laila looked down at her heaping plate of food. "I'm not sure I can eat. The idea of it all sounded good, but now that it's in front of me...." Her throat bobbed.

I waited for her to finish her sentence. My wrap was practically singing to me. The smell of the sauce was pure joy, and my stomach betrayed me by growling loudly.

Laila nodded her chin at my plate. "Go ahead and start."

"I'm not eating until you eat," I said, feeling feisty.

A smile finally twitched at the edge of her lips. She picked up a single onion ring and nibbled on it.

I lifted an eyebrow and ate one bite of my wrap.

We slowly played the game, bite-for-bite, until we were both giggling. Her shoulders relaxed a tad.

"What am I going to do, Josie?" she said, resigned. "I just want them to go back home and leave me alone already. I know it's awful saying that. But I also feel awful."

"I hear you," I answered sympathetically. "I wish I had the perfect answer for you."

Tessa's advice echoed in my head.

The truth had helped Tessa when she was in a tight spot. Maybe it would help Laila, too. Perhaps the truth would be a sturdy enough defense that her folks couldn't tear it down.

After a beat, I asked, "Have you tried just telling them the truth?"

Her eyebrows crinkled. "What do you mean?"

"Like, tell them that you don't want to get married and you don't want kids. Tell them that no matter what they say or do, whether they have a matchmaker arranging things or not, it won't change anything." I held my breath, waiting for her response.

She folded her hands in her lap and stared at her half-empty plate.

"I understand it's probably going to be hard," I added. "And they won't want to hear it. I know the expectations they've placed on you."

She shook her head slightly. "We don't do that in my family, Josie. I can't just say something like that. I'm supposed to do what I'm told. Make my family proud. Be a good daughter."

The silence stretched between us as we both picked at our food.

"I don't know what it's like to be you. Or how your family works. I get it," I admitted. "But the whole dodging arranged marriages hasn't worked. The only two options left are to bend the knee or hold the line."

She looked up at me.

I raised one eyebrow, and a smile tickled the edges of my lips. "And I know you don't want to bend the knee."

Her shoulders shook with a small, silent laugh. A fierceness danced in her eyes. "I do *not* want to bend the knee." Her voice was firm and resolute.

"So, try the truth," I nudged. "It's worth a shot. It can't get any worse than it already is."

She considered and then tilted her chin in a short nod. "Tonight. I'll do it tonight."

I reached across the table and gave her hand a quick squeeze. "Now, let's finish our food and talk about how we'll celebrate when they're finally on a plane."

"Ice cream and a game?" she offered.

"Hell yeah," I replied with a grin. "And *They Live*. Don't forget your promise."

CHAPTER
TWENTY-THREE

When I got back to work, there weren't any dead bodies waiting for me. Usually, that was a good thing, but I couldn't help but begrudge idle hands. I needed a distraction.

You wanted a slow week, I chided.

Thoughts of the pigs tumbled in. Everything with those three cases seemed to drag on, just like the crap with Laila's folks. Part of me wished I could fast-forward a few days to finally get closure. Feeling restless, I decided to hit Manuel up and check on the status of the PCR tests.

He was at his desk, fingers speeding across his keyboard. His office was the epitome of efficiency, and everything had a purpose. His desk was clear except for a picture with his family, a cup with pens, and a neat stack of papers that sat in a "finished" tray. The only pieces of flare in his office were his degrees and military awards, which were tastefully framed and neatly arranged on the wall behind his desk.

I knocked on the doorjamb. "Howdy, Dr. Rodriguez."

He waved me in. "Hello, Dr. Harjo. Checking on the pigs?"

"Yes, sir," I replied, taking the seat across from him.

"Beth completed the extractions on the case from yesterday. Everything is set to run overnight, including the Leptos."

"Awesome," I said. "Thanks so much."

Coming back from vacation and being short-staffed, I hadn't expected them to get everything going today. I was super appreciative and wondered what other cases had been bumped out of line or how much overtime Beth was pulling.

"Please tell Beth thanks for me," I said.

He nodded. "With three cases from the same farm in less than a week, I figured it was urgent. And you know how Beth is; she's a trooper. Always willing to pitch in to help the team."

"Yes, she's pretty amazing," I agreed, making a mental note to bring them some thank-you treats. They really were going above and beyond.

Gerald is going above and beyond, too, and you aren't bringing him shit, the self-deprecating side of me snarked.

But it's Gerald. That's different, the rational side of me countered.

Is it, though? The thought hung in my mind.

Shaking off the never-ending inner monologue, I smiled at Manuel. "Fingers crossed we get an answer soon. Thanks again."

"You're welcome," he replied. "I'll let you know as soon as the results come out."

We said collegial see-ya-laters, and I headed back to my office.

I flopped behind my desk, feeling a bit huffy. The chair creaked a warning as I rocked slightly, chewing on my cheek. Worried I'd gnaw right through the damn thing with my anxiety, I picked up a pen, twirling it in my fingers as I tried to puzzle through it all. The whole wait-it-out thing was killing me.

As my mind whirled, thoughts of Gerald kept popping up like a pimple that wouldn't go away. It just begged to be picked at, even though it would only make things worse.

He had been putting some effort into trying to be a better person in his own messed-up Gerald way. The fiasco with the tiger had changed him. It'd changed all of us. But he was still so acrimonious that it was hard to be nice to him.

Deep down, I knew I shouldn't have verbally scrapped with him earlier. Behaving like that only made things worse. I should've kept it polite and professional. Taken the higher ground.

But it's Gerald, I whined to myself.

I sighed and shook my head. The pen was still twirling in my fingers. If he was going to make an effort, as paltry and unsuccessful as it was, I should, too.

My anxiety was buzzing, and I was so jittery that I couldn't sit in my chair for a second longer. There was no way I would be able to focus on any real work. The uneasiness won out, and I pushed out of my chair to hunt Dustin down. Chewing the fat with my buddy would be a welcome distraction.

As soon as I exited my office, Gerald rounded the corner at the end of the hall, head down, looking harried. Like a startled rabbit exiting its warren, I stopped short and briefly considered a U-turn, sealing the office door behind me.

Seriously, Josie? Get your shit together.

Pulling myself up by my bootstraps, I took a slow step toward him. I didn't believe in fate or whatever nonsense, but I did feel like the nebulous "universe" was trying to send me a message. This whole cluster with Gerald needed to be tackled head-on.

At that moment, he glanced up, noticed me, and looked away quickly. His whole body tensed, and his mouth clamped shut. He hunched his shoulders, eyes to the ground, and made as if to go right past me without a word.

My palms instantly started to sweat as I walked toward him, trying to keep my steps measured.

"Hey, Gerald?" I hated myself for sounding so mousy.

His head jerked up, and a flicker of surprise crossed his face at my initiation of dialogue. As if catching himself, his usual haughty mask quickly fell into place, and his lips sagged into a frown. "Yes?"

Fuck, fuck, fuck. I did not want to be nice to this shitass.

Then, I heard Aunty's voice in my head, encouraging me to try to make peace.

"Yes, Dr. Harjo?" he repeated, starting to sneer. "People have work to do, you know."

Straightening my back, I slowed to a stop in front of him and met his eye. "Thank you for working through the storm and the holiday to get the cultures done on the pigs."

His eyes narrowed, searching for a hidden jab in what I'd said. Walls seemed to lock tightly into place around him. With a jolt of surprise,

I realized that he thought I was going to snark at him, and I couldn't help but feel like I'd been kicking someone who was already down.

"You're welcome," he said, cautiously.

His response completely floored me. In the past, he would have lashed out at me and said something hurtful. The polite reply had caught me completely off guard.

"I've rushed the cultures from the latest case," he added. "But I'm certain it's viral."

"I appreciate it," I said, the words almost catching in my throat like a nasty furball.

I certainly wasn't ready to bring the guy donuts tomorrow; there was too much bad blood between us for that. But I could extend the olive branch just a tad further.

"I'm sorry for what I said this morning," I managed to scratch out.

I was a bit sick to my stomach, apologizing to him, of all people. He was such a dick, and I couldn't help but feel like I was groveling.

But am I? Or am I just trying to help him be a kinder person? Lead by example and all that?

I watched him, waiting for his response. A part of me hoped he might even go so far as to apologize for calling me Pocahontas earlier.

He frowned slightly, and I knew then that an apology wouldn't be forthcoming.

Wish in one hand and shit in the other, I thought with a mental shrug. *I tried.*

With an almost inaudible *hmph*, he slithered away and left me standing in the hallway, feeling like a dope.

***

The interaction with Gerald had thrown me off-kilter, and I decided to skip hanging out with Dustin. I was in a weird mood and didn't want to drag him down with me.

I couldn't help feeling like I'd fumbled every damn aspect of my life lately. I'd been useless with helping Laila, the abortion storm at

Rising Sun Farms was still unsolved, and I couldn't even have an adult conversation with one of my coworkers. I felt like a trainwreck of a friend and a mess of a pathologist.

Feeling mopey, I hid in my office with my door closed for the rest of the day. When it was late enough that I could leave without catching any flack, I gave Dustin a heads-up that I was checking out early and fled home.

Relief washed over me when I pulled into my driveway and saw Yersi's kitty loaf perched in the window. I was somewhere safe. Somewhere that I couldn't mess anything else up.

Yersi greeted me at the door with purrs, forcing me to smile. I picked him up to cuddle, cradling him like a baby. He tolerated it for a bit before squirming free to demand dinner.

I tried to relax into my home routine: feeding Yersi, taking care of the chickens, and cooking a meal. But it all felt off in a way that I couldn't put my finger on.

Just as I sat down to eat my meal-for-one, Laila texted me.

> Wish me luck. I'm planning on talking to them after dinner.

She added a cringe-face emoji.

A burgeoning sense of dread washed over me, and I wasn't sure she was doing the right thing. I was worried about sending her down the wrong path. The one that led to a hungry wolf. Deep down, I knew I needed to be confident for her, tuck all the doubt into a black box, and bury that fucker.

I texted her back.

> You got this.

I sent her emojis of two fists bumping.

I'm around if you need me.

She hearted my text.

Hoping that was enough encouragement to keep her going, I locked my phone. I didn't want her to pick up a whiff of my doubt. I itched to do something, but I knew I needed to sit it out on the bench for a few rounds.

If my garden hadn't been a snowy wasteland, I would've gone out there and piddled around to distract myself. I toyed with the idea of going for a walk and quickly dismissed it, recalling my last altercation with a particularly malevolent crack in the sidewalk in front of the police station last September. That joyous moment had left me on my ass. The last thing I needed today was to go ass-over-teakettle on the slushy sidewalks.

Guess I'm stuck inside, I huffed to myself.

I decided to binge the rest of *Mindhunter* and pack away a pint of ice cream in what remained of the evening. It was a paltry attempt at soothing my frayed nerves and was completely ineffective. The doubt continued to spin in my head, turning into a whirlpool, threatening to suck me further into depression.

Dinner time came and went.

Even though I knew exactly how long each episode was, I couldn't stop obsessively checking the time on my phone. The minutes ticked by. And then it was hours. My phone stayed silent, and it was starting to creep me out.

Despite the acid crawling up my esophagus, I debated eating another pint of ice cream. Anything to quench the worry.

At half past nine, I couldn't stand it anymore and texted Laila.

You doing okay? How did it go?

My phone locked without a response.

The dread continued to build. Watching *Mindhunter* had not been good for my mental state. All I could do was imagine the million and one ways that her dad could fly off the handle and hurt her. I was so freaked out that I was ready to go over there to check on her if she didn't respond. I couldn't help but be a tad demanding, and I texted her again.

> I know you might be busy but give me a thumbs up that you're okay? Or a thumbs down if I need to come over to kick some ass?

My phone locked again without a reply. I'd give it until ten. At that point, I was going over, no matter what.

Just as my anxiety was reaching its peak, my phone binged with Laila's reply.

> I'm okay

I pursed my lips, and my eyebrows crinkled. That reply was very much unlike Laila: short and vague. She did say she was okay. But my mind kept skipping back into *Mindhunter*-land.

She probably needs space. She said she's okay. Trust her.

I took three deep belly breaths to calm my racing heart. Fighting the urge to fuss over her, I simply hearted her text and sent:

> Call me if you need anything.

She added a thumbs-up tag.

I chewed on my cheek. If I didn't cut that annoying tick out, I was going to gnaw straight through it. After all these years of grinding on it, I was shocked I didn't have a big, fat layer of scar tissue there.

Feeling a tad better that Laila was alive, I turned the TV off and went through the motions of getting ready for bed. I turned the volume up on my phone and laid it on my side table; I wanted any late-night texts or calls to wake me.

I snuggled under the covers, trying to calm my racing thoughts. As if sensing my inner turmoil, Yersi curled up into the small of my back. His steady purr started to lull me to sleep, and my eyes grew heavy.

Just as I was dozing off, my phone chirped loudly. I jerked up, heart thudding. Yersi scrambled off with an annoyed *merf* sound.

I frantically fumbled for my phone, unlocked it, and read the notification with mixed emotions.

It was a text from Armand.

After several deep breaths, I was able to get my hands to stop shaking and read the text.

> Are you still up? Can we schedule a call for tomorrow morning your time? I miss you.

Despite all the crazy shit going down right now, my shoulders relaxed a bit. It wasn't Laila texting me late at night with more bad news. It wasn't another case from Rising Sun Farms. It was Armand, and he missed me.

My face softened, and a smile tugged at my lips.

> Totally want to talk tomorrow.

I added a heart emoji.

> Usual time?

He sent a thumbs up.

My blood started thrumming in my ears. It was the first time he'd ever said that to me, even if it was just in a text. It felt warm. And soft. And *right*.

I wanted to hear him say it with his beautiful accent, holding me tight, the soft scent of his aftershave filling the air. I wanted to whisper it back to him, head pressed against his chest.

I promised myself that it would happen soon. But for now, all I had was a text. I slowly typed in a response and paused. Feeling a thread of nervous excitement, I hit send.

CHAPTER
TWENTY-FOUR

My sadistic phone alarm woke me bright and early Tuesday morning.

Nightmares of being chased through the dark woods had woken me repeatedly through the night, sweat dampening my jammies and heart racing. I would just manage to get back to sleep when they'd jerk me awake again. I was feeling blurry-eyed and tired.

Yersi seemed to have slept fine, despite my tossing and turning. As soon as he heard the alarm, an excited *merf* escaped, and he assumed his begging position.

I crawled out of bed, rubbing my puffy, dry eyes. I went through the motions of feeding His Royal Highness and making myself presentable for my call with Armand, which, on a day like today, meant combing my fingers through my hair and grabbing a cup of hot tea. I cradled my mug in two hands as my computer booted up.

I missed Armand, but if I was being honest with myself, I wanted to drag my ass back to bed and hide. Today was going to be a hot mess, I could just feel it.

After burning my tongue on the tea and wallowing in my self-pity for about five minutes, the ringing of Armand's call came through my computer.

I answered with a tired smile.

He smiled back, slight concern dampening his usual sexy grin. His dark curly hair tipped over onto his forehead, and a heavy five-o'clock shadow shaded his face. Despite being the middle of winter, his skin had a lovely tan and he looked relaxed.

Of course, he looks fabulous.

With a flash of mortification, I saw my video on the bottom of my screen and realized I looked as shitty as I felt.

Sigh.

"Hello, *iubita mea*," he said, voice low.

"Hey, babe," was all I could manage.

Just then, Ileana bounced into the screen, squeaky toy chirping in her mouth, and knocked his computer over.

He let out what I could only assume was a string of curses in Romanian. He righted the computer and said with a smile, "Just a minute."

"All good," I replied, smiling back, and took a tentative sip of my steaming tea.

He said some more words to her in Romanian in his sweet-dog voice. The toy squeaked a few times, followed by the skitter of excited toenails across the floor. From the sounds of it, he'd tossed the toy for her.

He came back into view, grinning. "Sorry. I haven't walked her yet. She is very insistent." The squeaking picked up again, and he looked over the camera on his laptop. "She will try to tear her bear apart for the next fifteen or twenty minutes. But then I will need to take her out, I think."

I smiled back. "I get it. The only reason Yersi isn't raising holy hell is that I fed him already."

I tilted the camera on my laptop so he could see Yersi curled in my lap.

"How's the Black Plague doing?" he asked.

I shrugged with a smirk. "As long as the food shows up in his bowl on command, he's pretty damn good."

I positioned the laptop back on the coffee table. "Working at home again?"

He nodded. "I have a lot of data I need to analyze before I leave."

He'd wrapped up his last few experiments a couple of weeks ago, clearing out his greenhouse before he left for six months.

"All the grading done?" I asked.

He nodded. "Finished yesterday."

"Wow! That was fast," I said, impressed. He had been co-teaching two classes at the university last semester, and each class had over a hundred students. Finals had been just last week.

Shrugging the compliment off, he said, "It was multiple choice."

"Ahh. Smart." I leaned back and took a sip of my tea.

Everything at his work was in a good place for him to leave, especially since the data analysis could be completed anywhere. He just had to pack, and then he'd be here. With me.

My stomach fluttered with anticipation.

As if reading my mind, he said, "I am counting the days. I've got everything just about wrapped up here. I found someone to lease my place. Most of my things are boxed up for storage.

"And the crate training?" I asked.

He shrugged slightly. "Still not so good, but I keep trying."

I just wanted to reach through the screen and pull him through. Feel his arms around me. My heart tugged.

Sometimes, it was easier to get lost in work and not think about his absence. These video calls reminded me that I couldn't touch him. Sometimes, these calls were harder than not seeing him at all.

Wanting to stay away from anything serious, I asked him about the data he was working on. His eyes lit up, and he described a gene he'd identified that changed the root-growth pattern in wheat. He was confident it would help the strain grow in nutrient-depleted, dry soils. He couldn't wait to try it out in Oklahoma.

I loved seeing him geek out, and I felt a warm flush of affection for him. I wished we were having this conversation at my table, bellies full of breakfast and steaming cups of tea in front of us. I wanted him here so bad it hurt.

"Enough about my work. How are you?" he asked. I could tell he'd noticed how tired I was but was too polite to say anything. Instead, he looked worried.

"Meh, strikes and gutters," I replied. The corner of my mouth turned up in a faint smile at the reference. "We all weathered the storm okay. The chickens are back outside. The roads were clear enough that Tessa and I could go on Friday, and the holiday was nice. I had to work on Sunday, though, so I missed brunch." After a beat, I added, "You should come with me sometime. Meet Aunty."

Introducing him to Aunty was a huge step, and he knew it. He smiled at the invitation. "I would very much like to meet your Aunty."

My heart fluttered. I'd given very few people the opportunity to meet Aunty; only Tessa and Laila had had the pleasure. I tended to hoard her like a cherished secret.

Am I really ready for him to meet Aunty? I reached out a hand to pet Yersi. *Yeah, I think I am.*

Armand must've seen all of the thoughts flicker across my face because he said, "How about after Ileana and I are settled? We can find a time that works for both of you."

He was giving me an opportunity to back out, which I appreciated. It made me love him all the more.

Yes, I think I'm head-over-heels in love with this guy.

"How are things with Laila?" he asked.

Surprised at the shift in the conversation, it took me a minute to catch up. A lot had happened since our previous call. And, the last time we'd talked about Laila, we'd gone on to some uncomfortable topics. I realized that I'd been subconsciously avoiding bringing up Laila's predicament because I didn't want it to lead to what might happen next between *us*.

"Um," I started. "Things haven't gone well."

I didn't want to share further details. Armand and Laila worked together, and the whole situation might just be a step too far into the TMI zone.

"She was going to have a heart-to-heart with them last night," I finally answered. "I don't know how it went. I was going to try to catch up with her today. I'm trying to balance being there for her and respecting her space."

He locked eyes with me through the screen and smiled softly. "You're a good friend."

My chest tightened. There was an awkward pause as I fumbled receiving the compliment.

I was afraid of where the conversation would go next. I wasn't ready to talk about things like marriage and kids, especially when I was trying to function with almost no sleep. Even when operating at full capacity, I hadn't tried to unpack those feelings.

His eyes softened as he watched me. I felt like he could read me like a book. I squirmed, unsure how I felt about him knowing me so well.

It was Ileana who saved me. She bounded back into view with her squeaky toy, proudly dropping it in his lap and then dipping out of view. He broke eye contact to look at her, rubbing her ears.

"I need to take my lady out. Want to call again in a couple of days?" he asked.

"Sure. Sounds good," I said, with a mixture of regret and relief.

He held the squeaky with two hands, his eyes piercing through the camera, caressing me from thousands of miles away.

"I love you," he said softly and with so much sincerity that my heart practically shattered right there.

***

I trudged into work, stopping along the way to grab donuts.

I was tired as fuck and felt like a trainwreck. The call with Armand had my heart bouncing all over the place. I was still fretting over those damn pigs. And then there was Laila's situation.

I'm not even sure I can make it through today, I moaned to myself.

On my way to my office, I noticed that Zoe's door was open, light pouring into the hallway. Surprised to see her back at work so soon, I poked my head in.

"You're back? I thought you were out this whole week," I said.

"Hey, Josie," she said with a sad smile. "We got back from Portland yesterday. I'd planned on taking the whole week off...but...." She shrugged.

"But?" I sidled into her office, closing the door behind me. I took a seat, keeping my purse still looped over my shoulder and setting the box of donuts on my lap.

"I've just got a lot to do," she answered, dodging the question.

"Want one?" I asked, lifting the box toward her. "I got them for the PCR lab, but I'm sure they won't notice if you took one.

"No, thanks," she said, not unkindly.

I watched her for a beat, unable to stop my sewing machine leg. I didn't want to pry, but I was also worried about her.

Instead, I offered, "Anything I can do to help clear the cases off your desk? It's been really slow."

She shook her head. "I'm good. Thanks, anyway."

Sensing she wasn't ready to talk about anything, I reached over to squeeze her arm and rose.

"I'm just down the hall if you need anything," I said.

"Thanks, Josie."

With an apprehensive goodbye, I left Zoe to it, hoping she'd join us for lunch today. Maybe I could suss out what was going on then. It worried me that she hadn't taken a donut, as silly as that was. If she came to lunch and refused one of Carol's treats, I'd call in the troops.

I dropped my purse by my desk and headed to Manuel's office. His door was open, but he wasn't in there. I assumed he was in the lab. I left the box of donuts with a quick note, thanking him and Beth for all their hard work. He'd ensure his team had their pick before leaving the leftovers in the breakroom.

As I passed the microbiology lab, I felt a tad guilty for not bringing any for Gerald and quickly brushed the thought away. That was yet another hefty load of feelings I wasn't ready to unpack yet. It was better to distract myself with work.

Back in my office, the first hour of the day crawled by. I waded through emails, trying to keep my tired eyes open.

Around half past nine, my desk phone rang. I was too exhausted to do anything but answer it.

"Dr. Harjo. How can I help you?" I answered.

"Hello, Dr. Harjo," Anna said. "A dog just came in from the vet school. Dustin's getting it out on the floor."

"Thanks, Anna," I said, unable to keep the weary sigh from my voice.

The cases coming over from the vet school were typically pretty easy, and cutting up dead things was usually an effective distraction. But I was so damned tired. I couldn't help but feel like I had an emotional hangover. Bucking up, I headed to the necropsy floor.

If there was one silver shaving in this last week or so, it was that I hadn't received any cattle or horses, and I hadn't had to change into full coveralls and rubber boots. Or go home smelling like *parfum de bœf mort*. I threw on a lab coat and shoe covers as I walked through the door.

The sound of Hank Williams crooning "Cold, Cold Heart" spilled out. I stepped over the footbaths and into the bright lights of the necropsy floor, the sharp scent of fresh disinfectant permeating the air. The familiarity of the room washed over me, and I felt the creases between my eyebrows relax a tad.

Dustin caught my eye and gave me a chin nod. "Mornin', Doc."

"Morning," I answered.

I took the submission form and skimmed it. The patient was a twelve-year-old, male neutered German Shepherd cross. He had presented to the ER with a sudden onset of lethargy. On exam, he had been pale with a thready heartbeat and had passed despite resuscitation attempts.

"Well, this'll be exciting," I said, with a bitter edge to my voice. I just hoped it hadn't been a poisoning or garbage-can gut; that would make for a pretty awful end to the holiday weekend.

Since the dog was on the bigger side, the necropsy would require more than a dinky scalpel, and Dustin handed my knife to me. The black-handled tool-of-the-trade had a six-inch blade. "Harjo" was spelled out in all caps on the handle. Since the piglets had only required a scalpel blade, I hadn't worked with my knife in over a week. It felt good to have it in my hand again and return to the usual routine.

Dustin and I made quick work of the carcass. After we opened the abdomen, I felt a surge of satisfaction. In the liver, there were approximately a dozen red, soft, raised, circular masses, ranging in size from one to five millimeters.

In a slight breach of necropsy etiquette, I pushed the intestines to the side to look at the spleen. It was against the rules of "the little gray book" to start mucking around before all of the cavities were opened, but I couldn't help myself. I was pretty sure I already knew what had killed this dog. I was confident I could walk off the floor with an answer.

When I exposed the spleen, Dustin grunted. It looked normal.

Dang.

Knowing where we were headed next, he handed me the loppers, and we crunched through the ribs to expose the heart and lungs.

"Jackpot," Dustin said.

Scattered throughout the lung were dozens of red, soft, raised masses, similar to the ones we'd found in the liver. These were larger, with some of the masses being as wide as one centimeter in diameter. The pericardial sac was filled with blood, obscuring the outline of the heart.

"Hemopericardium," I said, stating the obvious.

I cut the pericardial sac open to examine the heart. The blood seeped into the thoracic cavity, and the heart seemed to rise from the pool.

I rubbed my thumb across a large, multinodular, tan mass on the right atrium. It was a classic hemangiosarcoma that had ruptured and bled into the pericardium. The pressure on the heart from the fluid had led to cardiac tamponade and rapid death of the patient.

"Don't get more classic than that," Dustin commented.

"Yep," I said with a nod.

I didn't like seeing any animal pass, but cases like this were nice to have every once in a while. It was a fairly common disease, an easy diagnosis once the animal had been opened, and would send the owners home with peace of mind. No one had poisoned their dog. And there was nothing the vet or the owner could have done differently to save the dog's life. Sometimes, necropsies were about closure more than anything else.

Unlike the pigs, an evil voice whispered in my head. *There are still lives at risk with whatever is going on at Rising Sun Farms.*

I chased the train of thought away. I needed to enjoy this small win.

Representative sections were plunked in formalin in case the clinician wanted to run histology, but most ER vets just wanted an answer, and I'd already slam-dunked that.

Working together, Dustin and I bagged the dog for private cremation and washed down the table. All in all, it had taken less than an hour for us to wrap this case up. It felt good to get back into the normal flow of things. To be able to get a diagnosis the same day I did the necropsy.

Back in my office, it took another twenty minutes to type up the report and send it out. I allowed myself a moment to enjoy the high from an easy case.

It didn't last long.

As soon as I finalized the report, anxiety slithered to the forefront of my mind. I couldn't help myself, and I kept checking the pig cases to see if any new test results were in.

In my heart of hearts, I knew I wouldn't get any results back until the afternoon at the earliest. I also knew that if anything pinged positive, Manuel or Gerald would track me down to give me a verbal. But the obsessive part of me couldn't stop checking the system for the results.

When lunchtime rolled around, I grabbed my bag and headed to the breakroom, hoping that some time with my friends could pull me out of my loop. Carol was already there with Anna, playing gin and snacking on their meals. Dustin joined us just as I sat down.

"Howdy, y'all," Carol said.

She popped the lid off a tray of lemon bars and pushed them toward us. The sharp citrus smell hit me, and my mouth watered.

"Help yourself," she said with a smile.

"Those look delicious," I said, picking one.

Dustin was close on my heels, selecting a bar with a murmur of appreciation.

I took a bite and practically moaned. The custard portion was light and tangy, with just the right amount of sweetness. The crust was miraculously thin, flaky, and crisp. It was exactly what I needed. The zesty tang sharpened my senses and swept the tired feeling away.

"Carol, these are amazing," I said with a contented sigh.

"Yep, they are," Dustin agreed.

Carol beamed. It always made her day to feed us tasty treats.

I finished the first one and selected another. Who needed a real lunch anyway?

Just then, Zoe walked in and dragged over an extra chair. She slumped in her seat, putting a plastic bag with a sandwich on the table. "Hey," she said.

"Surprised to see ya' back, Dr. Smith," Dustin said.

"Yeah, I thought you were out until next Monday," Anna added. "Did you have a nice holiday?"

"Yes, Portland was nice," Zoe answered, her reply uncharacteristically short.

Sensing that something was off, Dustin pushed the lemon bars toward her.

Zoe paused for a beat and then took one, placing it on a napkin next to her sandwich. "Thanks," was all she said.

I was glad she'd come to lunch and equally pleased that she had taken a treat. But she hadn't actually eaten it yet. I knew people couldn't be positive and full of energy all the time, but Zoe was definitely not her usual self today.

"Gin," Carol called out, saving us from any more awkward conversation.

She fanned out the cards on the table for Anna to see.

"Gall darn it," Anna said with a frown and flopped her cards on the table.

"Language," Carol chided with a friendly smile as she swept the cards back into a pile. She expertly shuffled them with her knobbly hands and set them to the side.

The conversation shifted to the weather, the post-storm clean-up, and other light topics. I surreptitiously watched Zoe through all of this. She kept quiet, slowly eating her sandwich and, thankfully, the lemon bar.

Just as we were all thinking about heading back to our respective desks, Gerald slunk in like a black cloud. He stopped short, noticing us, and frowned.

Suspecting an imminent attack, my heart sank. The last thing Zoe needed was to be goaded by that shitass today.

A hush fell over the table, and everyone watched Gerald to see what he would do. His scowl deepened as his eyes jumped to each of us. After a tense beat, he swept past, moving to the coffee pot for a refill.

Dustin shot me a look, one eyebrow raised. I shrugged slightly. We still weren't in the clear.

Sure enough, with his coffee mug topped up, Gerald made his way over to our table, all of us silently tracking his movement. Zoe tensed. Carol pulled the box of lemon bars toward her and snapped the lid on, lips pressed tight.

Gerald positioned himself at the end of the table and watched us without saying a word.

After an awkward moment, Anna asked, "How can we help you, Dr. Richter?"

He cleared his throat. "I don't need any help."

Uh, yeah, you do, an evil part of me snarked.

Zoe fiddled with her plastic bag, avoiding eye contact. Dustin looked relaxed in his chair, but I could see the tension around his eyes. Carol straightened her back and rested both hands on the closed lemon bar box.

"I thought you were out this week, Dr. Smith," Gerald said.

His tone was a bit strained and uncomfortable. But to my surprise, there wasn't anything accusatory or nasty in the way he'd said it.

It slowly dawned on me that this was Gerald's attempt at making small talk. With a sinking feeling, I realized that I felt well and truly sorry for him.

Before anything could go sideways, I jumped in, and the words poured out. "Yeah, you know what it's like. When there's a lot of work to do, and customers are waiting for us, sometimes you don't take PTO, or you come back early to make sure they're taken care of."

All the eyes around the table shifted to me. It was a very uncharacteristic thing for me to say, especially to Gerald.

Gerald grunted lightly and said, "Good on you." He lifted his cup to Zoe in salutation.

Chip, chip, cheerio, lad, I thought, unable to stop mocking him in my head.

Everyone was frozen, unsure what to do with a Gerald who wasn't attacking us. He looked equally uncomfortable. He shifted his feet, and his lips started to tip back into a frown.

Before he could snap into villain mode, I said, "Would you like a lemon bar?"

Carol looked at me, slightly shocked. Then, she slowly peeled the lid off and reluctantly held it out to Gerald.

There was a moment—like a high noon moment—when I wasn't sure what would happen next. I thought he might sneer and mock her. Or make a quip about someone's weight. Do something evil.

I held my breath.

To my utter amazement, he took a lemon bar and said, "Thank you," before turning heel and fleeing the breakroom.

We sat in stunned silence for a good minute or two, Carol staring down at the lemon bar box in her hand with a dumbfounded expression.

"Well, *that* happened," Anna finally said.

The bubble of tension popped, and I let out a small nervous laugh.

"It's your lemon bars, Carol. How could anyone resist?" I said, forcing a big smile.

Carol looked thoughtfully down at her lemon bars and folded her hands delicately in her lap. Dustin watched me, one eyebrow raised and lips pursed. There was a flicker of surprise with a hint of admiration in his look.

I wasn't sure where things with Gerald would go from there. But we'd all somehow made it through an encounter without him dropping a slur or making a nasty comment. Maybe lemon bars were his kryptonite. Who the hell knew with that guy?

Maybe there was hope for him after all.

CHAPTER

TWENTY-FIVE

I'd never wanted a dead body so bad in my life.

After lunch, there was so much swimming through my head that I just wanted to be back out on the necropsy floor, knee-deep in blood and mind occupied by a case. At this point, I'd even take one with maggots.

Instead, I was stuck in my office, tapping my pen, thinking about all the loose ends in my life. They hung around me like broken cobwebs dancing in the wind: the pigs, Laila, Armand, Zoe, and the muddled feelings I had about Gerald. The list felt endless. Sometimes being caught in my own head was exhausting.

After about an hour of pushing digital paperwork around, my anxiety got the better of me, and I texted Laila.

When the bouncing ellipses popped up, I felt a hint of relief. My shoulders relaxed just a tad, knowing there was a live body on the other end of the text, available to reply.

I got up from my desk to close the door and dialed her number. My sewing machine leg started up as soon as my ass hit the seat.

"Hey," Laila answered flatly.

"Are you okay?!" I practically shouted, all of the pent-up worry exploding out.

"I'm alive," she answered, with a tinge of sarcasm.

"What happened? Should I come over? Are you safe?" I rattled questions off.

"Josie," she said softly. "It's fine. It's over." Now, she sounded firm but resigned.

What does that mean?

I wished I could see her expression, her body language, something. I was having a hard time reading her tone, and it was stressing me out.

Reigning in my emotions, I took a deep breath to center myself and gave her space to say what she needed to say. After what felt like forever, she began her story.

"We had a very long talk at dinner last night," she said in an even voice and sighed heavily. "I explained why I'd turned down Arjun and the other matches. I said it wasn't about them specifically. I said I just didn't want to get married."

"How did they react?" I asked, holding back the million other questions that were on the top of my tongue.

"As you'd expect," she said. "My mother was disappointed. She said the only reason they came was to find me a good match. She insisted I keep looking and that I was bound to find someone I liked. But I just kept saying I didn't want to get married, no matter who it was. She said I was just being stubborn and that I needed to see some sense."

Laila? Stubborn? No way. I tried not to huff a laugh; I was pretty sure it would've come out semi-hysterical.

"She went on about kids," Laila continued. "Saying I needed to get married to have children before I became too old. She was very insistent."

Laila paused.

"You'd be proud, Josie," she said, still sounding sad. "I put my foot down. I said I didn't want kids right now. And I said I might not ever want them."

"What did your mom do?" I asked, practically holding my breath.

"She said it didn't matter if I wanted them or not. She said it was my duty to have children."

"You thought she might say that," I said.

"Yeah, I know," she responded. "But I stood firm, and she finally backed off. She's still this dark cloud of judgment floating around the house. But, I guess, now I'm used to disappointing them, so what's one more thing?"

A silence fell over us. It wasn't awkward, just pensive.

"For what it's worth, I'm proud of you, Laila," I said. "You stood up for yourself in a very difficult situation."

"Hmm," was all she said in reply.

It slowly hit me that she'd only talked about her mom.

"How did your dad take all of this?" I asked hesitantly.

She sighed heavily. "At first, he was furious. Like fuming. He got so mad his face turned red. When I said I didn't want kids, he finally exploded...." Her voice trailed off.

"Exploded how?" I asked, hesitantly, unsure whether I wanted to hear the answer.

"He started shouting and pounding his fists on the table. He directed it mainly at my mother. Blaming her for not raising her daughter correctly. That kind of thing." The words caught in her throat.

"Are you safe?" I asked, my voice hushed.

She sniffed lightly as if she was crying. "Physically. Yes. I'm okay. He stormed off and hasn't talked to me since. When I went downstairs this morning, my mother said they booked a flight to return tomorrow."

My pen stopped twirling. I felt a surge of victorious joy. *We got them to leave!*

Then, the reality of everything settled around my shoulders. The implication of them scurrying away so quickly was huge. I couldn't imagine the cost of getting a last-minute flight like that, especially around the holidays. I suspected they'd be changing planes a lot. I couldn't help but think they deserved a miserable flight for all the crap they'd been putting Laila through.

Laila.

She'd told the truth, and they responded by treating her like an outcast. I wasn't sure her relationship with her parents could ever be mended.

"How do you feel about everything?" I asked softly.

She sniffed again. "Doesn't matter how I feel about it."

"Of course it matters, Laila," I said.

"I guess...I guess I'm okay with it. It hurts. I'm fairly certain they hate me. But I'm also glad I stood up for myself." After a long pause, she added, "It's messy."

"Fair enough," I conceded. I figured she'd be unpacking this for a while. Maybe her whole life. Nothing would be solved today.

"Can I do anything? Back you up at dinner tonight?" I offered.

"I'm not sure my parents will even eat dinner with me. They've been avoiding me. I'll probably grab something on the way home and hide in my room."

"Do you want me to go with you to drop them off tomorrow?" I had work, but I knew I could bump anything off if Laila needed me. This was important.

"They're taking a taxi," she said, her voice cracking.

Damn. The bad blood between them was worse than I'd thought. I was pretty sure her relationship with her parents was irrevocably damaged.

"Crazy how telling the truth has left me alone," she said out of the blue, a hint of bitterness lacing her voice. "It's what I wanted, in a way. But it also makes me feel a bit empty."

My eyebrows crinkled.

She caught my silence and said, "I think I did the right thing. But I'm not sure they'll ever talk to me again. I won't be forced to marry anyone, but I've also lost my parents."

I chewed my cheek, puzzling out the best way to respond. Forcing a smile into my voice, I said, "Well, you're not totally alone. 'Cause you know you can't get rid of me. Like ever. I'm gonna keep trying to crash your house with ice cream and tabletop games. I might even move in."

She laughed. *She actually laughed!* And then she said, "What about Yersi? You know you couldn't leave him."

I thought about my main man waiting for me at home, and my heart warmed. "Well, of course, he'd come, too."

"Umm. About that," she said playfully. "You know how I feel about cat hair. I'm not sure I want a cat in the house, even if it is one as renowned as The Great Slayer of Canned Food."

I let out a fake gasp of shock. "Cat hair is a *blessing*. Yersi has bestowed unto me the gift of all great feline leaders. You're just jealous."

She laughed again, this time with me right along with her.

"Want to come to Aunty's on Sunday? Get your mind off things?" I asked, somewhat shyly.

I could still see the hole in her heart where her parents used to be. Even though they would be halfway around the world, the act of completely cutting her out of their lives was brutal. I knew what it was like to be alone. I also knew what it was like to have found my own family. A family that I chose. One who supported me and loved me. I wanted to share that with her.

It took Laila a hot second to answer. She knew how closely I guarded my time with Aunty, and I think I shocked her.

"That would be wonderful," she said slowly. "Thank you, Josie."

My heart swelled. "You're like my sister, Laila. You'll always have a place with us."

CHAPTER
TWENTY-SIX

When Sally brought three cardboard flats of slides into my office a couple of hours later, it was like manna from heaven.

"Here they are," she said, all business-like when she handed them to me. "The glue is still wet, so just be careful."

"Oh, Sally. You're a gem. Thank you," I said, chomping at the bit to dive right in.

"You're welcome," she replied, laying the flats next to the scope.

Before she'd even left the room, I had the flats open, scanning them to find the tissues from the third case. The first few flats were the six mummified fetuses from last Wednesday, and I knew they'd be faded, unhelpful shmoo under the scope. I shucked them aside and flipped open the last flat. My eyes danced over the twenty-odd slides from the two piglets from Sunday, seeking the sections of the placenta, the only organ from all three cases that had a whiff of a lesion at necropsy. The little spirals of ribbon-like tissue practically smiled at me from the last slide.

My heart thudded with anticipation. *Please, please, please have a lesion.*

The glue stuck to my fingers as I guided the slide onto the microscope stage. My chest grew tight from holding my breath.

I didn't have to hold it for long. The faint irregularities that were so subtle on gross examination reared up and smacked me in the face when viewed under the microscope. Patchy areas of necrosis dotted the chorionic surface, the normal shag carpet replaced by debris from dead, shattered cells.

Finally!

I couldn't help but feel a tad vindicated. Not only had I finally found something, but it had confirmed what I'd thought I'd seen at necropsy.

I still didn't know what was causing it, though, so I flicked to higher magnification. After a few minutes of slow-crawling for bacteria or fungi, I came up short. My shoulders slumped, and a heavy sigh escaped. Unwilling to let these damn cases get the better of me, I continued to systematically scoot the slide across the microscope stage.

There aren't any inflammatory cells. Like zero. The dismaying thought pressed in, and my eyebrows wrinkled. If this was bacterial, I'd expect an inflammatory response. The amount of said inflammation varied from case to case, but there should still be the odd white blood cell trolling around, something other than the bland, patchy areas of cell death. I checked the large blood vessels, too, just in case, and there was no evidence of vasculitis.

Probably not fungal, either.

I tried to shrug off the last thought. I hadn't really thought it was a fungal infection anyway. Fungal placentitis typically caused sporadic abortions and didn't affect multiple sows at the same time.

Clicking to the highest objective on my scope, I scanned the cells lining the fetal side of the placenta, unwilling to give up, thinking maybe I'd find intracellular bacteria or something.

I sucked in a gasp and jerked back from the scope like I'd been bitten by a snake.

Heart pounding, I hesitantly leaned forward to look through the scope. Once my brain started really and truly processing what I saw, I froze. There was a large, faintly colored pink-to-mauve blob in the nucleus of a single trophoblast.

A viral inclusion. It has to be.

My heartbeat sped up to match the tempo of my sewing machine leg. Everything started to fall into place—or crash, more like. If the abortion storm was caused by a virus and said virus was what I thought it was, some crazy shit was about to go down.

I needed to be absolutely certain that what I thought I was seeing was real. I scanned along the edges of the necrotic areas. Viral inclusions could be tricky. Sometimes, those intranuclear blobs were just some weird artifact, put there by an evil pathology god to taunt us lowly mortals.

Turning the stage knob incrementally, the slide slowly moved through the field of view as I scanned the placental surface. The intranuclear blobs repeatedly popped into view. They weren't obvious, but I'd bet dollars to donuts that they were real viral inclusions. They had to be.

My chest tightened.

Gerald was right all along. It's viral, and PCR missed it.

I rocked back in my chair, trying not to panic. Intranuclear inclusions in the placenta of a pig were characteristic of one virus in particular, and it was one I wouldn't wish on my worst enemy: Pseudorabies.

At that point, I was really and truly starting to panic. Pseudorabies was a reportable disease and was seriously bad juju. If this was pseudorabies—and I was pretty damn sure it was at this point—the feds would panic, and the black helicopters would swoop in to control the spread of the virus. It was likely that Rachel would have to cull an entire building's worth of pigs, if not her whole farm. I didn't want to be the one handing out a diagnosis that would mean the death of so many animals.

I took a few deep breaths, trying to mentally talk myself off the ledge and keep a panic attack at bay.

Maybe you're wrong.

This was incredibly serious, and I certainly wanted to be wrong. Trying to focus, I found one of the liver slides from the third case and placed it onto the microscope stage.

Scattered throughout the section of liver were random areas of necrosis, little dots that were so small that they would have been impossible to see grossly. Smears of faded pink amorphous material replaced the normal architecture and were rimmed with purple flecks of nuclear debris. The revolving nosepiece clicked as I switched to a higher objective.

Acid trickled up my esophagus.

Sure enough, rare hepatocytes bordering the edge of the necrotic areas contained convincing intranuclear viral inclusions.

Fuck.

I fished out the other liver from the third case. Though less frequent, there were small areas of necrosis and rare viral inclusions in those sections as well. I couldn't escape the diagnosis that was staring me in the face.

Worried I'd skimmed over something, I fished through the flats to find the slides from the first case. The liver slide skated across the microscope stage. I quickly scanned the other organs just to be safe. Everything was completely normal.

I wasn't sure whether to be relieved that I hadn't missed something or continue with my burgeoning panic over the fact that there was evidence of a reportable disease in the third case. Regardless of how I felt, the lack of histologic changes in the first case didn't change the situation. I mentally gave myself a light smack on the cheek, trying to get my shit together.

The lack of any lesions in the first piglet was likely connected to the negative PCR in that case. The virus probably hadn't made it to the fetus before the sow had lost her litter. It could've been in the placenta, which we didn't get.

The first case was one pig, no placenta, no lesions, and no virus detected, I thought, trying to order all of the facts bouncing around my head. The second case was six mummified fetuses and no placenta. I hadn't even looked at those slides yet, and the PCR results were still pending. The third case had clear viral inclusions in the livers of both piglets and in the placenta. The PCR was also still pending on the last case.

First things first. Wrap up the histo on all the cases. Then, you can panic.

Sifting through the stack of slides, I found the livers from the mummified piglets. The tissues were faded smears with a lack of cellular detail. If there had been a histologic lesion, the mummification process had wiped it away. I scanned the rest of the tissues and didn't find anything of note.

I knew I needed to focus on the case from Sunday: the two piglets and the placenta with the viral inclusions. If any cases pinged positive on PCR, it would be those. Whatever had caused the abortion of those two piglets was likely the culprit in the other two cases, even if we didn't detect the virus with PCR.

I needed to talk to Manuel immediately and check on the PCR results. After that, I knew it'd be a difficult call to the state vet.

Don't forget Rachel. That call needs to happen, too.

The vomit trickled back up my throat. This was going to be a rough afternoon.

I found Manuel seated at a hood in the clean area of the PCR lab, pipetting samples. I hated bothering him when he was back there, but this case changed everything. I knocked on the glass.

He turned around, eyebrows raised questioningly. I waved to him to come out and put my hands together in a prayer position. I mouthed, *please,* hoping he'd understand it was an emergency. He gave me a nod and held up a gloved pointer finger to indicate he'd be a second.

I mouthed, *Thank you.*

Practically wringing my hands, I anxiously waited at the door as he got everything to the point where he could leave it in the hood. He made his way out of the clean area, removing his gloves, eye protection, and lab coat as he went.

"How can I help you, Dr. Harjo?" he asked.

"Hey, Dr. Rodriguez." I took a deep breath and went straight for the punchline. "The pigs. I'm pretty sure it's pseudorabies."

His eyebrows shot up, his expression quickly switching from bland curiosity to *holy fuck.* His face went slightly pale.

"Yeah. I know," I continued, keeping my voice steady, knowing he'd need a hot second to process. "There are intranuclear inclusions in both fetuses and placenta from the third case. The ones that came in on Sunday. I went back to the other two cases. I didn't see any inclusions in any of the other samples. But we didn't get placenta with those first two. And the fetuses were mummified in the second set."

I could practically see his mind racing to put all of the pieces together.

"That explains the negative pseudorabies PCR in the first case," he said, more to himself. "It probably didn't have time to cross over from the placenta."

After a beat, he added, "We need to call the state vet." His voice was firm with an edge of panic.

"Yeah." I nodded emphatically. "I just wanted to check with you first. See where the pseudorabies PCR is at in the third case. I'd like to have confirmation before calling in the troops."

He nodded, eyes bouncing around as his mind whirled. He rubbed at the wrinkles between his eyebrows. "Sally set it up yesterday to run overnight. The data is probably ready. Let's go check."

I followed him into his office and took the spare chair. My sewing machine leg started bobbing as soon as my ass hit the seat. My anxiety had me feeling like I was trying to crawl out of my skin. I needed to fidget with a pen, something to help me calm down.

This isn't really a calm-the-fuck-down moment, though. Is it?

I took three deep breaths as Manuel logged into the qPCR software.

There were only two cases on the pseudorabies run today, both of which were mine, and they were easy for him to find.

He clicked through the first one, looking at the graphs. "The pooled fetal tissues from the second case last week are negative," he said, hyper-focused on the screen.

I wasn't sure how I felt about that. Not having pseudorabies was a good thing for the farm. But, if it wasn't that, what the hell was it?

"A negative result doesn't completely rule out pseudorabies. The quality of those samples was questionable, if I remember correctly," Manuel said, echoing my earlier thoughts.

His mouse clicked several times. With a sharp intake of breath, he leaned back in his chair stiffly. "The third case is positive."

My chest felt tight, and I could barely breathe. "Oh, no..." was all I could whisper.

He looked at me, worry crinkling at the skin between his eyebrows. "We need to call it in right away."

It took everything in me not to blow partially digested lemon bar chunks all over his squeaky clean desk. This was one of the worst possible things that could've happened at the farm. It wasn't a foreign animal disease, but the outcome would be just about the same.

"I'll call the state vet and then call the owner," I said.

Maybe if I got into action-planning mode, I could get out of the swirl of panic that was swallowing me.

"Is there anything I can do to help?" he offered. The next hour was going to be pretty awful, and he knew it.

"Um...." I stalled, mind racing. "Can you give Fran a heads up? She hasn't been answering her phone, but we should read her in on this."

He nodded.

I chewed my cheek, running through the checklist. "And since I'll be on the phone for the next ten years, can you ask Dustin to get all the raw tissue in the digestor ASAP and do a deep clean? I don't want it leaking out of the lab."

I wasn't really worried about anything making its way off the necropsy floor. But I wanted to make a hundred percent sure any fresh tissue didn't leave the lab. Plus, if the state officials asked, I could say we'd buttoned everything up on our end.

"And Gerald," I added. "We need to let him know. You both keep a pretty tight lock on your samples. But if the state gets involved, I want to make sure everything has been done by the book."

"I'll connect with Fran, Dustin, and Gerald," he confirmed.

"Thank you," I said, slightly breathless with anxiety.

We parted ways with a hurried goodbye, and I sped to my office to call the state vet. I was dreading this call and what it would mean for Rachel.

And all of those pigs.

I could only hope that they kept each building isolated enough from the others that only the pregnant sow barn would have to be depopulated. I hoped the virus hadn't spread to the farrowing barn; that would be rough.

All of those animals.

I felt myself start to choke up.

Taking three deep breaths, I tried to regain my focus. The faster I made these calls, the sooner we could get a handle on the situation.

Back at my desk, I opened my resource binder. It wasn't often that I had to crack that puppy open to call anyone, much less the state vet. I think we'd exchanged all of ten words since I started here, and that was at a conference.

I found the number for Dr. Hannah Keating and dialed her direct line. I hoped she wasn't out for the holidays. If she was, I'd be working my way through the phone tree to try to find her assistant or the field vet.

A no-nonsense voice answered on the third ring. "This is Dr. Keating."

"Dr. Keating, hello. This is Dr. Josie Harjo from the state diagnostic lab," I said, trying to keep the panic from my voice.

"How can I help you today, Dr. Harjo?" she asked, skipping the usual weather chit-chat.

"I need to report a case of pseudorabies," I said.

This was the first time I'd had to call in a reportable disease. Usually, it was the microbiology lab calling to report the one-off tularemia-positive case or sending in their aggregated monthly *Salmonella*-positive results. I wasn't sure how to go about it.

"Come again?" Hannah asked.

"Pseudorabies," I repeated. "In pigs."

Come on, dumbass. Get your fucking shit together, I thought, kicking myself for mumbling like a preschooler.

"Apologies," I stuttered. "I'm just a bit rattled."

"You're fine," she said. "Start from the beginning. I'll be taking notes. But, once we get off the line, please email over the report."

I started with the basic information, sharing the address for Rising Sun Farms and Rachel's phone number. Then, I gave a high-level overview of the number of animals, the vaccination program, and the general biosecurity, as Rachel had explained them to me.

"I haven't informed the owner yet," I added. "I just found out myself and figured it was more important to call you first. Please give me a bit to call her before you connect with her after we hang up?"

This was going to pull the rug out from under Rachel. As much as I dreaded it, I wanted to do her the courtesy of telling her the awful news myself.

"I'll give you some time to fill her in," Hannah said, tone neutral.

I couldn't get a read on Hannah. Being able to stay cool in the face of a disaster was an important skill as a state vet. But I still hoped she had enough empathy to have a dialogue with Rachel without sounding like a robot. Rachel was going to be crushed.

"Tell me about the samples you received, please," Hannah prompted.

"The first case came in last week on Monday," I said. "One fetus and no placenta. Histo was within normal limits. Nothing was detected on the abortion panel PCR."

"Hmm," Hannah said.

"The second case was a set of six mummified fetuses. They came in on Wednesday last week," I continued. "Other than being mummified, I didn't see anything on gross. Histo and PCR had to wait until this week because of the storm and the holiday. Histo was normal. Dr. Rodriguez verbally confirmed that nothing was detected on the pooled tissues on PCR from that case either."

"No placenta?" she asked.

"Correct," I answered. "No placenta on the second case, and they were mummified."

I grabbed a pen and started tapping it.

"The third case was the positive one. We received that on Sunday," I pressed on. "Two fetuses. This time with the placenta. I was suspicious of placentitis on gross, but it was subtle. I just received the histo back. There are intranuclear inclusions in the placenta and liver. Dr. Rodriguez verbally confirmed that pseudorabies was detected in the placenta and fetal tissues with PCR. He's preparing that report right now."

"Have any other samples from the farm been submitted to the lab?" she asked.

"Feed and water were brought in and sent to the toxicology lab," I replied. "But no other fetal samples, no blood from the sows, or anything like that."

"Noted. Thank you," she said. "Any idea on a potential source?"

"No, ma'am," I answered. "The owner runs a pretty tight operation, from what I understand. I'm frankly a bit shocked that it's pseudorabies."

"We'll figure that bit out," she answered. "If you could email me those reports as soon as possible, I'd appreciate it."

"Yes, ma'am. I'll call the owner next and then get them out to you." After a beat, I added, "Sorry to drop this in your lap over the holidays."

"All part of the job," she said matter-of-factly.

The tapping of my pen sped up. Unable to help myself, I asked, "What's going to happen to all the animals?"

The question was virtually impossible for her to answer, given that she had very little information about the situation. But I had to ask; I needed her to reassure me that they wouldn't have to cull the fifteen hundred pigs that called that farm home.

"I'm not sure," she said, her voice finally softening. "It depends on how isolated the units are from each other and how good their biosecurity is. But given that pseudorabies somehow found its way into the facility to begin with, I'm not too optimistic."

"Oh," was all I could say. My heart clenched, and I felt myself teetering on the edge of a deep well of depression. This was almost as bad as some of the animal cruelty cases.

"I'm going to let you go," Hannah spoke up. "You give Ms. Hoskins a call and send over the reports. I'll get everything started on my end and give her a call at, say, three-thirty?"

"Yes, ma'am. Thank you," I replied, grateful to have my marching orders.

We said polite goodbyes.

I hung up the phone, reluctant to pick it back up. I didn't want to call Rachel, but I knew I had to. We'd started this journey together, and I wanted her to hear it from me first, no matter how difficult the discussion was going to be.

I picked the phone back up and swirled my pen in my other hand, using the end to poke at the numbers. The phone rang for an agonizingly long time, and I was worried I might have to drop this bomb via voicemail.

After what felt like forever, Rachel finally picked up.

"Rising Sun Farms," she answered.

"Ms. Hoskins? This is Dr. Josie Harjo from the diagnostic lab."

"Glad you called. We lost another litter just a few hours ago. I was just about to bring it over to y'all. Got anything?"

My emotions were all over the place. We had an answer, but it was going to completely shatter Rachel. I figured I had to cut to the chase. If I pussy-footed around this one, I would only be rubbing a fistful of salt in a ginormous wound.

"The third case was positive for pseudorabies," I stated matter-of-factly and gave her a moment to process.

"Pardon me?" she asked sharply, disbelief lacing her voice.

"Pseudorabies," I repeated. She'd been pushed into the deep end, and I could practically hear her mind working through everything. I waited a beat and then added, "We didn't detect it in the first two cases. Just in the fetus and placenta of the third. Despite that, I think pseudorabies is the cause of the fetal losses on the farm."

"I don't understand," she said, more to herself. "How on earth did pseudorabies get into the pregnant sow building?"

I was thinking the same thing myself, but it wasn't the right time to blurt that out. Instead, my pen picked up its tapping again.

I cleared my throat uncomfortably. "Pseudorabies is a reportable disease. I...um...I called the state vet just now. Dr. Hannah Keating. She'll be reaching out shortly."

"I guess I don't need to bring this litter in then," Rachel responded, still shell-shocked.

"I defer to Dr. Keating," I replied, my voice heavy with sympathy.

Anything that was found in the fourth litter wouldn't change a damn thing for the farm and would probably be a waste of Rachel's money. I suspected their focus would be on a test-and-cull approach if they didn't just shut the whole thing down.

My heart broke with the pain of it all.

At a loss for what to say next, I added, "I'll be issuing the final reports shortly, and you should have them in your email within the next twenty or thirty minutes."

I realized at that moment that I hadn't contacted her primary care vet. I wasn't too worried about it, though. They'd been radio-silent through this whole debacle anyway. They'd still get a copy of the report, and Hannah might have already reached out.

Back to the matter at hand.

"Is there anything else I can do for you, Ms. Hoskins?" I said, feeling a bit helpless.

"No, thank you," she said, sounding utterly wrung out.

"For what it's worth, I'm sorry this is happening," I said.

"Ain't your fault," she said. "It is what it is. Can I get the number of the state vet?"

As someone who did it routinely, I recognized when a person wanted to stuff the emotions deep down in a tidy little box and distract themselves with action. The least I could do was help her out.

I read her the phone number. "Dr. Hannah Keating is her name," I repeated, in case she'd missed it. "She should pick up, and if she doesn't, I'm sure she'll call you right back."

Eager to rush off, Rachel said a curt but not impolite "thank you," and then we said our goodbyes.

I hung up the phone, feeling the acid burble and tasting the burn at the back of my throat. That was one of the worst calls I'd ever had to make. Rachel had taken it pretty well. But I still felt like an angel of death, delivering a message that could wipe out a tenth of her herd, if not the entire thing.

I took a drink of water to chase away the nasty taste. My hands shook, and tears threatened to push in. Usually, getting a diagnosis on a difficult case felt good, like winning a challenging strategy game against an experienced player. But this was awful.

Focus, Josie. Deep breaths. Little steps. Eyes on the prize.

There was no prize here, though.

Since the third case held the key, I finalized that report before the others, adding the histologic findings and referencing the positive PCR. I immediately emailed the report to Hannah. She replied back instantly with a simple "received."

Then, I finalized the two remaining cases, linking them to the third case. I added some speculative comments as to why pseudorabies might not have been detected in those samples. At the end of the day, it didn't really matter; we now knew why the sows were aborting at Rising Sun Farms. But adding that information to the formal report unified the three cases for posterity.

With those tasks done, I no longer had anything to distract me, and the weight of the day settled around me. It was almost too much. I was mentally done and wanted to get the heck out of dodge.

Though the clock hadn't tipped to five, I decided to cut out early, with a message to Anna and Carol to text me if anything else came in or if Dr. Keating needed me. With that, I cut tail and ran.

CHAPTER
TWENTY-SEVEN

When I pulled into the driveway, I felt numb and wrung out. Clinging to my phone, I slugged around the house, going through the motions of feeding Yersi and tending to the chickens. I wasn't expecting a call from Dr. Keating, Rachel, or the lab. But I couldn't seem to put my phone down.

When it came time to feed myself, I wasn't feeling it. Acid was still crawling up the back of my throat, and I wasn't hungry. But if I didn't eat, I'd be a shaky, hypoglycemic mess.

I decided to eat a small bowl of soup and call it quits. I knew it wasn't the best choice, and I'd probably wake up in the middle of the night, hunger clawing at my stomach. But soup wasn't the worst choice, either; I could've snarfed down a pint of ice cream.

Ice cream was my solution to just about everything, but the thought of it made my stomach burn. I fell further into the spiral of self-flagellation over why I couldn't even use ice cream as a bandaid today.

Yersi brushed against my leg with a supportive *merf* sound.

I closed my eyes and took three deep breaths. I needed to get out of my head before I auto-digested myself.

"Come on, bud," I said, picking him up.

I flopped on the couch, placing him on my lap. He immediately started making biscuits, his throaty purr wet with happy-kitty drool.

I couldn't put my finger on why my mind was so unsettled. Laila's parents would soon be on a plane, so I knew it wasn't that.

It has to be the pigs.

We finally had a diagnosis, as awful as it was, and I'd passed it off to the powers that be to take it to the finish line. I should be done with

261

that hot mess. But the cases still nagged at me, and my brain wouldn't let them go.

I decided to call Aunty, hoping she could help me recenter. She answered on the first ring, saying, "Hello, sweety. I was just thinking about you."

"Hey, Aunty. Have a minute?"

"Always," she answered.

My heart warmed, and for the millionth time, I thanked my lucky stars that I had Aunty. "It's been...rough," I sighed.

"Work? Laila? Armand?" she asked.

"All of the above," I replied. After a beat, I added, "And Gerald."

"Deep breaths. Little steps. Eyes on the prize. Start with one foot first," she coached.

As prompted, I took a deep breath. My fingers brushed along Yersi's hair, further lowering my blood pressure.

"Well, we finally figured out what was causing that abortion outbreak in the pigs I was telling you about," I started. "It's a pretty scary infectious disease. It's really rare, and I'm not sure how it got in there. They're probably going to have to cull a significant number of animals." I sighed. "It's just hard."

She *hmmed* in sympathy.

"So, even though we have a diagnosis, it's still eating at me," I said.

"Be patient with yourself," she advised. "It's perfectly normal to feel that way. Acknowledge those feelings. Be right with them."

I wished Aunty was here so I could hug her. So many other people would've tried to cheer me up or brush it off. Her telling me it was okay to be sad meant oodles to me.

Next step.

"With Laila," I plowed on. "I think she's in a good spot. Well, as good as she can be. She was honest with her folks. They're pissed, but they're going home. I guess that's a good thing."

Aunty let out another soft *hmm*. "From what you've shared, I sense that resentment sits between them like a snake, ready to strike."

"Yeah, but they'll be half a world away," I said, grasping at straws, desperate to know that Laila would be safe.

"You don't need to be in the same room with someone to hurt them," Aunty said. "Laila will need you. It is good for her spirit that she has been true to herself. But the pain will still be there."

"Strikes and gutters," I said softly to myself.

"Yes," Aunty agreed. "But I think there are more good things here than there are bad. Family can be difficult. It has roots in us. Even when we are true to ourselves, if our family doesn't like that truth, it can hurt."

The wisdom in Aunty's words settled over me.

"Thank you for being *you*, Aunty. You're the best family I could ever have."

"The families we choose are sometimes better—and healthier—than the families we are born into," she replied.

My thoughts drifted to my mom. If she had been alive, she'd be part of my found family along with Aunty and Tessa. But death had taken her, and it wasn't an option anymore.

"I invited Laila to brunch on Sunday," I said, feeling a little shy. "I hope that's okay."

"Absolutely," Aunty said. "She's welcome to join us any time."

My heart warmed at her welcoming tone. "Thanks, Aunty."

I paused, trying to find the words for what I wanted to say. Aunty gave me space to get to the next topic, which I was trying desperately to avoid.

"Armand told me he loved me the other day," I said, voice hushed.

There was a beat of silence.

"How does that make you feel?" she asked gently.

"I think I love him. Like a lot." I paused, tasting the words. "It's just scary. His visa is only for six months."

And I think he wants to get married. And have kids. And I don't know if I want that.

Even though it was Aunty, I couldn't say those words out loud. They just felt too heavy.

After a long pause, Aunty asked, "Remind me. When does he come back?"

"I pick him up from the airport next Thursday," I said, feeling a nervous tickle in my stomach.

"Then, that is all you need to think about right now. The rest of it can wait. Cross that bridge when it appears in your path."

From anyone else, that might have sounded flippant. But from Aunty, it was just what I needed to hear. I didn't need to make any decisions now. All I had to do was be at the airport on Thursday. And hold him. And smell his aftershave.

"Bring him to brunch, too. I want to meet him," she said, not unkindly.

"Yes, Aunty," I answered, a smile tugging at the corners of my lips.

"And what is this about Gerald? Is he being a shitass again?" Aunty asked with a hint of snark.

"Actually, he's not. And that's the bit that's messing with my head. I think he's trying to be a better person. He's still totally weird, don't get me wrong. But he's not being cruel. Does that make sense?"

"Yes," she said. "It does."

I sighed. "I've actually started to feel sorry for him. But it's hard to forget how truly nasty he's been. It's really confusing."

"Has he apologized?"

I snorted. "You haven't met this guy. Gerald'll apologize when hell freezes over. I'm not holding my breath on that one."

She *hmmed*.

"It's just weird feeling sorry for someone so awful," I said, my thoughts whirling.

"People aren't inherently evil," she replied softly. "There's probably a reason he is the way he is. It's okay to pity the villain. Accept those feelings and move forward on your true path."

My shoulders sagged in relief. I didn't realize how much I needed to hear that it was okay to feel sorry for someone who was such a jerk. I still didn't like Gerald, and I probably never would. He'd done too many terrible things. But Aunty had made it okay for me to feel sympathy for him and about wanting to help him be a better person.

"I love you, Aunty," I said. "Thank you for always being there for me. Always saying the right thing."

"I love you, too, Josie," she answered, and I could hear the smile in her voice.

When we said our goodbyes, I was in a good spot and wanted to stay that way. I turned the TV on and opened the Netflix app, hoping to distract myself. I deliberately steered clear of *Mindhunter* and anything sort of violent. I settled on a nature documentary. David Attenborough's voice could calm anyone, and if that didn't work, I figured I was doomed anyway.

Slowly, the soothing cadence of the narration and Yersi's purring forced my shoulders to relax. Before I knew it, I was pulled into a heavy, dreamless sleep.

CHAPTER
TWENTY-EIGHT

The next morning, I woke up still feeling exhausted. I'd spent half the night on the couch, and I had a crick in my neck. Plus, it had been a roller coaster of a week, and I had a lingering feeling the ride wasn't over yet.

I went through the motions of caring for the animals and getting ready for work. Despite several cups of tea and some ibuprofen, I was still feeling off when I pulled into work.

The snow had melted, and the landscaping around the lab was a wet, brown mess. The parking lot was still half-empty. Gerald's truck sat by itself, parked a few spots away, looking lonely.

This last week and a half, he'd come in early, stayed late, braved a storm, and worked over the holiday to make sure the tests were getting done. A small part of me admired his tenacity.

And he hasn't ambushed me in the parking lot in forever. Not once.

Was there a path to redemption for our resident troll? I wasn't so sure. I had no idea how long this lull in the storm would last. But for now, I planned on enjoying a harassment-free workplace for as long as I could.

On my way to my office, I found Zoe's door open.

I chewed my cheek and hesitantly knocked on the doorjamb. "Morning," I said, offering a small smile.

Zoe leaned back from her scope. "Hey, Josie. Come in."

I slipped into her office, leaving the door open behind me. Flipping my purse to the front, I took the seat across from her.

I nodded my chin to the stack of glass on her desk. "How's it going?"

"Slowly but surely," she sighed. "I think I can finish up the last of it today and take the rest of the week off."

"You're on duty next week, right?" I asked.

She nodded.

"It'll be nice to be all caught up," I offered.

She shrugged.

I hesitated and then said, "How's everything else?"

She took a deep breath. "It's been rough. Jayden's parents want us to move to Portland. We can adopt in Oregon, so there's a lot of pressure to go there."

Every single muscle tensed, and I practically had a heart attack right on the spot.

I'd worked for a couple of years without Zoe as a peer. But now that she was here, I couldn't imagine working at the lab without her. It was a selfish thought, and I immediately tried to brush it aside.

"A lot of people are leaving Oklahoma," she added. "And Texas."

"And Florida," I added, my heart sinking.

It still blew my mind how some of the most religious states were also the most intolerant. What happened to loving and accepting others? It wasn't like Zoe was hurting anyone. If anything, she brought more love and care into the world than the devils waving Bibles at her. Even though it hurt, I understood why she might want to leave for a more friendly place.

"Do you really think you'll leave?" I asked, concern lacing the edges of my voice.

She frowned slightly and shrugged again. "I don't know. It's a big decision. But Jayden has started job hunting in the Portland area."

Jayden was in HR and had buckets of experience. I was pretty sure Jayden could get a job in two seconds. It would be more difficult for Zoe. The only vet school in Oregon was in Corvallis, which was an hour and a half from Portland. If they didn't want to move there, she'd have to try to find a job in commercial diagnostics or with a CRO.

"What other options are there to adopt here?" I asked, not wanting to think about Zoe leaving.

"There's one more agency we can try. We could also try adopting from overseas. I just…. It would be nice to help someone local. There are lots of children who need a good home right here in Payne County."

I nodded sadly. "If there's anything I can do to help—provide a reference, whatever—let me know."

"Thanks, Josie," she said, smiling sadly.

I reached over and squeezed her hand.

"Well, I'll leave you to it," I said. "If you need anything, I'm right down the hall. Otherwise, see you at lunch?"

"See you at lunch," she answered.

My heart went out to my friend and coworker. I left her office, feeling awful that I couldn't do more for her.

Back at my desk, I went through the motions of starting my day. I didn't have any voicemails. My emails were also fairly *blah*. There was nothing about the pigs. I figured my part was done, but I couldn't stop wondering what was happening at Rising Sun Farms.

The morning slugged by. I busied myself with revising some lectures and prepping for rounds once the students returned. When lunch came around, I grabbed my sack and headed to the break-room.

Everyone was already there, Zoe included. They were playfully placing bets on how slammed she'd get next week, given how slow the last two weeks had been.

I dragged an extra chair over to the table. "Hey, y'all."

"Howdy, Doc," Dustin said.

Carol pushed a box of peanut butter cookies over. I selected one, taking a bite before I even opened my lunch.

"These are amazing," I said around a mouthful. "Thanks, Carol."

She beamed in reply. Anna and Zoe continued their conversation at the other end of the table, both enjoying their cookies.

I turned to Dustin. "Think anything'll come in today?"

"Doubt it," he said and then nodded his chin at Zoe. "I'm thinking it's all gonna come in next week when Dr. Smith is back on."

"Lame sauce," I empathized.

"Yup," he half grunted. He'd have to deal with the rush of dead bodies no matter which pathologist was on duty next week.

"Get everything all cleaned up from the pigs?" I asked.

"Yes, ma'am. I tossed the parts in the digester yesterday and bleached the heck outta everythin'. Should all be cleaned up now."

"Thank you," I replied, still distracted.

Hearing our conversation, Zoe asked, "Why did you have to bleach everything?"

"Just gettin' everything sparkling clean for you when all of the cases start rolling in next week, Dr. Smith," Anna teased.

I was surprised that word of the pigs hadn't spread. Given the severity of the diagnosis, I was shocked that the lab's gossip tree wasn't on fire with it.

"The pigs were positive for pseudorabies," I answered.

Zoe's eyebrows shot up.

"Yeah, exactly," I said and pressed my lips in a firm line.

"Were they out on pasture?" she asked, eyebrows creased.

I shook my head. "Commercial farm. All-in, all-out."

At her incredulous look, I nodded and said, "I know. I can't figure it out either."

"Why can't a commercial farm get it?" Anna asked.

"Pseudorabies has virtually been eradicated from commercial pig farms for almost twenty years," I replied.

"Huh," Anna mused.

I leaned back in my chair, thinking. "It's now so rare, they stopped vaccinating commercial pigs ages ago. It's still in feral pigs, I guess. But the owner runs a tight ship. There's no way her pigs could've come in contact with a feral pig."

"Well..." Dustin started.

My eyes jerked up. "What do you mean 'well?'" I asked as my chest tightened.

"Well," he repeated and then paused to roll his lower lip over his mustache in thought.

I circled my hand to keep him going, feeling like I was on the edge of a precipice.

"What if one of the guys hunts wild pigs?" he asked.

"What do you mean?" I replied, trying to catch up.

Zoe leaned forward, studying Dustin.

"Just thinkin'. Pig season ended 'bout three months ago. Can't imagine it bein' on their gear or nothin'. But maybe there's somethin' there?" he mused.

My mind could not make the leap from wild pig hunting to an outbreak of pseudorabies in a commercial pig operation.

"I'm not sure the virus can live that long on surfaces," I said hesitantly. "Plus, I get the impression that the biosecurity is pretty tight there. I bet they make their employees wear coveralls and rubber boots. Make them use footbaths and stuff. I haven't been out there. But—" I shrugged, "—I get the impression that Ms. Hoskins knows her stuff."

"Having the virus survive that long on clothing is a long shot," Zoe chimed in.

Dustin lifted an eyebrow and fiddled with the end of his beard. "What about meat?"

"Meat?" I asked, still totally confused.

"Yeah. Meat. If one o' the guys made sandwiches or somethin' from the meat, and it came in that way," he said. "I had a cousin who'd feed table scraps to his hogs."

I shook my head slowly. "I don't know. No one eats raw pork. I'm pretty sure any curing or cooking or whatever would kill the virus."

Zoe whipped out her phone. "Yeah. Dr. Google says the virus is inactivated with heat."

My sewing machine leg picked up. I felt like Dustin was on to something, but I couldn't get the puzzle pieces to fit right.

"Maybe," I started. "What if one of the workers fed raw meat to the pigs? Scraps like Dustin's cousin."

"At an all-in, all-out facility?" Zoe asked doubtfully.

"I know. But what *if*? Like someone new. Someone who didn't know any better?" I pressed. I felt a thread of memory pulling somewhere but couldn't follow it.

Dustin shrugged. He'd sowed a seed and had decided to sit back to see what grew.

Even though Zoe looked unconvinced, I felt the familiar tingle that I was on the right path. Urgency nipped at my heels.

"Thanks for the idea, Dustin," I said hurriedly. "I'm gonna go check in with Dr. Rodriguez. Stay tuned."

He gave me a friendly salute.

I shoved the last bite of cookie in my mouth and left the break room without touching my lunch.

I thanked my lucky stars when I found Manuel in his office. He was at his desk, eating his own meal.

"Howdy," I greeted him.

"Hello, Dr. Harjo," he replied. "Quite the excitement yesterday."

I huffed a bitter laugh. "Yeah, just a bit. Have a sec?"

"Sure," he answered. He put his fork down and rested his elbows on his desk.

I grabbed the seat across from him.

"Something's bugging me about the pigs. I can't figure out how they got infected."

He shrugged. "That'll be up to the state vet to figure out."

"Sure," I said, unwilling to let it go. "But Dustin said something about how feral pig hunting season ended a few months ago. And maybe someone brought in some meat."

"The virus can't survive in cooked meat," he replied, repeating what Zoe had said just moments earlier.

"Yeah. But what if the meat wasn't cooked?" I asked.

He answered me with a skeptical look. No one was dumb enough to eat raw pork, and we both knew it.

"I know," I answered his look. "But what if it was for the pigs to eat? Like feeding them the internal organs or something. Scraps."

His look grew sharp. "You think they fed the sows raw, feral pig meat?" His voice was incredulous but not rude.

"Well, not Ms. Hoskins," I said, back-pedaling a bit. "Or any of the employees who've been around a long time. But what about someone new? Who maybe didn't know any better?"

He considered it. "Swine feedback has been reported as a cause of outbreaks in other countries," he said, more to himself. "It's possible." He still looked doubtful.

But that tingle, the one that said I was on to something, had grown.

"Thanks," I said, itching to move. "I'll leave you to your lunch."

I rushed back to my office. It wasn't my job to suss out this piece of the puzzle, but if we had a possible lead the state vet could follow up on, I should share it.

I dialed Hannah's number and got her voicemail. I wasn't surprised; I figured she was probably crazy-busy right now dealing with the outbreak. I left a message, quickly laying out one possible route of exposure.

Still not feeling a sense of closure, I called Ms. Hoskins. Though she'd answered every other time I'd called, I got her voicemail, too. I felt a hint of frustration. I left a similar message for her.

I leaned back in my chair. I'd done what I could. Now, it was in the hands of the state vet.

With a start, I realized that I wasn't chewing my cheek or tapping my pen.

Maybe this was the last puzzle piece. Maybe I was finally out of the damn woods.

***

A few hours and one routine necropsy later, I was back in my office, typing the report, when my phone rang.

"Dr. Josie Harjo. How can I help you?" I answered.

"Hello, Dr. Harjo," Carol said. "I have Ms. Hoskins on the line for you. Shall I put her through?"

"Yes, please," I said, heart skittering in my chest. "Thank you, Carol."

After a couple of clicks, Carol said, "Ms. Hoskins? I have Dr. Harjo here for you. Have a nice day." There was another click as Carol left the call.

"Dr. Harjo? It's Rachel Hoskins from Rising Sun Farms."

My stomach clenched. "Hello, Ms. Hoskins," was all I could manage.

"Thanks for callin' and leavin' that message earlier. Dr. Keating was out here this mornin'. We asked 'round. It turns out the new guy in the pregnant sow barn is a hunter. He hunts wild boar, to be more precise."

My heart started racing. I kept silent, waiting for it.

"He brought some liver he'd saved in his freezer," she continued. "Thought it would be good for the pregnant sows. Full of vitamins and all."

Holy. Fucking. Shit.

She sighed and said, "There's no more of the liver left to test. But Dr. Keating confiscated the rest of the meat in the freezer. I suspect it'll be comin' your way for testin'. She said that'll let us know for sure what the source was."

I was still in shock over how the last puzzle piece fit so well, and I was essentially speechless. All I could squeak out was an unhelpful "Wow."

"I wanted to thank you for all your hard work," Rachel said.

It was pretty damn magnanimous of her to be thanking me. Most owners would be raging pissed, blaming me for the inevitable depopulation of their farm.

As if reading my mind, she added, "We'll have to cull all the animals in the sow building. That'll be rough. But Dr. Keating said we can test and decide what to do with the animals in the other buildings, including the farrowin' barn, since we haven't had any stillbirths or neonatal deaths in there. I'm just hopin' the virus stayed in the one building."

There was a very slim chance the virus hadn't moved between units. But a very slim chance was better than none at all.

"I'm crossing my fingers and my toes that the rest of the buildings come up clean," I said.

"Thank you," she said with deep sincerity. "Anyway, I gotta get a move on. We got a lot of work to do over the next few days. I just wanted to let you know how it all shook out."

Flabbergasted that she would be thinking about keeping me in the loop during this shitshow, I said, "Thank you, Ms. Hoskins. I appreciate it."

After hanging up the phone, I stared at it, trying to process everything. The last puzzle piece had fallen into place. At least, I was pretty sure it had. We'd have to test the rest of that wild pig meat in the freezer to confirm it. But still.

And yet, the normal pride in a job well done was overshadowed by the implications of the diagnosis.

One tiny, innocent mistake was going to wipe out several pigs. Maybe even the entire farm. Even with the subsidies, Rising Sun Farms might never recover. And that was just the financial piece. I couldn't imagine the heavy emotional burden Rachel was carrying right now.

Even though I'd finally solved the case, it weighed heavy on me and would for a while.

***

As the clock ticked close to five, I made a beeline for Dustin's office. The dude was a gem, and we never would've figured this last bit out without him. I was eager to share the news before he cut out for the day.

After all the negativity in the lab a few months back, it had taken a hot second for him to feel comfortable at work again. I didn't blame him. If several fingers had pointed at me as the thief, I'd be damn salty, too. He needed to hear that he'd knocked it out of the park with this one. I wanted him to know that he was a valued member of the team.

As I rounded the corner to Dustin's office, voices trickled through the half-closed door. I stopped dead in my tracks, still out of sight.

Gerald's nasally voice was unmistakable. "I need to speak with you."

Unable to decide if I should interrupt or skedaddle off, I ended up frozen like a rabbit in its hidey-hole.

Dustin cleared his throat, and his chair creaked. "Sure ya don't want to sit, Dr. Richter?"

"No," Gerald replied curtly.

There was an awkward pause, and I held my breath.

"The situation with the stolen tiger pelt was challenging," Gerald said.

This was met with a long stretch of silence.

I held my breath. I couldn't see Dustin, but I could only assume he was stiff with anger. And hurt. And the center of it all was standing right in front of him, picking at the half-healed wound. Just when things were starting to get better for Dustin, the shitass just had come in here to dredge everything up.

And we gave you a lemon bar! I huffed irrationally.

"I apologize for erroneously telling the police that you were the culprit," Gerald blurted. It was a loud, rushed, and uncomfortable statement that was met with the creak of Dustin's chair.

I figured Dustin was probably as shocked as I was. He must've recovered quickly, though, because, after a beat, he said, "Apology accepted."

Before I could even move, Gerald sped out of the office, stopping short to avoid running into me. Our eyes met, his going wide. I tried to wipe the shock off my face, pretending like I hadn't heard. His eyes bounced back to the ground as he swerved around me and fled the scene.

Heart racing, I took the last few steps to Dustin's office and lightly knocked on the doorjamb before entering.

With my eyebrows raised, I met Dustin's gaze. "What the hell just happened?" I whispered, flabbergasted.

His chair creaked again as he leaned back, passing a hand over his beard. "Did y'all just see a pig fly by? 'Cause Gerald Richter just 'poligized.''

ACKNOWLEDGMENTS

How did y'all feel about Gerald in this book? When I first sat down to write the Josie series, I channeled all of the mean shit I'd heard and experienced from men into his weaselly character. And boy is he a shitass. But I also knew from the start that I wanted there to be a reason for him to be such as asshole. The way we behave is a product of our experiences. How we act is a choice, and Josie sees that. Will Gerald get the memo and be able to overcome his personal baggage to start behaving like a decent human being? Only time will tell. For some villains, there is no redemption.

Enough about Gerald. This book is really about motherhood, and it only scratches the surface of the societal pressures that all professional women face. Whether you want to have kids or not, remember that it is your choice. There is no right or wrong answer, and no one should have to conform to expectations around getting married and having kids. There are lots of versions of a fulfilling life and what family looks like.

I also want to send a shot out to all of the DVMoms out there. In most partnerships, women do the heavy-lifting when it comes to raising a kid. It is hard to balance child-rearing and a successful career. You all are badasses!

To the UC Davis DVM Class of 2004: we did it! Even though the faculty thought we were nuts for having more babies than any other graduating class, we all came through the other side as successful veterinarians. I can't help but toss a chin flick at all those smug gents in administration.

I also want to send a warm thank you into the ether to Dr. Linda Munson. She was the toughest pathologist I knew, and I looked up to her. When I was eight months pregnant and we were finishing up a large project, she didn't judge me like the other faculty in the vet school. Instead, she was all bubbly and even bought a "Got Milk?" onesie for my son. Seriously, y'all, that's like Furiosa buying a onesie for one of the pregnant ladies on her truck. It was so unexpected. And so kind. I still have that onesie in my son's memory box.

And now to all of the wonderful people who helped make this book happen.

Thank you to all of the talented women who polished everything up. Thanks to my copy editor, Caryn Pine, for sticking with me through our fourth book together. Her input always puts more heart into the stories. Yasmine Bonatch served as proofreader-extraordinaire, catching every missed comma. Angela Caldwell designed the cover. The tilt of the pig's snout is absolutely perfect.

I huge thank you to Dr. Karyn Bischoff. A veterinarian and toxicologist, I often lean on her for the toxicology-related facts in the stories. She also serves as a beta reader. I struggled with the right tone for this book, and couldn't figure out why it was bugging me. When she pointed out that the original draft had a Lucy-and-Ethel-shenanigans vibe, I was mortified, but I also instantly knew why the book wasn't sitting right. After some hefty rewriting, Josie and Laila are now true to themselves. Thank you, Karyn, for helping me keep the women strong in this book!

To my oldest son, Derek, you sat through vet school lectures *in utero* and joined the outside world before senior year. You were there through all of the trials and tribulations of my anatomic pathology residency. And when I passed pathology boards and collapsed in tearful relief, I remember you saying "You can play with me now, mommy!" To my youngest son, Tyler, you spent many hours on the pathology floor *in utero* and made it through the cortisol-heavy days of the board exam. To both of you: thank you both for always bringing joy to my life, tolerating your mom "cutting up dead things," joining me on business trips, and always being cool with me being a career mom.

Finally, thanks to my mom. She raised me as a single parent, and made me into the woman I am today. She was my Ripley, and I was her biological Newt. She blasted her way through many bad guys to help me survive. She died when I was eighteen, and I still miss her almost thirty years later. I released this book on my mom's birthday, in honor of her and all of the other single moms who work their asses off to create a better life for their kids.

ABOUT THE AUTHOR

Catherine Sequeira was born and raised in the Bay Area. She obtained her BS and DVM from UC Davis and completed an anatomic pathology residency at Cornell. Throughout her career, she has lived and worked in Switzerland, New York, Oklahoma, and Scotland before returning to California. With over twenty years as a veterinary anatomic pathologist under her belt, she now writes and teaches. In her spare time, she enjoys reading sci-fi and fantasy, playing tabletop games, and gardening. She lives in Northern California with her partner, cat, and dragon (the bearded kind, that is).

She can be found online at www.catherinesequeira.com.